telephone love

Dedicated to: Foluke and Mahalia.
The loves of my life
and to Elaine who raises them so well.

Credits and thanks

Cover Photography	Mike Williams
Cover Design	Andrew Evans (875 Design)
Cover Models (L to R)	Donald Noble
	Barbera Scott
	Joseph Greenidge
	Althea Dixon
	Herman Grant
Editing	Helen Fittock
Production	Mike Taylor
Comments, assistance and encouragement	Elaine Anglin
	Caroline Grant
	Malcolm Hinds

telephone love

John Sailsman

Published by Twin Flames
123–125 Oxford Road, Reading, Berkshire, RG1 7UH

Published in United Kingdom by:
Twin Flames. An imprint of Creative Development & Consulting
123–125 Oxford Road Reading, Berkshire, RG1 7UH
Tel: 0118 9508534

ISBN 0 9533858 0 9

British Cataloguing in publication is available.

Printed by Antony Rowe Limited

Distributed in UK by Turnaround Distribution,
Unit 3, Olympia Trading Estate, Coburg Road, London N22 6TZ.
Tel: 0181 829 3000 Fax: 0181 881 5088

"Stolen waters are sweet, and bread eaten in secret is pleasant. But he knoweth not that the dead are there; and her guests are in the depth of hell."

Proverbs 9: 17,18

prologue

David Adams pushed his 190E anxiously around the block. His urgency almost got the better of him as he took the corner into Brunswick Road a little too sharply and mounted his back wheel on the curb.

'Calm down,' he told himself. 'You'll find one soon.'

He hadn't been back in his home town for very long and whilst he knew the streets, he had forgotten half of the places where all the phone boxes were. He had stopped at two already and they were occupied. One had a queue of people waiting outside and the other had two people inside and another three outside, so he hadn't bothered to wait. He was convinced that there was a phone on Brunswick Road and sure enough, after driving for a couple of yards, he saw one. But he was disappointed again.

A young punk-rocker type girl was in there and it looked as though she was pretty distressed. She was going to be in there for a long time. He thought he'd take a chance anyway, figuring that he might end up driving around all night looking for another box. Anyway, it was getting late and he didn't want to upset anybody by calling after hours. So he waited. He looked at his watch. It was ten thirty. He decided that he was going to get a mobile phone. He had just moved into his new house and the phone people were taking ages about installing a phone there. He'd better get on that case tomorrow too, and then he wouldn't have to be dealing with this shit anymore.

Before he knew it, it was ten forty-five; the girl was still in the damn phone box and still talking and now looking more distressed than ever. He kissed his teeth, revved up and sped off. He was now mightily pissed. He drove on and headed for the town centre. Surely there must be boxes there, he reasoned. When he hit the centre, he pulled up outside of a pizza take-away. The high street wasn't very far away; it was a pedestrian-only zone so he decided to walk. After a short trek he found a string of them. Four boxes, nicely arranged in a little square, smack dab in the middle of the street opposite Macdonald's which was just shutting down for the night. Only one of them was occupied. He pulled the door and hurled himself in. Eagerly he picked up the handset and pressed the necessary digits. He took a deep breath. Then blew out in disgust. It was engaged. He slammed the handset down with venom.

'Fuck!' He murmured to himself angrily.

He tried again. It was still engaged. He waited. Then tried again. Still engaged. He rested his head against the window of the phone box, kissed his teeth and pushed his shoulder against the door. A slight gust of wind hit him as he came out. He zipped up his jacket and headed for his car. He was not amused.

'Fuck it!' he thought. 'I'm gonna have to try again tomorrow.'

one

Elisha Road was a hot spot. A row of old dilapidated 1930's terraced houses and a couple of shops had been transformed over the years, from a busy road that was occupied by lower middle class English families to a ghetto area now inhabited mainly by Blacks, Asians and poor white trash.

By the end of the nineteen fifties many of the white middle class families had started to move out as the black people continued arriving. Many had been in the country for some years by that time and had struggled their way to buying a property. They wanted big houses to live in to raise their big families and also to house other migrants that came over from the West Indies and Asia. Once the Blacks moved in, the house prices went down with the area scoring very highly on the social deprivation charts – not for the level of poverty, but for the number of 'minorities' that lived there. By the nineteen seventies the area had begun to attract the worst kind. Slum landlords moved in, made their money and went. Others couldn't command enough rent to keep the houses in good condition, so they were repossessed.

By the end of the nineteen eighties, not even people looking for cheap accommodation would live in Elisha Road, because by then it had such a bad reputation. So some houses stayed in disrepair. Then the pimps and the hustlers, seeing in Elisha Road a window of opportunity, stepped in. Cash buyers, some of them. Having property was as important to them as a car is to a travelling salesman, or a saw to a carpenter. You couldn't work without it. Drugs needed to be sold, music needed to be played and hookers needed to be fucked. So soon, Elisha Road became a series of blues houses, shabeans, brothels, and gambling houses. It was a kind of underworld Bond Street or Fulham Road populated by tenants, shopkeepers and home owners who didn't give a shit because their lives were shit.

Mr Singh did give a shit. He was a frowzy, dirty old man. As he walked around his little corner shop with legs bowed from rickets and his back bent in an almost perfect arch shape, he coughed. His turban was dirty. Yellow and brown stains made it look as if he had neither changed nor washed it for days. He stank, he never wiped his arse when he took a shit, never shook the excess piss off his willy after he urinated and never, ever washed his hands. He would bathe now and then, but he never dried himself properly or creamed his skin, so it was dry, hard and peeling. His feet were so dry, from an extreme case of athletes' foot that they itched, and he would often sit behind the counter of his shop, working his already dirty fingers between his toes, sometimes so incessantly that the skin between them would peel off and they would bleed. He picked bogies from his nose endlessly and would roll them up into little balls before flicking them. He would regularly draw snot or the cold from his chest and spit wherever he felt like it. He would pick his bottom, scratch his balls and pick his ears with matchsticks, wiping the emerging earwax onto his trousers. He was a mess. A thin ageing man, he had a long drawn face that was littered with wrinkles and his long grey beard was brown at the edges around his mouth from his sixty a day smoking habit. He coughed profusely, seemingly bringing up his guts as the whirring noise of his respiratory problem echoed around his untidy retail store.

He fumed as his side-to-side swagger took him out of his corner shop to bring down the shutters, not only on his windows, but also on a busy nights' work. All he ever seemed to sell nowadays was packets of cigarette paper, condoms, a few drinks and a few curry patties that he had wisely invested in. His customers would take them out of the fridge personally and insist on heating them themselves, so he moved the microwave to the other side of the counter to keep his few patrons happy and to make sure that he didn't get beaten up for touching them. This was, after all, his best trade. This and bottles of Dragon Stout. He ordered them by the busload. He wondered if this was all that Black people lived on. Maybe, he figured, that was why they were always so angry, because they didn't eat properly. He was fed up, business generally wasn't going so well. The lease had just gone up again and those blasted Black dope dealers had driven all his best customers away. He dreamed of being back in India, rather than here on this cold wispy night, spending all hours that God had sent trying to beat out a living that was hardly worth it. He swore to himself in Hindi, then surveyed the street ahead of him.

'Get away, get away, why don't you go somewhere else and ply your trade? This is decent area, decent people live here!' he shouted angrily in his distinctly Asian accent at the crowds of people as they wallowed outside his shop. 'I come to this country forty years ago to make my living! Now I can't make my living because of you! Why don't you go away?'

'Fuck off Singh!' came the reply from an oldish looking man with a sharp Jamaican accent.

'I want to work here!' he challenged. 'Why you ply your dirty trade in front of my shop? Everyday every night, why you no go somewhere else? I try to run clean business here!'

'Man me seh fuck arf an' stop badda we! Nuh mek none a we affi come over deh to you. You likkle bloodclaart! Gwaan back inna you house an' wash yuh rassclaart kin!'

Upon noticing the seriousness of the mans' threat, by simply clocking the anger etched on his hard face, Mr Singh continued his complaint, but this time with only a faint mutter, once again in Hindi, as he extended his pole to reach the blinds and pull them down. He then scurried angrily back into the shop and, slamming the door behind him, settled down for the night.

Elisha Road was a hive of criminality. It was now a home for what society considered the worst kind. Like nocturnal vampire creatures, a cluster of prostitutes, pimps and drug dealers would make their way to Elisha Road if they didn't live there already. Every night without fail this was where they all plied their trade. It wasn't just dealers and pimps that frequented the area though. Hard gamblers, drinkers and soundmen were there too. It was the most popular venue for a blues party, so practically half the town's Black population would reach there at some point during the night.

On this particular Friday night things were just getting started and over 30 people were milling about. Some sitting in their rides, others just standing around either selling or buying something. Cars would often drive through very slowly and on the odd occasion – a very odd occasion – a police car would wander by. Not that they could do anything about what was going on there. Countless dawn raids on the area had come to nothing because the pimps and their hookers, the dealers, the soundmen and the gamblers just kept coming back. Elisha Road had been officially dubbed a no-go area. Rumours abounded throughout the town that it was the place to go if you wanted to get killed. This was hardly the case. It was the place to go if you wanted to get weed or drugs, take in a blues party, eat Caribbean food or pay for a fuck. But like everything else it had received too much hype, too much adverse publicity.

It was a long road and in seemingly every house there was something going on. There were two brothels and sometimes blues parties might be happening in three different places at one time. From one house, Caribbean food was sold and another house simply sold drinks and had space for the endless games of dominoes that punters would play, often all night long. There were two shabeans or gambling houses, one of them, Reggie's, had only recently opened for business and it had quickly become a popular hangout.

It was now 11 o'clock and the place was beginning to get busy. Eight guys were unloading gigantic speaker boxes from a van into a house, preparing for the evening's blues. An almost endless stream of coke heads and ganja smokers were talking to different dealers. Some, with expert knowledge of the goods, bartering for the best deal whilst others, almost afraid, settled for what they got, whipped out their money, paid for their goods and were off. Hookers lined the streets, leaning up against lampposts and walls. They would run to the first car that drove through or display themselves seductively for passers-by, trying to coax them with sexy words or passionate X-rated banter.

The place was beginning to become more active. Before long a police car drove through. Detective Inspector Kirk had been entertaining the new Chief Constable. He had been the keynote speaker at 'Community Policing into the Millennium', a conference that had been organised by the local Race Equality Council. He had decided to take him on a tour of the patch that he presided over, part of which included Elisha Road. The residents were undeterred by the sight of the police car coming their way. The drug dealers simply put their hard drugs out of sight, whilst the ganja sellers merely carried on smoking and carried on selling. Worried punters hid their faces as Kirk drove slowly by whilst hookers, knowing that they were in no danger from the policemen in the car, shouted obscenities and stuck fingers in the air at them.

'This is a tough spot,' said Kirk

'I can see,' replied the Chief Constable, who was visibly shaken by what he was seeing. This made Kirk smile to himself.

'Got to be tough to work these streets,' he said. 'These bloody niggers are hard as nails. They grow up hard, poverty makes 'em that way. Their cultural habits from back in the Caribbean mean that they don't appreciate authority. They can't live in an organised social system like we have in this country. They don't value order. Jamaica, y'know sir, was the only Caribbean island to resist slavery. Hard fuckers they are.'

'Equal opportunities, Detective Inspector, equal opportunities now,' broke in the Chief Constable. 'Remember your training. The force didn't spend twenty thousand pounds on training you just so that you could forget it all. Come on now, they're disenfranchised black people, ethnic minorities. Many of them didn't ask to be here and those that did were fooled. Oh we taught them to love the Commonwealth and to come and work for the mother country, only to greet them with the worst jobs, the worst living conditions and the most intolerable racism.'

'Of course sir, of course.'

' I mean racism is a terrible thing and we are all guilty of it. Discrimination causes situations like this, and we, as keepers of one of this country's institutions, need to recognise that at all times. We have such a bad relationship with these people and we really must do what we can to bring about some trust and work together.'

'You would trust these people sir?'

'That's hardly my point, Detective. Some live within the law and others live outside of it. They all have their reasons. Those that live outside the law don't always choose to, but it's all they know to do. They're all victims of discrimination and some of it is caused by us. I think we all have to admit that.'

Kirk was stunned. He could hardly believe what he was hearing coming from a policeman, a higher ranking one maybe, but a policemen all the same. The Chief Constable hadn't made conversation with him, but had just blurted out a series of sound bites. But then he reasoned that perhaps these were the sorts of things that one needed to say in order to get himself up the ladder in this profession. The Police Commissioner of the Met was always going on about combating racism in the force but did fuck all about it. Maybe that was it. He surmised that the Chief Constable was nothing but an educated twat, who had probably seen a minimal amount of real action out on the streets. He had probably never seen a dead body, had probably never even grappled with a small-time thief. He probably just said all the right things at all those seminars, conferences and training courses that he so often attended. So much so that he had lost contact with the real world of policing, the hard brutal reality of the Black underworld that was riddled with hookers, dope dealers, yardies, players, pimps and hustlers. Because this is what Black people were. They were a misguided and uneducated lot, whose only way of living was anarchic, anti-establishment and violent.

'Let's have a look at the town centre now then,' said the Chief Constable. 'Think I've seen enough degradation for one night. My God, she's a big girl!' He said as they meandered past a busty hooker, who, holding both her breasts in her hands, shoved them his way, pouting and blowing kisses at him. Kirk remained silent except for the 'Bitch!' said under his breath.

The Chief Constable's vibe was all so much crap to him; these people were simply a bunch of troublesome wogs and niggers. Trouble makers as far as he was concerned and they needed to be put away. The force needed new draconian measures to deal with this type of problem. As far as he was concerned they had come to this country and had initiated a wave of crime and underworld racketeering the likes of which Britain had never known. He had joined the force to do something about it personally. His quick rise through the ranks had put paid to that desire somewhat, for now he was working homicides. But oh, how he would have loved to be in the Chief Constable's shoes, because then he could do something about places like Elisha Road. As the police car pulled away, a few of the hookers brazenly ran behind the motor shouting more obscenities at them. One turned her back to the car, bent over and pulled up her skirt to reveal two large bare rounded buttocks which she accompanied with a shout of 'Have some of this copper! You know you want it!'

As the police car pulled away another car pulled in. It was a slick dark blue BMW 840, an outstanding luxurious sports coupé that in the dark tranquil night was simply a wonder to behold. The motor car personified elegance; its engine could hardly be heard as light alloy composite wheels with star-shaped styling rotated majestically. Its peerless muscular design won many admirers and most if not everyone on the street watched in awe as the wonder of modern car-making technology glided slowly past. Eventually the car ground to a halt. Usually a car like this turning up at Elisha Road would have everybody wild with enthusiasm, because they would know that someone's luck would be in. But as it was, everybody knew who the owner was and whilst the car created a modicum of excitement, that's all it did. The car pulled up outside a house that had a red light in each of the windows. This was Pum Pum's hang out and place of business, a brothel, and Tony Morrisson had come to see him.

Tony was a tall, slim man with an athletic build. He was quite stunning, and turned heads as he emerged from the car, pushed the door steadily behind him and pressed the small triangular piece of plastic on his key ring which applied the central locking and the alarm simultaneously. As his indicator lights flickered to register the application, Tony was immediately accosted by a fit, well built middle aged hooker christened Doreen Digmeout, who ran her jewelled hand up her strong, fishnet-covered thighs as she spoke to him.

'W'happen Tony baby? When you gonna buy the best pussy in town?'

'Me nuh haffi buy it Doreen, you know dat,' he replied smoothly.

'Well tek it fi free den nuh, den me an' you can spen' all dat lovely money you have.'

'Mine you know, no mek Pum Pum hear you seh dat.'

'Pum Pum a mi pimp, not me man.'

'Neither am I.'

'Chuh man, you always a do me so. A long time me a watch you y'know? Inna you big sport car an' ting. Man I beg you, dash weh the likkle gyal wah you a deal wid man an' try out a real woman.'

'Maybe one day yeah?'

'Me can give you real lovin' y'know.'

'Maybe one day Doreen.'

'Remember y'know, wanty wanty can't getty. Anyway hole it down rude bwoy. I will see you later.'

With that, the hooker turned away to once again apply her talents to the streets. Tony turned, paced slowly to the front door and entered the house. The front door was unlocked and once inside he stood in an empty living room that had large speaker boxes standing in its four corners. Two men stood in the centre of the room, watching highlights of the cricket on a small T.V. that rested on a coffee table below the window. It was the only piece of furniture in the room. They were both mature men, one slightly ageing and shorter than the other. Both spoke with heavy Bajan accents.

'Look how de rasshole man coulda ketch he out na man!' exclaimed the tallest one.

'Fuckin' guy like he bline!' replied Pum Pum.

'You right deh man, the guy nuh even make a effort to dive for the rasshole!'

'Pum Pum, w'happen?' interrupted Tony. At which the short mature man looked up and noticing him, bellowed across the room.

'Come in na man, close the rasshole door, it cole out deh yeh.'

Tony closed the door and locked it.

'Wha de arse you doin' man, you don' want we have no business tonight? Tek off de rahtid lock na man!' shouted Pum Pum, arms splayed in disgust.

Tony kissed his teeth and took the lock back off.

'Mek we talk nuh?' he said.

Pum Pum took his cue and excused himself, whilst walking through the living room door into the back room. He swaggered as he walked, he had never abandoned his old pimp strut from the seventies and the way he dressed made him look like something of a relic. The seventies were his best days. He believed himself to be something out of a blaxploitation movie. Those were the days when he had long relaxed hair like Superfly or an afro like Shaft, when his mink coat dragged on the floor every time his platform shoes touched the ground. When the interior of his Rover was made of fur and when those same platform shoes had heels that were so high that he had to work hard to perfect his pimp strut or risk broken ankles.

Now, some twenty years on, his hair was receding. He had been able, at least, to decipher the fact that in the nineties afros were out, even though those American rap boys were steadily bringing the long relaxed hairstyle back. This night he wore a black silk shirt that was smartly tucked into a pair of well-cared-for slacks, held up with a belt buckle so big that it commanded one's attention. Pum Pum liked gold and he was covered in it. Eighteen-inch chains with various insignias and symbols rested on his short light hairy chest that was exposed from to the fourth button down. Every finger but for his thumbs had a gold ring on it and even the buckle of his well cleaned shoes seemed to be gold. His mouth was littered with gold teeth; he had five in all, one holding a ruby inside it. A gold ring hung from both ears. He had a slight figure; years of hard hustling had taken its toll on his body and although small in stature, it was easy to tell the effects of endless late nights on his now quite bony frame. Once in the back room he swivelled back to Tony who had followed him and immediately began the banter.

'Fuck pussy last night till a mornin' boy,' he began, running his hand from the top of his brow down to his chin as if tired.

'Man you always fuckin' pussy,' replied Tony.

'Got a new girl, had to try it out. Emily Honeycunt, that's what I gon' call her.'

Tony laughed. Pum Pum was always coming up with imaginative names for his prostitutes and like Doreen this one was no exception.

'Girl got a fat arse boy,' he continued. 'Nineteen years old and she got a backside like a fuckin' horse. Man, you know I had to get right behind that and make like I was John fuckin' Wayne!'

Tony looked at him knowingly. Pum Pum was about to tell one of his famous 'pussy fucking' stories. They were good for a laugh and even though he had more important business to attend to he suffered it.

'Skettel ting man, pure Skettel. Only one way she did want it boy. I was lying down on it, sucking up the titties and ting.'

Pum Pum was now becoming animated.

'Bitch push me off, tell me I got a stiff one and how she want to feel the full extent. Back off she draws and lay down pan she front. Me barely know what she want, then the bitch tell me, nibble she ears. So me take out de boy and lay it between them giant size buttocks cos' me nuh ready to enter hyperspace yet you understan'? When I start nibble them fuckers. Fuckin' hell man she went wild.'

Pum Pum was now demonstrating his movement by winding his waist slowly as if fucking.

'I juicing up the earlobes now right an, man, before I know what's goin' on I'se chewing rasshole ears ring. When I realise is what, I spit the fuckers out and start nibble again. All the time, she waving that backside around like a fuckin' rasshole underneath me. I barely wanted to shoot up the batty crease but I says no, hole yuh horses man, the best is yet to come. So I pull offa she see, an' tell the bitch to hit the all fours. When she do dat, man I had to get up an' switch on back the light, because I got to see this backside work. Half the excitement y'know, just wanted to see them great big fuck arse buttocks waving at me while I bangin' away in between. Fuckin' shit gets me goin' every time man. Ain't nothin' like fuckin' a bitch wid a big boxy, trust me. Boy listen. When I sen' the starship into the docking bay and start shiff my prick into dat pussy, man I tell you, I wasn't disappointed. She start bellowing like a fuckin' cow! Me a hit it hard now!'

Pum Pum was standing arms open wide as if he were holding her waist in his hands. Shoving his trouser front in and out to mimic his action.

'Harder and fuckin' harder. Buttocks slappin' me either side of my dick and jumpin' up and down, hittin me in my stomach they was so rasshole big. Bitch screamin',' – he raised the pitch of his voice to sound feminine – ' "Ohh ohh Pum Pum, that's the biggest prick I've ever had. I fuckin' love the big prick." Well that just mek me fuck harder right. So I says' right, manual overdrive, hyper fuckin' space. I gon' mad now, killin' the li'l bitch wid fuck. I'm fuckin' it so hard man, I'm outta breath cos I ain't eat yet, my stomach so full up of gas man every stroke makin' me fart. I'm fartin', fuckin', fartin', fuckin fartin' fuckin'. Place start to smell like a fuckin' cowshed. She can't take the fuck no more right, 'cos I killin' it. So she grabs for the nearest thing. My fuckin' curtains.'

Tony was in stitches; he was enjoying this one.

'My eldest daughter bought them things for me from Ikea last year. Good fuckin' curtains man. Make the bedroom look pretty. I'm proud a dem curtains, I love dem so much, I don' wanna lose them and this bitch got dem in she han'. First she hold on with one hand. I 'fraid she gon' pull them down. Look man. I got one eye on the backside, the other on my fuckin' curtains right? But holdin' the curtains give she more leverage, so instead a she just takin' the fuck an' ballin', she workin' harder now too an' by now she got she both hands on dem fuckers, tuggin' away like she fuckin' mad. Rollin' the boxy around like there's no tomorrow. It only make me feel sweeter, I start tearing my wood into this pussy even more. Cos now I want depth.'

Pum Pum bought his hands forward, and clenched his fists

'I hold onto the batty right, stretch them fuckers aside like plasticene, to make my way in further. I tell myself, if I rip sumptink up in there it's the bitch fault for makin' the fuck so sweet. She scream, louder an' louder.'

Pum Pum applied his girly accent once again.

' "Ooh ohh Pum Pum, this is the best fuckin' I ever had, it's just so fuckin' good," an she start wildin' out again. Man I felt like fuckin' Dolomite or some shit cos this time, never mind hyperspace, we in the fuckin' twighlight zone! I lost my fuckin' mind, she lost hers too. I couldn't imagine nothin' sweeter, she backside sweatin' by now, make the tings feel sweeter. Then before I know wha'. Whack!!'

'What happened?' asked Tony in surprise.

'The bitch only pull down the fuckin' curtains man. Curtain rod, lick me right across the side of my head.'

'Shit. So what did you do?'

'What the fuck could I do? I shoot my load up the bitch get up and check my bruise an' tell she it comin' out she first wage packet, She must be at Ikea now lookin' for the same curtains.'

Tony laughed and so did Pum Pum. 'Boy that was a rahtid sweet fuck though. Sexy li'l thing had me drippin' boy,' he concluded. 'Hey look here man,' he said, starting on another subject. 'I got a new poem for you to hear.'

Pum Pum stuck his hand in his pocket and drew out a crumpled piece of paper. He unravelled it eagerly. Tony threw his eyes to the ceiling and let out a gust of air.

'Go on let's hear it then,' he said wearily.

He knew what was going to happen next. Pum Pum was in entertainer mode. He was like a little child about to show off something. Pum Pum liked to write poetry. He was a man blessed with inspiration. Poems would come to him out of the blue and he would recite them or write them down. In another life he would have been a Dylan Thomas or a Wordsworth. Maybe a bit closer to Linton Qwesi Johnson or another dub poet. But he was a pimp and therefore, more often than not, recited about his chosen profession. He never sought to publish his work, but maintained a dead-end fantasy that some day he was going to be the Poet Laureate.

'This one 'gon be big. Hear 'dis.' He stood, with back arched leaning forward, holding the paper out in front of him. Adopting a strangely pathetic pose as he began to read. All done somewhat dramatically as if he were on stage.

'Would you pay for pussy?' he started.
'Would you pay for the delights, under Brenda's watussy?
'When the nights get long, and the days get lonely,
'When the whisper of depression sends solemnity to you soul.
'When you're lonely, cast out and sorry,
'And the burdens of this miserable life cause you nothing but worry,
'Would you pay for pussy?
'Would you pay for the delights under Brenda's watussy?'

Tony yawned, he was tired. Pum Pum continued.

'Long hot summer days, become long cold winter nights.
'The dew drops from the tree in autumn and the birds fly home for the spring.
'Life's water is dripping from between your legs.
'And life itself takes on a new quality.
'As the heavens open and the vastness of the seas betray the nobility
'Of the masters sovereignty.
'But would you pay for your pussy?
'Would you pay for the delights under Brenda's' watussy?'

Tony yawned again. He hadn't realised how tired he really was.

'Cos when push comes to shove you know you've only got one choice
'When you're sick of makin' your right hand moist
'When you crave for the feel of human flesh
'Against the tip and the walls of your nature.
'When the Titanic rises once again

'Hoping to sink once again to depths of the Atlantic.
'I know you would pay for your pussy.
'I know you would pay for the delights under Brenda's' watussy.'

'Wha you tink?' Pum Pum asked enthusiastically.

'Wicked man, wicked,' replied Tony, 'Whole heapa vibes.'

He lied, it was pure shit.

'I know you would like it man, I gon' publish dis one next week.'

Crap. He said that about all his poems. Tony let the vibe slip nicely before getting down to business. Pum Pum, was way ahead of him though and began, albeit rather sheepishly.

'How much you lookin' for?' he asked crunching up the piece of paper and stuffing it back into his pocket.

'Three.'

Pum Pum exploded.

'What the fuck you talkin' bout man? How de arse I gon' mek three gran' in one night?'

Tony exploded too.

'Pum Pum don't give me this fuckin'shit, you do it all the time! Three grand man, that's what we need to make the deal go down. You knew about this deal two fuckin' months ago! What the fuck!?'

'Alright man alright, I gon' see what I can do.'

'I'm gonna be back here tomorrow, over at Reggie's gambling house. I'll there in the afternoon.'

'What, the new shabean?'

'Yeah.'

'Alright. Luck gon' pass round here later anyway so I gon' check see what he saying'. So what you doin' tonight'?

'Going out.'

'Wid de lady?'

'Yeah.'

'So you don' wanna lick no domino wid me tonight man? Wha you fraid to lose you money?'

'We'll do that tomorrow man.'

'How's Jean?'

'She's alright.'

'Give that girl my regards. Tell she, when she ready I lookin' a wheels same like yours.'

'Get your hustle right man, you won't need no woman buyin' you no big car if we score tomorrow night, trust me. Anyway look I gone, tomorrow yeah?'

'Yeah man. Easy.'

As quickly as he had arrived Tony was gone. His car sped off down the road as the hookers and dealers looked on once again in admiration. Tony didn't like Elisha Road, it was too downmarket for him. He wanted to buy drugs but even for him Elisha Road was the last place that he was going to buy it from. He figured he'd circle across town and get something there, the drugs were better, cleaner and sold by a different level of supplier.

two

It was a peaceful night. The cool breeze swirled around the town as Tony twisted and turned the steering wheel of his precious coupé, speeding almost desperately to his destination. His woman, Jean, had bought this motor car for him at nearly sixty thousand pounds brand new. In it he felt like a king. Rap music was blaring incessantly from the four furthest corners of his cockpit. The heavy-duty speaker in his car boot was doing its best to add to the atmosphere, but could only spurt distorted and cracked bass notes due to the slight rip in the speaker that he had meant to have repaired during the week. But with his constant runnings and 'business' ventures, he had neglected to do it.

Tupac was rapping in his wild and uncontrollable fashion, wailing as he tripped about he and his girlfriend. It was a wild track, undiluted, with all the rawness that had become custom with the young rappers' lyrics. Tony loved hearing this artist and in many ways likened himself to the deceased rapper, who throughout his life and even in the days of his riches lived perhaps a little too close to the edge. Never afraid to curse, never afraid to confront those that upset him, those that reviled him and those that stabbed him in the back, he was unafraid and considered death a gift. This was Tupac, and as Tony drove, he wondered if someday he too might share the same sort of fate as his young mentor and go out in the sort of blaze of glory he consistently fantasised about.

Eventually, he pulled up at a set of traffic lights and as he sat bobbing his head, a slick red R-reg Honda Prelude pulled up next to him. Four pretty young street urchins, Ragamuffin homegirls, occupied the motor. The girl in the front passenger seat was the first to notice him, she revealed a gold tooth by smiling at him and he did the same by smiling back. It was an action that motivated her to inform her friends of the handsome young man that was opposite, which she did with gusto, causing a large degree of excitement among the all-girl posse. He wanted to get a number. Any one of the four would have been sufficient because they were all so fine. He began to fumble for a pen, wondering how the hell he would be able to get those precious digits under these circumstances. But when the lights turned green and the traffic behind him began to get impatient, he let it go, with the comfort that the woman waiting for him at home was pretty enough, and at least for now she was all that he needed. He sped off with a slight wave at the ladies in the car, who returned his motion emphatically as they waved and pounded on their car horn.

Soon enough, his journey was coming to an end – but not before a police car coming the other way grabbed his attention. Two beast boys, one plain clothed and the other quite official looking occupied the souped-up Vauxhall Vectra. It was Detective Inspector Kirk and the Chief Constable. Kirk appeared to try and stare him out. Tony thought he recognised him. Probably had been stopped by him at some point, but with a loud chups of his teeth, he allowed him to fade from his thoughts as the police car drove on. How he would have loved to just pop one of them, they were feisty and stink and were always doing what they could to make life difficult for Black people. In his music, Tupac had often referred to the police as the 'Po Po'. He didn't know what that meant, but as he drove along steadily, he held two of his fingers together in the shape of a gun, aimed it at them through his back window and made as if he was letting off shots whispering,

'Po Po beast boy, Po Po.'

Eventually the sound of his motor ground to a halt as he pulled up outside a West Indian Take Away a couple of corners away from the high street. The Caribbean Food Shack was different from most self-respecting Caribbean take-aways' because it fronted for a dealer. From the view through the main window of the shop it seemed to be quite busy, but he was undeterred and immediately, almost in a mad haste, he was out of the car and into the shop.

As the slight tinkle of hanging bells trickled through the heavy smoky atmosphere, he eyed the people standing around in the shop who were either eating, chatting, or waiting to order. He glided past a queue of customers and made his way up to the counter whereupon instantly recognising him, the man serving the food raised the counter, pulled open the lock of the western-style gate and let him through with a slight but appreciative nod of his head. There was only a quick exchange of glances before Tony made his way through a set of swing doors and along a dark corridor to a dimly lit room situated at the end of it.

Inside was a kitchen. It was really a back room and was the place where most of the food in the shop was stored. There were boxes and a couple of fridge freezers loaded with food. There was also a cooker and it was here that a lot of products on sale from the shop were prepared and not just those that got eaten. There were two people in the room. One a young man, perhaps in his early twenties. He was white and dressed in a suit. He looked like someone that probably worked as a salesman or even on the stock market.

From his crisp appearance, Tony surmised that this geezer was probably loaded. His haircut was neat and his complexion suggested that he regularly spent his time on sunbeds and in saunas. Either that or he was abroad in sunnier climes for a good part of the year. He was frantically thanking the other man and placed a small wad of money in his hand before turning, whispering a sheepish hello to Tony and making an eager exit, leaving him alone with the other man. This man was Black, youngish looking and dressed in fine apparel. Dark shades hid his eyes and a small goatee beard worked its way neatly around his mouth. He had dark lips and a large flat nose that was spread evenly across his face. His complexion was a very dark chocolate brown and he wore a leather baseball cap from which short thin dreadlocks peered.

Enviously, Tony clocked the amount of gold that adorned him. Rings, chains and even teeth began to shine as the smile acknowledged Tony's presence. It was evident that his man was a drug dealer, and it was clear that he was doing very well in his chosen profession. He wore a long coat with deep pockets, which were evidently full of something unsavoury. He dipped his right hand into one of his pockets before asking Tony what his preference was.

'Half ounce, I beg you,' was Tony's eager reply.

The man reached into a small bag and pulled out a small parcel of white dust wrapped in cellophane. He poured a small section of it onto a set of mini scales that were positioned on the table in front of him, carefully readjusting the tiny weights in order to properly balance it out. When he was satisfied that he had measured a half ounce he mildly poured it into another bag, wrapped it, and passed it onto Tony who then handed him another wad of money. The man counted it and thanked Tony who in turn thanked him before making his way cautiously back up the corridor, past the counter and out of the shop.

Once in his car he took a look at the cocaine that he had just bought and opening his glove compartment he placed it gently inside.

'Yes bwoy,' he said to himself. 'I'm gonna get high tonight.'

As he was about to drive off, a high pitched ringing tone issued from his waist. It was his pager. After having to adjust himself to pick it up, he pressed a button twice to read the message.

WE'LL BE READY SOON. DON'T BE LATE. JEAN, was the message. Tony kissed his teeth and pressed another button on the pager.

SAVE PAGE? It asked.

Tony pressed the button again.

ERASE PAGE? It asked.

Tony pressed the button one more time.

PAGE ERASED. It read.

Placing the pager back in the neat holder hanging from the side of his waist, he smiled to himself, engaged the accelerator and sped off.

Jean was ironing in the living room of her flat. It was a large, spacious uncluttered room. A large pine dining table occupied the far wall whilst a pine coffee table filled the centre. There was a large elegantly framed full-length mirror on the facing wall that also housed an old fireplace that she never used. There was a leather three-piece suite that made its way around the large room adding to the luxurious surroundings. Large windowed double doors with a view of the quiet street led out to a balcony, where she would often sit and relax. Jean lived in a very posh residential area of the town. Her flat was one of four in a block of converted Victorian mansions that someone had spent a lot of money on and was obviously making a lot of money from.

She regularly ironed in her living room. There, she was close to the stereo and could listen to music as she worked. The living room contained the only full-length mirror in the house, which in her eyes was a very important and necessary commodity. As she ran the hot iron over her little black number, she contemplated the night ahead.

She looked forward to going out with her friends, but wondered why the regular DJs at the club that they were going to couldn't find anything more constructive to play. A short section of Jungle music was fine, but why she had to listen to it all night was beyond her knowledge. That's the way it was the last time she was at the Crescent Moon Club and the time before that and even the time before that. Whatever happened to the likes of Johnny Gill? or Freddie Jackson? What happened to cool easy going soul music or those mid-tempo 70's rare grooves? Groups like Side Effects, Patti and the Lovelites, Ashford and Simpson, Bobby Womack. What happened to Lovers Rock? The likes of Gregory Isaacs, Winston Reedy, Carol Thompson, Louisa Marks, John Holt and tunes like 'Caught You In a Lie', 'Sixth Street', 'Paradise' and all those great Studio One tunes that she used to rub to at blues parties. They were always good for a night out she thought but now it seemed that she could only ever get that kind of musical fulfilment at wedding receptions and revival dances.

Were the kids of today all without musical taste, or was it just her? She favoured a more romantic style of music, a kind that, whenever she listened to it, would make her feel wanted, romanced and appreciated. Maybe she was showing her age and just had to get with the nineties groove a little more. It didn't matter that much anyway she concluded, as she pressed the steaming iron over her dress and mused over the prospect of hitting the town with her friends.

This Saturday night ritual was one that she really enjoyed and tonight was going to be just a bit more special. Tony was going to be there and that was really all that mattered. She loved this man very much although she was often forced to wonder why. Their relationship had been going strong for nearly five years now despite his bad boy image, and she was pleased to have stuck it out – much to the amazement of Shakela, Juliette and even her closest friend Sheila, who for the life of them could not understand just what it was that they saw in each other.

They were such different people. He was rough, wild and uncouth. She was gentle as a kitten. He was a broke street rebel; she was a successful and financially secure Black woman. But still, she was his and although they'd been going through something of a rough patch recently, she figured that it might be good for them to be going out together that night. It had been a good while and she was confident that at the end of the day he loved her as much as she loved him. On that basis, she thought, they still had a few more good years to spend together.

She reminisced over the day that they first met. He had come into the department store that she was working in at the time and was looking for a decent aftershave. She remembered being completely taken by his handsome appearance, but contemplating how much she could improve it if this man were hers. She remembered taking his hand and spraying Hugo Boss onto his wrist for him to smell. She remembered how they laughed and giggled together having gone through Armani, Calvin Klein and Christion Dior only for Tony to ask, 'Have you got any Old Spice?!'

She remembered the day that he came back into the store, said nothing but slipped a bit of paper into her hand with his phone number and a note that read WANT A TELEPHONE LOVE? RING ME. She called the number as soon as she got back from work pretending to be the BT operator.

'Hello, I'm calling from BT. May I speak to my telephone love?' She began. They talked for ages, laughing and joking enjoying the simple pleasure of getting to know each other. They spoke on the telephone for days afterwards. Jean had christened him her Telephone Love and kept the tag, because they spent so much time on the phone together.

When they did finally date, she took him to an expensive restaurant and he took her to a pool hall where he taught her to play pool. Over the next few weeks, they couldn't be out of one anothers pockets, for the endless night-clubs, dance halls, wine bars, restaurants and shopping trips that they made together. She must have spent a fortune on him, but she didn't care. It was weeks before they made love but when they did, it was the absolute bomb. She remembered what it felt like feeling Tony inside her for the first time. This thought bought a wry smile to her face. A smile that she quickly had to hide or risk undergoing the third degree as her musings were blown apart by the distinct sharpness of Shakela's interruption.

'Jean, aren't you ready yet? Come on, we're late enough as it is, we ought to be thankful that he hasn't arrived yet!' she erupted as she entered the room, fixing her earrings whilst quickly pacing towards the mirror.

'I've been trying to get these damned creases out of my skirt, it's not an easy piece to iron you know!' Jean replied dryly, almost as if to indicate to her young and rather boisterous friend that she wasn't pleased about having her daydream upset, particularly in such an abrupt manner. But this was Shakela's way. At 21 years old she was young and impetuous. She had seen a lot in her short life, but it hadn't dampened her spirits, in fact her experiences had given her an even greater lust for life. She wanted to live life to the full and live she did.

She was a short girl, shapely and stunning. Her hair was long and relaxed with a band at the back of her head that covered the joining of a long extension piece, which ran down behind her neck and rested on her left shoulder. She had beautiful eyes; they were Chinese looking and slight, accentuated with cute curly eyelashes that took years off her already youthful appearance making her even more pretty. Large round gold earrings dangled from each ear, cleverly accentuating the straight shape of her face. She had a dark brown complexion that highlighted strong facial features. Her cheeks were high and the bone clearly visible. Her sensuous lips sat like brown cotton wool beneath a straight and perfectly formed nose that had a stud in it. She had a voluptuous figure; firm 36d breasts rested comfortably beneath a sheer see-through shirt that stopped just above her waist gracing a firmly rounded protruding derriere that gave her the look of a honey. Her short skirt did little to hide the powerful legs that supported her perfectly proportioned frame.

'Well just hurry up and get on with it will you? Because according to my watch it's twenty past eleven and he'll be here soon,' she retorted.

Now Jean didn't need this; for a long time she had wanted to tell Shakela a few home truths about herself. How, for instance, she was young and fresh and needed just a little more patience. She was always in a rush, especially when they were going to a club. She was the youngest of the four-girl posse and Jean felt sometimes that she needed reminding of it. It had only been through her association with Shakela's elder sister, now married and living in the States, that they ever started moving together at all and there were times when she wished Shakela had gone to the States too. There had certainly been enough reasons to tell her some home truths in the past, but this time she waved away the urge with a quiet 'Yeah, yeah OK? I'm coming.'

Shakela though, as ever, was persistent.

'You know how he is, you know that he doesn't like waiting, he's a merciless man, he'll leave us,' she warned.

Jean was on the verge of fury, particularly at that last statement. But instead of pursuing her frustration she decided not to yield to her motherly instincts but rather challenged Shakela to a verbal joust. She felt as though she had to remind her brazen young friend of an important detail and that she didn't shirk from.

'Now hold on,' she said in a tone more befitting her twenty-nine year old status. 'Anyone might think he was your man not mine. Just cool your heels darling. I've been seeing him for some time now and I think I know him well enough to know that he'll wait on me.'

Shakela caught the vibe. She had slipped up and sensibly decided not to pursue the issue in the same way as she had begun. She understood that next to Jean, she was young and excitable, over-emotional sometimes and even aggressive, but she was learning. In an effort to diffuse the situation she adopted a slightly less hostile and more playful tone.

'Oh yeah?' she shot back. 'Remember the time he left us and we had to get a cab even though we didn't have any money? Remember how the cab driver was vex and he nearly made us walk?'

'I remember it very well, but if you remember, that was your fault.' Jean snapped back.

'Mine? How so?'

'You don't remember do you? The guy from Birmingham? Blair Underwood on a good day? Mr Fitness? Remember now? What was his name? Junior? If you hadn't stopped to get his phone number Tony wouldn't have driven off.'

Shakela went quiet. Jean remained calm and wondered where Shakela would go next, knowing full well that her next words would signal the beginning of another verbal contest. Shakela was not one to take defeat lightly.

'Anyway,' said Shakela half-dancing, half posing in front of the mirror. 'How do I look? I mean, do I look good, or do I look good?'

'You look good,' replied Jean. 'But check this out, you haven't seen what I'm wearing yet.'

'Am I going to knock them out, or am I going to knock them out?'

'Yeah, yeah, you're going to knock them out. Have a look at what I'm going to wear tonight.'

'I'll tell you one thing though babes, all the man dem are gonna want a piece of this tonight.'

'And this.'

Jean tired of the game quite quickly. Much as she liked Shakela, she was easily frustrated by her youthful bragging. She longed for her to realise that life was not a game. That it was not always about 'catching' a member of the opposite sex or indeed the pursuit of sex. Besides, she was going out too and wanted to do some bragging of her own. She had struggled to be heard. Her last statement was virtually said under her breath.

She hated Shakela when she was in this sort of mood, when she would just carry on regardless and not pay anyone any attention. It was her way of feeling important. Jean wanted to show off her dress too and show it to Shakela in particular and she wanted her to like it.

She hardly knew why, but there was something about Shakela that just made her want to seek her approval. Maybe it was her youth and the fact that she was more hip, more trendy and more with the fashionable youth culture that dominated the style of the day. Or maybe it was the fact that out of all the members of the crew, Shakela was by far the prettiest, by far the sexiest and easily the most unconstrained. She attracted admirers like flies and it made her easily the most popular person of all the crewmembers.

Jean shook herself, wondering why she had to be so envious of her friend. Why couldn't she be satisfied with herself without feeling the need to compare herself to everyone? Why was she always so quick to notice her own shortcomings?

'Anyway,' came her half-childish quip. 'You still haven't seen what I'm wearing yet, I know one guy that's definitely gonna get a hard on when he looks at me.'

Jean figured that she might win the little boasting joust yet, but only if she got down to Shakela's level. It worked, but perhaps not in the way that she had expected.

'Yeah, but he always gets a hard on when he looks at you,' was Shakela's glib reply.

It was a response that Jean was totally unprepared for. She wondered whether she had detected a hint of jealousy in Shakela's tone and quickly scanned her memory for further evidence to justify the notion, before claiming her victory.

'I know!' She smiled victoriously. 'You see darling, that is why I have a constant smile.'

Jean checked again for a reaction, again to justify the feeling, and why not? Shakela was young and wayward. Perhaps she saw Tony as some sort of a father figure. Jean couldn't blame her if she did, he was a man to be admired and she knew that he attracted a lot of women. She cast her mind back to the first time that she had introduced Tony to Shakela, recalling her own gut feeling at the time. The ever-so-false handshake that Shakela gave him had appeared more like a desperate attempt to just touch him rather than greet him. The intense look in her eye, the complete swoon, not to mention the flirting. It had angered her at the time but she eventually shook it off, convincing herself that this was simply the way that Shakela was. If she did have a secret lust for Tony, it was understandable. But anyway, she thought, it was of little consequence because he was spoken for and even as a father figure, he wasn't available. Shakela broke the momentary silence with a frenzied scream.

'Oh my god! Shakela what's wrong with you? Are you all right? What's happened?' cried Jean, half concerned and half-frightened to death.

'Me figett fi cream mi foot!' was Shakela's reply. It was all rather comical, but she was deadly serious as she dashed out of the room, leaving Jean half amused and half wanting to strangle her. In seconds, Shakela was back upstairs whilst Jean put away the iron and the ironing board before changing in the living room in front of the full-length mirror. Call it vanity or call it egotistical, but she welcomed the opportunity to look at herself, just to assess whether at just a few months away from the big three-0 she could still handle the competition.

The years since her teens had broadened her frame somewhat, but she concluded that at a voluptuous size twelve she was not yet too far-gone. Jean was a beautiful woman. A straight-relaxed bob slightly curled at the ends was her favourite cut, but she was trying out extensions highlighted with gold, just for a change. Her long egg-shaped face was highlighted by a sexy figure that was majestically crafted, half by nature and half by the hours that she spent in the gym and taking the right vitamins.

She had a sharp look, almost supermodel-like, that was both innocent and seductive at the same time. Her eyes were sexy, her nose long and sharp and her lips broad. She had high cheekbones that made her perfectly even light brown skin tone a gorgeous sight to behold. She was tall. Straight, well cared for legs held up a stunning figure that oozed desire. Once fully dressed in her backless satin dress, legs sheathed in sheer black ten eenier tights and finished off with four-inch leather heels, she concluded that with a few more step classes and bit more work on her bumper section, she would be irresistible.

Once she arrived back in the room, even Shakela echoed the emotion.

'Wow, you look nice man, you really do, dig the crazy skirt man! Wicked!' she said.

'Well I did try to warn you,' was Jean's triumphant response.

Shakela decided not to get into another game, perhaps a feeling that she couldn't hope to compete with the beauty queen in front of her, inspired her next reaction.

'Listen, don't you worry about me,' she said quietly. 'I'll be safe tonight.'

With that, they both realised that all hostilities for the night had ended. Jean felt quite happy that she had managed to put her young adversary in her place. At least for now.

'It's getting late, where the hell is this blasted guy man?' Shakela wondered aloud.

'Dunno, he must be on some kind of runnings, you know how he stays.'

'Yeah, yeah he's always on some kind of blasted runnings,' snapped Shakela. 'Do you know what he's into nowadays?'

Shakela had fed her that question with all the cunning of a viper at the helm of a stealth bomber. It signalled the beginning of round three and the stakes had just been dramatically raised.

'No I… Well I… you know actually I don't.' Jean replied sheepishly. 'Why? Do you?'

'Well you know… I mean, haven't you heard what people are saying outta street?'

'No, erm, I don't really. I mean… well… Just what are they saying?'

'That he's been selling drugs. Not just selling it either, I've heard that he takes the stuff too. I mean like… not any little rubbish. Hard drugs.'

'Oh Shakela! That's just total bull!'

'Well, I'm telling you Jean, there are enough people that are saying it! Someone told me just the other day that he was in a blues party and all he did was stand in a corner sniffing.'

'Shakela please! I mean that can't possibly be true can it? I really don't know how people can tell such bloody lies!'

'Listen Jean I don't.'

'Shakela, just drop it OK? We've been over this enough times already. I've been seeing the guy for five years OK? And yes, I know that he is a bit streetwise, a bit of a loose cannon, but I know he wouldn't either sell drugs or use drugs. He'll smoke weed but nothing hard. He's just not that kind of person, so please just drop it OK? Just leave it out.'

'Sure, I'll drop it, I'll leave it out, but it's what you need to know. Your lover boy's not all that he's cracked up to be! Excuse the pun.'

Now they were both upset, perhaps Shakela the more, she couldn't comprehend the totality of Jean's denial. She knew deep down that Jean didn't want to accept the extent of her lover's imperfections. It was like she lived in a dream world, operated in a vacuum all to herself and had closed herself off to all the harsh realities of the world, especially the one that exposed Tony as not being the absolute picture of flawlessness that she wanted him to be.

It made Shakela sick to her stomach. Sick because this was a woman eight years her elder. She had expected better from her. A tougher and more positive approach to life. This certainly wasn't how she expected a woman older and more experienced than she to behave. She saw no real desire in Jean to even confront the matter, no real wish to take any advice on the subject and certainly no intent to confront Tony about his extracurricular activities. What about the danger of AIDS if he was injecting? Was she totally prepared to ignore even that aspect of it? That her drug dealing, drug-taking lover had exposed himself to these sorts of dangers? Was she so naive and so much in denial that she would ignore even this possibility? If so, then Jean was in a worse state than even she could have ever imagined.

She smiled inside gently telling herself that Jean knew nothing about Tony's secret life and that even if she did, she'd probably just pretend it wasn't happening. She wasn't, however, prepared to hide her disgust at Jean's sorry performance.

'Look I… I'm just sorry I spoke OK?' she said sarcastically.

It made her smile in her heart once again when she noticed that Jean had carefully avoided looking at her throughout the whole ordeal and had almost heard her wondering just what it was that she knew. She pitied Jean. She'd known all along that Tony was not the man for her. She was honest, kind-hearted, good natured and pure, she needed to love and be loved in return. She certainly gave love, but what Tony was giving her in return was only as real as he made her believe. Sure he loved her, but she yearned to know just how much and wondered why he should keep such secrets from her. Still, she concluded that Jean only had herself to blame. She needed to grow up, get with the real world and understand the mind of her man as she herself felt she did.

In the silence that ensued Jean put on her make up, using the opportunity to consider the issues in question. She thought about Tony and the stories about his drug habits. She had heard them all before and had often wanted to question him about it, but always neglected to do so, afraid perhaps of what his reaction might be. It wasn't so much his anger that scared her as the possibility that it might all be true.

Her thoughts were interrupted at that point by the sudden blare of a car horn that seemed to rip through the building, shattering its walls asunder like the thunder of Jericho. Or at least that's what Shakela's reaction seemed to suggest. Her young legs propelled her into immediate action as she rounded the settee and raced to the window.

'Jean, he's here!' she cried, half peering out of the large bay window and over the balcony outside.

Jean sprinted to the window, her heart thumping as she went. It was he. Like clockwork the two women began a ritual. An almost war-dance type of manoeuvre that sent them across the length and breadth of the living room.

'How does my hair look?' asked Jean, tossing her head sideways so that her long extensions swished before resting just above her shoulder.

'Fine,' came the reply. 'My shoes. Jean how are my shoes, how do they look?'

'Good,' replied Jean nervously. 'They look good. Ear-rings Kela?'

'Beautiful, nice, where'd you get them from? Can you see my pantyline? Does it show? Shit, my pantyline's showing.'

They were in full swing now, resembling two partners working a samba beat on 'Come Dancing' as feet rolled in and out for the other to view and heads turned around for immediate inspection.

'No it's beautiful, but your booty's looking kinda round though, kinda robust you know? Cock.'

'Get stuffed that's just how the guys like it baby, de man dem love a big batty gyal seen? Jean, have you seen my handbag?'

By now the ritual samba dance had not only began to make its way not only across the room, but also in and around the furniture. Settee cushions began to fly and tables were moved in the frantic search that ensued.

'Kitchen.'

'No, I wouldn't leave it in there.'

'Bathroom.'

'Never.'

'Spare room.'

'Not been in there.'

'Oh I don't know where it is! Why don't you look upstairs in the bedroom?' cried a bewildered Jean eventually.

'Good idea, upstairs it must be in the bedroom,' came the response and with that Shakela was out of the room. The stomping of her shoes was still audible as the doorbell went. Jean, ever the pro, composed herself in front of the mirror and ran her hands from the top of her head to her thighs, almost as if to straighten out the creases, not only on her skirt, but her whole body, before striding to the front door with all the confidence of a catwalk queen. Shakela was sexy, but she had already acknowledged her own strengths in that department. She had a thing or two going on herself and she was always ready to show it to her beloved. She was ice cool as she pulled the door open exaggerating the swing to expose to her lover the absolute bombshell that he would behold.

'Hi baby how are you doing?' she asked in a sexy voice as she opened the door to him.

'Cool,' was his dry matter-of-fact response as he brushed past her and made his way into the living room.

Undaunted by his lack of interest, Jean followed and caught up with him just as he was about to sit down. She stood behind him, threw her arms around his neck resting both her hands on his chest and slapped a great big kiss on his left cheek.

'How's my lover boy? Did you have a good day?' she asked in the deepest and sexiest voice that she could muster.

'Yeah you know, was cool still,' he replied grasping one of her arms, releasing himself from her. Tony, still unimpressed, merely took a handkerchief from his pocket and wiped the lipstick that had stained his cheek, an action that made Jean wince with embarrassment.

'Which part Shakela deh?' he asked rather aggressively.

'Oh she's upstairs. She's just looking for her handbag.'

Tony kissed his teeth.

'Bwoy oh bwoy, every minute she a lose sumting! Fuckin' 'ell.' he muttered in his makeshift Jamaican accent before turning to the mirror to admire himself.

Jean soon forgot about her own attempts to win his attention and watched in awe. She adored every inch of this man, and there he stood, tall dark and extremely handsome. He had the body of an athlete from his closely shaven head with its slight hint of waved hair, to the soles of his alligator-style shoes. To her he was a living god. His superbly tanned Nubian features only accentuated that god-like aura. She wondered what the ancient Greeks really ever fussed about, because neither Eros nor Hercules could ever have compared to what stood before her and the fact that he was hers only made her life that much happier. He was cool, sassy and sexy, an amazing dresser, whether tucked into his street gear or whether, like tonight, he was dressed up.

He was a sight to behold. Standing at exactly six feet Tony had a thin but muscularly well defined body, long arms and long legs held together his frame. He was dark and his long face seemed to shine as he stood in the light. Dark, slightly reddened eyes shone from beneath a rather square forehead. His nose was long and his lips thick. He had a stud in one ear and a ring with a tiny cross hung from the other. Jean knew that she had won this man despite competition from his many admirers and she knew that if she ever let him go, he would be lost forever in the clutches of those envious vipers. Those sad, hopeless bitches that always had so many bad things to say about her because they were jealous of her association with him. She was not about to lose him, not for anyone or anything. He was too gorgeous and too much in demand for her to do a stupid thing like that. For the third time that evening, Shakela abruptly interrupted her thoughts.

'I found it!' was her triumphant bellow upon re-entering the room, proudly waving the missing handbag around. It had been sitting on the toilet seat where she had left it.

'Where'd you find it?' asked an interested Jean.

'Never mind,' responded Shakela cautiously. 'Anyway, I'm ready now.'

'Cool,' responded Tony. 'Let's make a move. We're late already.'

Jean began to switch off lights, place magazines back in the rack and sort out the array of make-up that she had left on the coffee table to carry in her handbag. Shakela meanwhile, brushed Tony away from the mirror in order to make a final check on her appearance. Tony shook slightly as if he had caught a chill.

'Hold up a minute, I soon come,' he said in a commanding and authoritative tone. He made his way out of the living room up the stairs and into the bathroom leaving Jean and Shakela little the wiser as to his intentions. Once inside the bathroom, he hurriedly locked the door and in seconds had taken the small cellophane bag from his jacket pocket. He unravelled the top of the bag to reveal the half-ounce of fine white dust which he carefully poured out onto the side of the bath.

He took a half-split razor blade that was carefully wrapped in paper from his wallet, and separated the powder into three thin lines. Then he rolled up the gift token that came with the cigarette packet in his shirt pocket to make a tiny tube just big enough to fit into his nose. He got on his knees, held one end of the tube to his nose and the other onto the powder before pushing his face towards it and quickly sniffing each row up his nose. He sounded like a pig as he drew his nose up a couple of times. The cocaine had stung him and it made him feel uncomfortable. He then stood motionless for a while whilst the immediate high settled. Finally, he screwed up the makeshift tube, flushed it down the loo, wiped the excess powder from of the side of the bath, and brushed the tip of his nose. He composed himself and as calmly as possible made his way back downstairs.

He lost his footing on one stair and tripped, but managed to control himself without arousing any suspicion from the two women patiently waiting for him in the living room.

'Relieved?' asked Jean.

'Yeah, you know,' was his tense reply.

As they all headed out of the door, Tony last, the telephone began to ring. A simple and everyday occurrence that seemed to attract greater attention from both Tony and Shakela than it normally would have done. Jean responded in her normal way when this sort of thing happened.

'Oh leave it.' She said. 'If it's the girls, tough, we've left already. We'll see them at the club anyway. Anyone else can call back tomorrow.' With that, she pulled the door to. Tony held his breath. He wanted to say something, but decided not to bother. Shakela also wanted to urge Jean to answer the phone, but eased her way into a sense of satisfaction at Jean's response. So as it was, the shrill sound of the telephone ringing disappeared eventually, as did the three excited travellers, deep into the breezy night.

three

David Adams was a tall, handsome, but very lonely Black man. He pushed a Mercedes 190 E, had bought a beautiful country house and a penthouse by the sea, and had money in the bank. Eight hard years of selling computers had paid serious financial dividends. He was rolling in it. He had all that he wanted. All, at least, that money could buy.

The old phrase 'money can't buy love' rang true for him. He knew and had known countless women, but none of them ever made him feel like settling down. None of them he considered perfect for him. He desperately wanted someone to share his world. At 31 years old he longed for companionship. He was not the stereotypical Black man – an image that he could easily have perpetuated because of all his money.

No, he was a family man. He yearned for love, yearned for someone to spend his life and his money and his heart and soul with. That someone was difficult to find. Most Black women that he had met only dreamt of having the sort of lifestyle to which he was accustomed and dream was all that they seemed to be able to do, for to live in it, to fit into it, was impossible for them.

He was bitter at the way that most of his relationships had gone and for a time had had a couple of white girlfriends, thinking that maybe, like so many other successful Black men, his ideal partner should be white. That at least they might be able to understand and appreciate the pampered and privileged lifestyle of eating out at the best restaurants, enjoying the opera or the RSC. He liked taking holidays to places like Goa, and the Seychelles or taking a shopping break in Manhattan, not just visiting with family back in the Caribbean. Perhaps he was right, and a white woman would be better able to share his taste in some things – but he had trouble reconciling this with his own identity as a Black man.

Ultimately, when he imagined his soul mate, she was Black. He preferred Black. It was his culture. He wanted a Black woman to love, who loved him in return not for what he had, but for what he was and this had been missing in all his relationships. All but one. As he shifted his mind to his days studying at university he remembered Jean Samuels. This was a woman that he had loved. He loved everything about her and particularly her giving qualities. She gave of mind, body and spirit when they were together. But he was young and impetuous then. He had deceived her with another woman. She found out and now it was over. He regretted that mistake, regretted the fact that he had ignored the silent whisperings of his youthful and tormented heart.

He should have stayed with Jean. Should have treated her better, for she was a good woman, angelic and virtuous. He remembered the timely advice that he had been given once about St Vincentian women, that they were easy going, committed faithful and generous. Jean had Vincentian parents and she epitomised that spirit. He remembered though, that she was soft and that it was this quality above all that led him to deceive her. She had been too easygoing, too emotional and almost childish in the way that she had approached the relationship. But he paid little attention to that. He reminisced on their life together, how they talked, spent time together, confided in each other and generally made the most it. It was pure love, shrouded in youthful innocence perhaps, but it had been real. As he lay in his bed alone staring thoughtfully at the ceiling for lack of sleep, he longed for a return to those days.

The hot air that swirled around Tony's car as he drove highlighted the eerie silence as he and Jean sped quietly back to her flat. She was sorely vexed and he knew that he had been the cause of it. She wore a blank expression throughout the journey only, every now and then, turning to him and throwing him a dirty look. Tony grew tired of the heavy atmosphere in the car and pushed in a tape that protruded from his cassette player. It was Tupac again, but somehow he figured that rap music might not suit the occasion. As he drove, one hand on the steering wheel, he dug under the cassette player where the rest of his collection of music tapes lay.

Once satisfied, he pulled out a tape that he had named 'Slow tempo', a collection of soft soul tunes that he figured would probably appease his unhappy lover. Wrong. As R. Kelly sang passionately about keeping it on the 'Down Low', Jean merely chupsed her teeth, threw him another cold look and stared at the passing traffic through the passenger window. Tony took a deep breath and let out an anxious gust of air, before settling back into his seat, concluding that the ride back to her flat was going to be a long and difficult one. He touched her thigh, she moved his hand off with another even colder chups of her teeth. Tony steadied himself, deciding finally to focus on nothing else but the road ahead of him.

Before long they were outside Jean's flat. As he ground the car to a halt, he took a longing and almost sorrowful look at her, perhaps hoping that by now she had calmed down. No good. The passenger door clunked louder than usual as Jean slammed it and stormed out of the car. In foul mood, she strode along the cobbled walkway to the entrance door, arms held firmly around each other at just above elbow length to shield her from the cold.

Once up the stairs it wasn't long before she had reached the front door of her luxurious flat and took no time in getting the key into the lock, shoving the door open and switching on the living room light. Standing almost in the dead centre of the room she swivelled, hands on hips, brushing aside her hair from her face as she waited for Tony to arrive. Calm as ever he entered the room, completely ignored her and walked straight over to the mirror to begin admiring himself. This was Tony through and through, he knew that he was about to enter into an argument.

Jean was going to try and curse him out, but he knew how to deal with it by not getting involved and generally taking the Mickey. He knew that he was a good looking guy and almost needed to remind himself of that fact at every opportunity that he possibly could and this, perhaps more than any other, was a perfect time. He was the sort of person that could remain unmoved in the midst of someone else's tantrum, particularly when that tantrum was directed at him. He was generally unconcerned that in a few seconds he would be called upon to justify a misdemeanour. He answered to nobody but the hidden voice that guided his own soul.

Hardly a man of great principle, but certainly headstrong enough to want to do his own thing without fear or worry of external influence. So his foray to the mirror was just as much a statement as anything else because it told Jean that whatever grievance she wanted to pursue with him, he was indifferent to it. Tony looked himself over from top to bottom, giving himself both full frontal and profile views just to make sure that all was in place and just how he liked his appearance to be at all times. Once satisfied with his appearance, after straightening both his lapels and rearranging the cuffs on his shirt, he began shadow boxing with his reflection. This was a playful recourse for him, a means of letting himself know that he was still the best. He'd never boxed with any serious intent before but there was something about the sport that he had always appreciated. It was for him, the greatest endurance test that any human being could undergo. That's why he held people like Mike Tyson and Muhammad Ali in such great esteem.

He had sparred once or twice when he was younger, but lacked the desire or the will power to pursue a career in the profession. But he liked to shadow box regularly, it kept him alive and in touch, not only with his childhood perhaps, but also, it gave him something of a stake in the world at large. Maybe it provided him with a sense of belonging. He knew that intellectually he could not hold his own but boxing was something that he knew how to do and it certainly provided a place for him. It also kept him fit. He regularly remembered the instructions that Belly, his one-time boxing tutor, said to him. Try shadow boxing for three minutes, which is the same time as a round of boxing and see how tired you get. Tony did this whenever he could, knowing that it would give him the necessary stamina to out run a policeman or chase a basshead that didn't want to pay him.

Jean, however, was still grieving. Once she felt ready to begin her verbal assault, she did so with alarming venom.

'Why?' she bellowed, trying to curtail his arrogant behaviour. 'Why does this shit always have to happen? Every time! Every single time we go out you have to act up and end up in a fight! What are you, a damned child!?'

'Well,' was Tony's cool reply as he ducked and shielded. 'That likkle bastard shouldn't have been looking at you should he?'

Jean was bewildered by his response. His ignorance was getting to her. There he stood in the mirror acting out some fantasy whilst she desperately tried to reason with him and deal with what she considered to be an issue of ethics. What an insult. Here he was trying to justify a completely unjustifiable action. She had longed to have that kind of intellectual, intelligent debate with the man she loved and she was increasingly disappointed that such conversations only ever took place in moments like this. What frustrated her more was that whenever such an opportunity arose, the response that she would get from him, just like now, was always cold and minimal. Her anger however could not lay the issue to rest. She pursued him some more.

'What the hell do you mean he shouldn't have been looking at me? They're his eyes! I should think he's entitled to use them he's entitled to look at what he wants!' she snapped back.

'Not at my woman!' Tony was now southpaw.

'Well you just tell me what were you going to do about it? Cut his eyes out?'

Tony stopped his shadow boxing, the discussion as far as he was concerned had gone on long enough. It was time for it to be over. He had grown tired of the matter and felt as though he had to do something pretty drastic to bring the farce to a close. After all, there were other things that he was interested in doing on this particular night, especially as the club hadn't turned out to be a sufficient evening's entertainment. Particularly also, as Jean was looking so sexy in her little black number. He used his brain and turned to her sharply.

'That's what I should have done! Hold up, I'll soon be back.' He said turning and walking across the living room floor towards the exit. Jean watched in amazement as he made his way to the door, she couldn't believe that he was serious and the very thought of what he appeared to have in mind threw her back, helpless into the settee. Once again Tony had triumphed in a battle of wits.

Jean really was not cut out to mentally challenge him. Her hopeless attempts to show him her anger and frustration were always easily, and with alarming regularity, quashed. She just didn't have the stomach to continue to argue with him for she knew that at the end of the day he made her weak. Day by day she walked a tightrope with her often over-sensitive lover. She was too afraid to upset him, knowing that the slightest pressure or stress might see him heading for the door for good and she feared this. It was the basis of her very worst nightmare. The very act, the very movement towards the door that Tony made, particularly in a heated or sensitive situation filled her with dread.

She loved this man and she could not imagine what her world would be like if she ever lost him. He knew this and this was why he always tried never to seriously bring about an argument with her. Whenever she tried to deal with an issue that was affecting the smooth continuity of their relationship, he would treat the matter lightly, perhaps mock her, knowing that it wouldn't take much for her to give in. But there was another reason also. Somehow Tony had to deal with the fact that Jean was quite an intellectual person. She was educated. The sort of person that he definitely was not. She had studied at university and had graduated quite easily with a degree in management. He loved her but he consistently had a nagging feeling that somehow she was above him in the mental stakes, and that if ever, perhaps during a difference of opinion, she bought that power to bear, he might end up the loser.

Now this was certainly not a position he wished to find himself in, least of all with a woman. His over-inflated male pride just wouldn't allow it. Jean was aware of this and except for specific occasions, when her passion would consume her, she rarely resorted to the greater power of objective reason that she knew lay dormant within her mind. There was too much at stake for that. She knew it was a weakness, but it was a sacrifice that she was quite prepared to make for her loved one. Why, she knew not. All that she ever really understood about their relationship was that he transported her to another world. She felt comfortable with him despite his often brutal and sometimes rather primitive outlook on life. To her, he was the pillar of strength that she – and perhaps every other woman – sought in life. In him, she had found her rock, her comforter, and her man and was happy to do all in her power, even go to the point of self-denial to keep him.

'Tony, please, I don't want any more trouble.' She pleaded. Her right hand resting against the side of her forehead with her extensions hanging over her fingers as she began to weep. This was Jean's most apparent weakness. Whenever she was distressed the tears flowed too easily. She was a sensitive and often very emotional person. The childlike innocence of her charming personality was almost too childlike. Ever since she was young, she was unable, at these times to control her passions. She had gotten into the habit at a very early age from watching her father beat the living daylights out of her mother whenever they argued. Feuding with her sister over toys or which kids' T.V programme to watch after they had arrived home from school. Even the difficulties she had when she was studying for her degree would cause her pain, and those tears would simply flow. She was a gentle thing and not cut out for a rough or difficult life. She had great inner strength and when things got difficult she could handle them, but it was those small things that she couldn't handle. Jean would only buckle, lose it, emotionally drain herself, all in a matter of seconds allowing the painfully warm feeling that lay just below her diaphragm to take control. She would heave and tremble just like a child and then the tears would flow and they wouldn't stop. As a child she would often cry herself to sleep and now things were no different. She was no good at funerals, no good at weddings, no good in front of a good film and certainly no good when quarrelling with Tony. Oh, she'd fight, she would put up some kind of resistance but it would never last long. She would give in too easily. She hadn't the stomach for it. She would feel every lash, every blow that her drunken father would inflict on her helpless mother and this somehow weakened her, made her lose all her strength at crucial times and simply concede. Tony stopped at the door, rolled his eyes to the ceiling before looking at the ground once he noticed that Jean had gone into one. He spoke quietly.

'Shit, just stop crying all right. I was only joking.'

Jean merely continued sobbing.

'Honey bunch,' he pleaded.

No answer.

'Sweetheart.'

Again there was no reply except for the soft and persistent rush of tears and sniffles.

'Cherry pie.'

Once again no good. Tony had been embarrassed by the words that had just come from his mouth. They were difficult words to use and he was damn sure that he would not be made to have to use them again. He slammed the door loudly.

'Lard stop barl nuh man! Me tell you seh me was only joking. Bloodclaart! Wah do you man?'

With that Jean rose out of the chair, approached him and with arms open wide, she gave him a hearty hug. A gesture he reluctantly received. She was easily pleased and Tony never ceased to be amazed by the apparent child likeness with which, in almost an instant she was able to switch emotions.

'But if I see that fool again I gwine buss him head seen?' he said in one final act of defiance.

Jean was unconcerned by his last outburst, she knew it for what it was. Mindless bravado. She proceeded only to study him.

'Where did he hit you?' she asked gently.

'Here.'

He pointed to his forehead. She kissed it.

'Here.'

He pointed to his right cheek. She kissed it.

'Here.'

He pointed to his mouth. She gently kissed his lips.

'And here.'

He held his crotch. She slapped him playfully against his chest.

'Oh you are so disgusting.' Jean said playfully. All her tears, anger and disappointment gone. 'Are you hungry'? She asked pulling herself away from him and heading for the kitchen. He pulled her back.

'Yeah, give me one Jean Samuels, lightly cooked, ready salted and boiling hot,' he said. He tried to kiss her, but with a slender hand placed firmly on his chest she eased him away.

'No Tony, not now,' she protested. 'I'm sweaty.'

'Sweat smell sweet sometimes, you know, cherry pie.'

'Tony please,' she pleaded. ' Just let me bathe first.'

Tony gave up and turned his attentions to the stereo.

'Put arn likkle music den no?' He asked turning away from her and resting on the settee.

With a flick of the remote control, the room was awash with the mellow sound of Blackstreets, 'Before I Let you go'. It was Jean's favourite song and it made her feel romantic. She slid across to Tony who by now was well relaxed with his feet cocked up on the arm of the settee.

'Take your blasted shoes off when you're on my settee. How many damn times have I told you?' she said playfully but with enough seriousness for Tony to know that this wasn't just banter. Reluctantly he used each foot to kick off the shoe on the other foot and in an instant they were felled to the ground.

'Why you nuh go have you bart?' he said, slightly vexed at being rebuked.

Jean merely planted a sensuous kiss on his lips to calm his increasingly frustrated spirit.

'I will,' she said softly. 'Of course…' she continued more seductively, '…you could always come and bathe with me.'

She didn't wait for an answer but instead pressed her mouth onto his. Tony wasted no time and in seconds they were embroiled in a long hot steamy kissing session. Then the phone rang.

'Who the hell is calling you at this time of the morning?' Tony snapped.

'Believe me I don't know. Probably one of the girls, Sheila always calls to find out if I'm OK,' replied a genuinely cheesed off Jean.

She stretched over. Not wanting to let go of her lover she picked up the receiver and dropped it violently back onto the phone.

'Whoever it is they can wait till a decent time to talk to me,' she said brazenly. Then looked at Tony seductively. 'I'm busy,' she told no-one in particular.

Tony was worried. The idea of Jean getting a phone call at that time of the morning was disturbing but he was in no mood to further investigate the matter, at least not when there were more pressing demands on his physical and mental energy. He brushed the matter aside, swearing to raise it again in the morning and instead wasted no more time. He immediately threw himself back into her.

After five steamy minutes Jean raised up. Her lipstick had left her mouth and had grappled itself around his mouth. But this was of little consequence for as far as she was concerned there was much more kissing to be done.

'Come,' she said, leading him of the settee.

Tony obliged. They didn't even turn off the music or turn out the lights, they simply wanted each other and under the circumstances there seemed no time like the present. They climbed the stairs quietly, anticipation written all over their faces. They slid past the bathroom, almost as if the subject of having a bath together had never been raised. As they entered Jean's bedroom it felt like entering paradise to Tony. She flicked the light on to expose a very well kept room that was tidy and well arranged. Her wardrobes were mirrored and the soft lighting emphasised the sort of mood that they were both in.

It was the sort of moment that Tony relished. His partner certainly knew how to make love and no more so than when she was in the sort of mood that he knew she was in now. They had just argued and made up, she let off her steam, now it was time for a spot of damage limitation. He knew that she would want to express to him, that despite everything she still loved him and no other woman that he ever knew was as good at doing that as her, so it was best not to even trip off the argument that they had had. Arms held firmly around his neck, Jean once again dropped her lips eagerly onto his. He himself returned the action and soon they were once again locked in wild passion. As they kissed they moved steadily back onto the bed. The movement was fluid and in seconds, still kissing, Tony was on top of her, his lips working their way all over the lower part of her face and neck.

Jean placed the tip of her right foot against the heel of her left shoe and kicked it off and did the same to the other. Her groans began as did his. She felt his erection lying brutally against her vagina. The slight but ever-increasing movement of his waist and the subsequent rubbing of himself against her began to make her feel even more horny.

Slowly she guided his top half away from her in order to undo the buttons of his shirt, to which he responded and before long she was kissing his bare chest and licking and biting his nipples. With vigour, he placed both his arms around her and with a wispy spin turned over and pulled her to lie on top of him. In seconds he had pulled down the zip on the back of her dress and the gap exposed her bra strap which he undid with ease. She paused to de-robe, an action that took no time at all.

Their writhing was now more frantic and their groans became louder as she lay on top of him, naked but for her panties. She figured that now was a good time to raise the stakes and so, she slowly directed her kisses further down his body until she reached his trousers. With the expertise of a woman well used to enjoying herself between the sheets she undid them. Gripping the trouser waist and his boxer shorts she pulled them down, slowly, allowing her well-rounded breasts to slide elegantly over either side of his rock-hard cock.

She slid back up, once the trousers and his boxers had reached his ankles. Once back up, she stopped at his penis again and without remorse slowly held it in one hand and stroked it gently before peeling back his foreskin to lick the tip. Slowly at first, she remembered that he had not bathed and wanted to assess its freshness before going at it hammer and tongues, as it were. Once satisfied that he was clean enough for a blowjob she licked it frantically before taking the whole thing in her mouth and sucking sweetly to the sounds of restrained but ecstatic moans from her man.

When she was finished she crawled up to his face and proceeded to tease the erogenous zone of his neck. She knew he was ready for her and without further ado, proceeded to relieve herself of her tights and panties. She sat upright on top of him, leaning forward to purposely throw her breasts in his face. She cleverly grabbed his erection whilst he held her firm breasts in his hands and proceeded to suck her nipples. As they both writhed in sheer delight, she placed him inside of her. Their groans were parallel, ecstatic and loud. The night was going to be a long one, this they knew.

The hours passed away to the sounds of heavy bumping and grinding, licking and sucking, moans and groans of sheer delight and pleasure and screams of sweet pain. Sweat flowed for a couple of hours as the two lovers remained embroiled in a joyous act of lovemaking and when they both eventually fell asleep they slept smiling both happily satisfied and very much in love.

four

Tony entered the living room steadily. He looked up at the clock on the wall before falling back into a chair. He was shattered even though he had just woken up. For some strange reason, it didn't feel like a Saturday morning. He had taken longer than usual to get dressed and he wasn't interested in either the T.V. or the stereo for neither the X-men, Spiderman nor TuPac held any sway for him this particular Saturday morning.

He was famished and desperately wanted to eat but didn't even have the energy to make himself any breakfast. All he could think about was the way Jean had totally sexed him out. She had performed like a woman possessed and he knew what it meant. Jean rarely gave blow jobs but the one that she had given to him that night seemed to suggest that it was more than just a sexual act, more than just a means of making up for upsetting him with an argument. It was her way of telling him how much she loved him and how much she wanted to please him. Almost as if, this time, it was relevant to do so more than at any other time in their relationship.

He wondered what the reason might be. He knew that Jean loved him very much. He wondered if he really loved her, then backed off out of it. This was already getting too deep and too sensitive for him. He knew what love meant and the thought of the commitment attached to it was just a little too much. The thought that someone was dearly in love with him, or that he could possibly love someone didn't worry or faze him. The truth was that he held an amount of affection for Jean that had surpassed any relationship he had been involved in previously. Anyway how the hell do you stay with someone for five years without feeling something even akin to love for them? He knew that he loved her but he did have difficulty reconciling to himself the fact that love would have to be returned and often in a physical and public manner. He dealt with that by reasoning that, after all, he was a man and he would not allow himself to get into any smutty business. No holding hands, no kissing in the street, no smutty shit like that. They hadn't done it before and they sure as hell weren't going to start now.

Anyway, he reasoned, Jean knew him well and he felt confident that she wouldn't start to impose herself upon him in any intense kind of manner, especially not in a public place. Deep down, Tony knew that he needed Jean. He did love her, there was no doubt about that, but he'd never before quite reasoned that concept through thoroughly enough. He had always refused to contact that side of himself and yes, Maxi Priest's love songs always registered, but they were a surface job, entertainment and not a reflection of how he felt about anyone, or at least he liked to think so. He had a space within his soul that had a no entry sign on it. That was the piece of himself that was for him and him alone. A dark place that even he sometimes was terrified to enter. Jean had perhaps laid a claim to that space but he rationalised that if he had to bar her from it, he would.

There was, of course, another reason for his defensiveness and it was this more than anything else that caused his heart to pound. The prospect of being let down in love was one that he just would not take and though he had done it many times to other women, having it done to him was just not on. He had thought about it before and had wondered just what he would do if Jean ever did the dirty on him, but he shook himself out of that thought too. For what he would do to Jean, he didn't want to imagine having to do to one so fair and so innocent.

But she wouldn't be innocent would she? He thought. Leave it, just fuckin' leave it, another other voice told him.

An equally flaked-out Jean eventually entered the room. Hair untidy, eyes half asleep, she tied together her dressing-gown as she stepped in, dragging her bare feet across the floor making a track in the thick shag pile as it warmly caressed the soles of her feet and wrapped itself around her toes.

'What time is it?' She asked in a rough voice as she scratched her head.

'Half twelve.'

'Oh come back to bed,' she begged.

'Uh-uh no way. I got enough of that last night thank you.'

Jean flopped her tired body into the single settee opposite him. She sensed that Tony was in a playful mood. She knew by his groans of passion the night before, his moans of sweet joy and the way he swiftly fell off to sleep after making love, that he had arisen a tired but well-satisfied young man. His mood reflected this for it resulted in a greater feeling of endearment from him to her, manifesting itself in a playful tone of voice. So she took the bait.

'Thank you very much. I hasten to remind you that you also got just as busy last night,' she responded in game-playing mode.

'Yeah, but you didn't hear any horny moaning from me though.'

Jean threw a cushion at him.

'Now that's not fair, and actually I did, you obviously didn't hear yourself!'

'Not for your groaning though. I mean the noise. Sounded like I was at a blasted football match. I could have sworn that Ian Wright must have just scored.'

She threw another pillow at him.

'You're just insulting. Anyway, you fuck like a madman. I know a wild stallion when I see one.'

'Nah baby, no wild stallion, just a cool and easy rider seen?'

Jean quickly tired of the game. She could never outsmart Tony, mentally he was always too quick and had too much of a silver tongue and it made her want to divert his attention, calm him down a bit more and perhaps whilst still in a pleasant mood get a bit more serious. She wanted to just sit down with him and have a long conversation, about, well anything really. Just as long as they talked seriously.

It had been such a long time since they did this and somehow she felt that time was running out, that somehow if they weren't connecting mentally as they used to before, maybe they never would. Still keeping the vibe though and in a pleasant even manner she put an end to their toying.

'Yeah right Mr Stud man,' she responded dryly. 'You want some breakfast?'

'Wondered when you were going to ask.'

'Bacon and eggs?'

'Nope.'

'Scrambled eggs?'

'Nope.'

'Fried dumplings and plantain? Yes?'

'Cool with me.'

Jean left the room. Tony reflected for a second on how good he felt being with Jean, but he barely had enough time to recompose himself when the telephone rang. Despite his fatigue he rose briskly up out of his chair, moved across the room and picked up the receiver.

'Yo,' he said.

There was no answer.

'Yo!' he snapped.

Again no answer.

'Yo anybody deh deh?' he asked in his typical yardie accent, a move he often adopted when he wanted to appear tough.

There was a short silence before the caller replaced the receiver. Now Tony was baffled, an emotion that quickly turned to anger. What the hell was going on? A caller hanging up the phone on him at his girlfriend's place was a sign of just one thing. He seethed as wicked, almost uncontrollable thoughts ran through his head, but he was able to compose himself in time as Jean re-entered the room.

'Who was on the phone?' she asked.

'Dunno, mystery caller,' he replied shrugging his shoulders sarcastically. 'Whoever it was they just hung up.'

'They hung up? Why, that's strange,' responded a somewhat bemused Jean.

'Well strange, who was it?' The retort appeared distinctly more aggressive than Tony's mood had suggested, it gave Jean a slight start.

'I don't know. They didn't leave a name did they?' was her innocent reply.

'Uh-uh that's not what I mean. You had a phone call last night before we left for the club. You get another call when we come back from the club. Both of them you didn't want to answer in front of me. Now somebody rings, I answer and they hang up.'

Jean stiffened.

'What do you mean?'

Tony made himself even more composed.

'Listen, I just hope that you don't have no undercover lover, toyboy or anything like that you know baby.'

'What the hell are you talking about Tony?'

'You know what I mean, me juss a deal wid reality man is man and woman is woman...'

Jean was fuming. Anger flashed across her face. Here he stood virtually accusing her of infidelity without any apparent justification. She flipped.

'Oh don't try to philosophise, you sound stupid...'

'Me juss a deal wid reality...'

'Well in case you didn't notice darling, the reality is that I happen to be in love with you. I haven't got a clue who was on the end of the phone yesterday, or today. I mean God, I don't see you for days even weeks sometimes, and do you ever hear me complain? Huh? Have you ever heard me complain? For Christ's' sake I could just as easily accuse you of having another lover.'

'You coulda neva!'

'Oh you heartless pig! Don't you ever listen to anything I say to you? I'm trying to tell you that… oh just forget it. Look, just press 1471. Let's get the number then we'll see who my mystery caller is.'

'De plantain dem a bun up.'

'Let them bloody burn. I'm trying to talk to you! Press caller I.D! Don't you want to find out who it is?'

'De plantain dem a bun up.' Tony was now in ignorant mode.

'Well I'll do it then!'

Jean walked over to the phone and picked up the receiver. Eagerly but nervously she pressed 1471, then dropped her head in disappointment upon hearing the reply.

'I'M SORRY THE LAST NUMBER THAT CALLED YOUR LINE WAS WITHHELD'.

'Number withheld,' said Tony knowingly. 'Bitch!' Tony's voice level raised considerably by a few decibels. He darted across the room and grabbed her arm.

'Now you listen the fuck to me!' he shouted, finger pointed firmly in her face. 'Don't mess around pan me or me will do you bad!'

'Don't threaten me!'

'It's not a threat it's a promise!'

Jean tried vainly to tug herself away from his strengthening grip.

'You bastard just get out!'

Tony let go of her arm, took one step across the room to grab his jacket that he had left on the settee from the night before and headed for the door.

'Me juss a go,' he said standing by the exit.

'Well move faster, the sight of you is beginning to make me sick!'

Tony calmed himself down in order to give his next words greater effect.

'Just remember what I said,' he said in a voice that made Jean shiver. 'See you tomorrow.'

In a second he was out of the door slamming it brazenly behind him. Jean, quite astonished at his display, was hardly able to believe what had just happened. She paced solemnly over to the settee, her heart pounding, her breathing unsteady. Gently she sat down, leaned forward and placed her forehead in the palm of her hand as her elbow rested on the arm of the settee. She gazed blankly for a lasting second at the floor. Her thoughts became dazed, more and more unfocused. The tears were inevitable and she was unable to stop them as they began a steady flow.

Soon, she had dug her head deep into the crevice created by the joining of her two arms on the arm of the settee, which soon became saturated with her eye water. Her crying became louder and before long she was hugging the arm of the chair which soon enough became more and more soiled with her tears. The pain in her stomach wrenched her from side to side and her face was awash with the tears that signified her sadness. She was torn, but the gut wrenching agony was almost refreshing, as she let it all out, unable to comprehend or even believe what had just transpired.

She was helpless and no one but Tony at this time could help her. But he was gone, gone to perhaps the only thing that he loved more than her. The street.

Shakela, Sheila and Julie jumped off the bus that stopped just around the corner from where Jean lived. As they made their way down the street, they laughed and joked. Shakela was in a good mood.

'No honestly, it was hilarious,' she said excitedly. 'I swear to God, the man must have been about five foot two and skinny like he ain't eaten for days! She was six plus about 20 stone with breasts like two blasted hot air balloons! He was at the bar now right, enjoying himself right, him and his other sixty-year-old veterans…'

'Oh he wasn't that old?' enquired Sheila, surprised.

'Fifties at least,' argued Shakela. 'Honestly, no less than fifty.'

'So carry on. What happened?' Julie said, eager for the joke.

' He's at the bar now right, orders a rum and black or some shit like that, you know how those old boys like their drink? He's about to knock it back now right, then all of a sudden, tap tap tap on his shoulder right. It's his missus. On the dance floor now she says, and I swear he looks scared as fuck now you know. No, he says, woman can't you see I'm with my buddies. I'm having a drink!'

Shakela placed her hands on her hips for greater effect, imitating the woman.

'She is vex now you can see it on her face. "On the dance floor now, I've had enough of this standing around waiting on you. This is the first time you've taken me out in ages, and what do you do? You completely ignore me, make me sit down, half the blasted night on me own! Get your skinny little backside on that floor with me now!" she says. "Bitch fuck off!" he says.'

'No!' interjected Julie with alarm.

' "Woman fuck off an leave me in peace nuh?" he says. So she grabs him round the neck right? In big big club you know! And this little guy, he's wrestling her but you know, no way is he going to get out of that grip, because she's just too flippin' big, and he's too flippin' small!'

'So what happened?' cried Sheila through her chuckles.

'She's got him on the dancefloor now right, everybody's shocked. And I swear, me and the girls were having a fit, it's just so funny. She holds him. You know trying to hug him and you know, smooch. He's trying to get away, but she's just too flippin' strong for him. She's dancing with him and he's struggling trying to get away so she holds the back of his head and pushes his face down her cleavage. Meanwhile, she's holding him with the other arm. She's just looking at the ceiling whining up her self on him and him, honestly, all you can see is arms and legs struggling for dear life it was hilarious and she's paying him no mind at all. I'm telling you, girlfriend just wanted her dance.'

'Then what happened?' enquired Julie further.

'I noticed him just go limp. I swear he just stopped struggling. After a while she was holding a limp body and she didn't even notice. It was only when then the record finished now, she realised. He wasn't moving. When she let him go , he just dropped to the floor.'

'What!?' bellowed Julie in sheer amazement.

'The guy was out cold!'

'Was he dead?

'Heart attack.'

'Oh my God.'

'The living heart attack. Ambulance had to come for him everything.'

'How was she?'

'Julie, she was parrow, crying everything. You should have heard her. Me tek me two big bress dem an' strangulate me man. She was crying man. Some heavy tears. I hope he's alright though,'

Sheila kissed her teeth. 'Serves him right if you ask me,' she said. 'You know how these man dem stay. Want to keep the missus in doors while they're gallivant chasing skirt. Good for her if you ask me.'

'Yeah but you've got to feel some kind of sympathy for him,' argued Julie.

'Yeah, some I suppose. But not much.'

'I ain't even getting into no argument. That was just the best joke I've had all week,' concluded Shakela. 'Here we are anyway,' she said opening the door to the large building that housed Jean's flat. As the women climbed the stairs they looked forward to a good day out. Shakela knocked on the door once, twice, three times. The knocks on the front door became louder and noticeably quicker as Shakela began to get more and more agitated. The feeling had spread and became shared by the other girls Sheila and Julie who were also were unable to comprehend why Jean either wasn't opening the door or why she had gone out without letting them know.

It was about 2.30 in the afternoon, Jean had abandoned breakfast, had not bothered to get changed and had fallen asleep on the settee. The first knock had woken her and she knew very well who it was at the door but somehow just didn't feel like facing anyone today. However, Shakela's typically incessant shouts of her name through the letterbox became too much for her to bear and she reluctantly and rather sluggishly rose up out of the settee to greet her three friends. The trio of ladies stepped in cautiously, aware that there was something amis. Sheila's immediate reaction was one of concern.

The emotion was etched all over her face as she tried to decipher just what if anything was wrong with her closest friend. Julie was a little concerned too, but not overly. In fact she already had an idea as to what the problem was. So she aimed just a quick glance at Jean, the sort of glance that checked to make sure that the problem wasn't any more serious than she had figured it out to be. Once satisfied that it wasn't she found herself a comfortable space on the settee with a magazine that she wasn't going to read, but just look through whilst keeping her ears open during the inevitable ensuing conversation. In due time it was Shakela that broke the silence. Her brash and often impatient streak would often get the better of her, giving her the appearance of someone without emotion, without feelings or without concern, diplomacy or sensitivity. She too had an idea as to what the problem was but she was hardly fazed by it. She had worked through her feelings regarding Jean and Tony and she had little sympathy for her in times like this.

'Jean,' she said half-lost and half-angry. 'You're not dressed! Aren't you coming shopping?'

'No,' Jean replied. 'I'm staying in.'

Julie interjected.

'But you were going to buy something for the party tonight. Aren't you coming anymore?' she queried.

'No. I just don't feel like it.'

Sheila and Jean had been through a lot together. They grew up with each other. They went to the same schools and colleges. Ambitions had sent them on different courses in life.

Jean, the more business and career minded of the two, made her way into the private sector securing herself a senior managerial position with a large chain store. Sheila became a vegetarian, grew dreadlocks, would visit WOMAD, Glastonbury and Reading Rock Festival every year, hung with the hippies, dated white men and listened to indie and other forms of alternative music. She only worked if she had to and would often do, whenever she needed to finance a trip abroad. She was a thin wiry woman in her late twenties.

She wore sandals and sarongs in the summer and heavy knitted cardigans and fleeces with jeans in the winter. She was a good time girl with a feminist philosophy that would fall somewhat short of radicalism whenever she was dating.

Red, gold and green beads hung from one of her dreads. Along with those dreads, they symbolised her connection with her roots, for although she dated white men, she had no problem with Black albeit they would have to be cultured and refined. Which was why she had a problem with Tony.

Cultured and refined he wasn't. He was no good for her best friend. Sheila loved Jean: at one time she'd wondered whether it was more than friendship, and if her affection could even be interpreted as lesbianism. But no, Jean was her best friend and she cared for her. If anyone knew what Jean was about, she did. She wasn't afraid to acknowledge the situation and certainly would not shy from confronting the matter so, as it was, her first question hit right on the nose.

'OK Jean,' she said, arms folded. 'What's he done?'

There was a nervous silence as the realisation sank in that Tony was about to destroy not only their plans for the day but for the whole evening. All of their fears were confirmed. Almost simultaneously Julie and Shakela half rolled their eyes to the ceiling. Shakela clasped her hands, sighed and looked towards the heavens or at least took another look at the ceiling before making herself comfortable by finding a seat. Sheila's instinct was to offer her comfort.

Jean was her friend and it cut her to the bone to know that she was distressed. She was even the more agitated to know that Tony, once again, was the source of her distress. This just wasn't a union made in heaven, at least not in her eyes and by God she would tell her so whenever the chance arose, not in a cruel or malicious way but as logically and sensibly as she knew how. It wasn't out of hatred or dislike for Tony, it was just the fact that her closest friend was so hopelessly in love. A love that made her blind and rendered her completely blind to the pitfalls that were before her. Pitfalls created purely and simply by the fact that she loved a man who, even if he honestly loved her, had great difficulty in showing it. Jean was often left in this condition and she, more often than anyone else, would be left to pick up the pieces.

Sheila wanted to comfort her just like she had done so many times in the past, but not until she knew exactly what had happened, so she took a seat too, preparing herself to demand answers.

'Jean!' she ordered.

Jean was startled. She was hardly used to Sheila speaking to her in such an aggressive manner. It made her jump slightly and immediately initiate a reply.

'He was just being a bastard that's all,' she said calmly, desperately trying to shrug the matter off.

'Did he hit you?'

'No Sheila, he wouldn't do that.'

'Don't be so sure, I wouldn't put a single thing past him.'

Julie had finished flicking through her magazine. She was hardly interested in Jean's problem. After all, she'd been here too many times before and frankly she was getting fed up of it. This particular scenario was becoming too much of a regular occurrence. She prided herself, being born under the star sign of Aries, with an innate ability to reason things out logically and to be emotionally detatched if ever she needed to. This was one such time.

This situation, especially of late, for her, had only one logical conclusion and why Jean was unable to make the decision to ditch the pretentious little so-and-so that dared to call himself a man was beyond her. Julie knew though, that she might not be beyond reproach in her judgement. She didn't want to condemn Jean too much because as a woman she sympathised completely with the fact that here was a woman who was in love and that being in love was very difficult, especially with a rat like Tony. So she rather aggressively flicked the pages of the magazine back to the beginning, pledging herself not to speak in any way that would offend their host. Shakela though, hardly felt the same way. This for her, was the perfect opportunity to convey to Jean just exactly what she thought of the situation. More perhaps, her disgust in Jean that she would even allow herself to become so upset over a man. Also, that in the immediate, she would have the possibility of a pleasant and enjoyable Saturday afternoon ruined because she would rather sit and sulk over him. Over what she considered was a hopeless case. A case of love walking down a one way street.

She got out of her chair and walked menacingly over to where Jean stood.

'How many times have I told you Jean? That guy's just a bag of sh... '

Jean saw it coming and cut her off immediately. She wasn't going to have that sort of thing said about Tony, at least not from Shakela. She was upset, but there was no way that she was ever going to have this young Miss Thing dictate to her or even try to advise her on what she ought to do with any aspect of her life.

'Shakela, please, just leave it out,' she interjected cooly.

Shakela though, was adamant.

'I'm telling you Jean, one day that guy is just gonna beat the crap out of you. You need to get his sorry, down-trodden, black backside out of your life for good! Count your losses girl. OK, I wish I had the money, but forget the sixty grand motor you bought him and get out intact man! Shit! He's just no fuckin' good!'

No matter how much Sheila agreed with Shakela, her first allegiance was to her best friend. She immediately realised that the situation was getting out of hand and that Shakela, if anyone, was the more direct and insensitive person in the room. She had noticed Jean try to fight back but concluded that in her state she wouldn't win and that if she didn't do something about it, Shakela would only upset her more. She had definitely been out of order, no matter how much she spoke the truth, and right now Jean didn't have the strength for a slanging match. So she quickly jumped to her defence.

'Shakela, you heard what she said, leave it out OK?' she said in a commanding tone of voice.

She walked over to Jean and put her arm around her. Shakela wanted to persist but one look from Sheila was enough to let her know that she needed to cool off. She went back to her seat mumbling under her breath. She was angry now. They were good mates, but there were times when Sheila really aggravated her and this was a case in point. There should be no reason just because she was her best friend, for her to be shielding Jean from the truth. She reasoned that it was unethical, rather typical and ever so slightly pathetic.

'You all right babes?' asked Sheila warmly of Jean.

'I'm fine. I guess I'm a bit shook up but I'll be OK.' was her reply.

Julie tossed her magazine to the other side of the settee as if she been given a sign.

'Good. Now that's all over,' she said, 'are we going shopping or not?'

Sheila turned to Jean.

'How about it kid?' she asked.

'Oh, I really don't know if I feel like it you know.'

'Oh come on Jean,' cut in Julie. 'Come, come out with us man, we're your friends. The last thing you want to be doing is to drown yourself in misery.'

'That's right,' agreed Shakela. 'Plenty more fish in the sea you know.'

Julie muttered something under her breath which bought a giggle from Shakela before they slapped palms in a rather feminine hi-five. Sheila ignored it because she knew that it was derogatory towards Tony and that Jean may not approve, so she simply held her shoulder ever the more tightly.

'Jean?' she asked. 'What you saying?'

There was a momentary silence.

'OK,' Jean said finally. 'I'm sorry. I'll just go and get ready.'

'Atta girl!' replied Sheila.

As Jean left the room the mood instantly became less tense. Sheila grabbed the remote control for the television and tossed it expertly into Shakela's lap.

'See what's on T.V.,' she said.

Shakela threw her an evil glance that made Julie laugh. Sheila proceeded to look throughout the T.V. guide.

'Nothing on, just sport.' Shakela reported after quickly scanning the T.V. channels to see what was on offer.

'Wait,' Sheila interrupted, 'Cable are showing repeats of Buddies.'

'Quick get it on!' squealed an exited Julie. 'I used to love this show. American sitcoms are so much better than British ones.'

Shakela reluctantly flicked the remote and there was one of the lead characters playing away in his inimitable fashion.

'Seen this one,' Shakela said.

'Yeah? Well just keep it to yourself OK?' Ordered Julie.

'Shelly's gonna walk in and catch them… now!' said Shakela, who was right on cue as Shelly had walked in on her two-timing lover.

'Look if you don't want to watch it find something to do!' ordered Sheila.

'OK, ' challenged Shakela. 'I'll watch sport. Sports channel's showing basketball.'

'Don't you dare touch that remote!' commanded Julie.

'Well for Christ's sake!' snapped Shakela. 'All right,' she said. 'I'll make a phone call.'

'Just keep it down OK!' warned Sheila.

Shakela picked up the telephone that was sat next to her, and walked to the furthest part of the room that the telephone cord would allow. She dialled, waited, then spoke.

'Is Badman there?... Put him on please... It's Shakela... hi baby, hear you got problems... coming out tonight?... Party... I'll call you later then we can make arrangements... OK then... love you baby... later.'

Clearly pleased with herself, Shakela replaced the phone and resumed her seat. Julie and Sheila had exchanged knowing glances to each other throughout Shakela's brief but revealing conversation. She certainly had not spoken to her boyfriend. This wasn't odd, more rather typical of Shakela, whom they knew to be just a little too much on the wild side.

It was Julie that spoke first. From her point of view, rather more interested in hearing a piece of gossip than anything else. She certainly wasn't interested in offering her any advice, just like with Jean and Tony, they had long since tried that and failed.

'Who, were you talking to?' she enquired.

'Someone,' was Shakela's arrogant reply.

'Making arrangements with another guy?' asked Sheila. 'What's Mr Pum Pum going to say?'

'Believe me, Pum Pum 's safe. He does his thing, I do mine,' said Shakela confidently.

'Sounds like a nice arrangement, I'll just ring him and tell him that you're here making arrangements with some other guy. What's his number again?' retorted Julie just as confidently.

'Don't even go there miss goody two shoes!' warned Shakela.

'Just you be careful.,' cautioned Sheila.

'Yes, mummy,' replied Shakela, mimicking a child.

That was the last of the conversation until Jean reappeared.

On seeing her, the ladies flew out of their seats in a hail of excitement.

'Shoes and a new handbag,' proclaimed Shakela.

'Frock and hat,' announced Julie and then both together they shouted; 'It's gonna be good today!' before jumping up with hands meeting each other some eight feet off the ground in another triumphant hi-five.

Shakela and Julie bolted for the door. Sheila eagerly slung her bag around her shoulder and followed them, but Jean beckoned her back.

'The two of you carry on.' She said. 'We'll catch you up.'

'Don't be too long!' Ordered Shakela.

Sheila waited for them to go before she approached Jean. She became quite concerned when she beheld the intense and thoughtful expression on her friend's face. She had never seen her like this before and knew that something big was going to happen. It was, for Jean, one of the most crucial moments in her whole life and didn't her expression show it. Sheila held her breath, rubbed her fingers, then breathed softly as she nervously meandered around the furniture over to where Jean stood.

She knew that Jean was going to confide in her. She tried to kid herself that it was nothing serious, but she knew in her heart that it would be – and the knowledge scared her. This thought died quickly though. Her very feelings and the love for her best friend propelled her all too easily into a space that made Jean feel even more comfortable and safe. She cast a needy glance at Sheila before she spoke. But Sheila was the quicker. Maybe it was her curiosity, maybe it was her concern or maybe she just wanted to get the matter dealt with as easily and as quickly as possible. But she spoke softly.

'What's up?' she asked cautiously.

'Sheila, I think Tony's seeing someone else,' struck Jean.

'How do you know?' came Sheila's concerned reply.

'I don't. I just have a feeling. For all his bad ways he's never treated me the way he treated me this morning. I mean, he got well shirty and didn't even care about what he was saying.'

'Yes, but that doesn't mean he's seeing someone. I mean, what about this drugs thing? People have been saying…'

'Oh come on Sheila, woman's intuition. It's not a drugs' thing. You know what men get like when they begin to lose interest.

Anyway, he virtually accused me of seeing someone behind his back, you know what they say…'

'…He accuses you because he's either doing it himself or thinking about doing it,' replied Sheila nodding her head.

'Exactly.'

'Well anyway… Jean look. Why don't you just let it ride? You'll find out soon enough, a phone number in his pocket maybe. Perhaps he might want to talk to you about it, when he's ready and mature enough to.'

'I might wait forever for that to happen.'

'Gossip then. You know how news spreads like wildfire around here.'

'Yes but I just don't feel that I can wait that long.'

'Well what else can you do? Why don't you ask him then?'

'Sheila it's just not that easy… look…'

Jean paused tentatively. Sheila felt the air fill with expectation. She knew from the slight depression in Jean's voice, her flickering eyelids almost fighting back tears and the pained expression on her face that she was about to be hit with another bombshell, a bombshell that didn't take long in coming.

'I'm pregnant,' announced Jean beneath a thick gust of outgoing breath.

Sheila recoiled in horror. For once she was dumbstruck. Her mouth gaped wide open as did her eyes as she surveyed the sorry sight helplessly standing with her head in her hand before her. She barely found her next words.

'Have you told him?' she asked.

'No,' replied Jean, who by now was in tears.' I have to do a test first. Sheila I just don't know what to do, I'm having his baby'.

Sheila moved towards Jean, gently put her arms around her and softly laid Jean's head on her shoulder.

'Baby, don't worry,' she said reassuringly. 'It'll be all right, believe me it'll be all right.'

Sheila held on to Jean tightly stroking the back of her head as she did so and as the heaving started and the tears rained, she rocked her gently.

five

'Fuck me! Fuck me! Oh baby, fuck me! That's it right there, hmmm that's it, now, harder baby harder! Oh yes that's good! Ooooh baby ooohh. I love feeling your dick inside me! Ride me baby ride me!'

The atmosphere was electric as Luck worked his rock hard nature into the young girl Nicole, who by now was ecstatic. He had met her the night before at the swanky Desdemona's wine bar in the town centre. They had fucked the night before, slept until the late morning, woke up and were at it again. He worked her expertly and with grit. He had figured that she liked it rough and that's how he gave it to her. She was no novice either, she bubbled under him sweetly and with exquisite rhythm. She knew exactly how to use her waist, working it so that her pussy got the best out of the stiff prick that Luck was giving to her. She talked through it too and that's what Luck liked about her.

She had no inhibitions, hardly afraid to let her most sensitive feelings show. As he pumped away at her, she grabbed both her naked breasts in her hands. They were quite large and soft and quivered like mounds of jelly as her whole body rocked to the elastic motion of their intercourse. She squeezed them together, trying to shove her nipples to his mouth, but although she was large, he was taller than she was so it gave her difficulty. Luck however caught on to what she wanted, so by the time she pleaded:

'Suck me baby! Suck me while you fuck me!'

He had already grabbed them from her, bowed his head to meet them and was sucking her nipples for dear life. But Luck had another trick up his sleeve. He could only do it with well-endowed girls like Nicole here and he knew that it would drive her wild. He pulled both of her breasts together so that her nipples met at one point and expertly placed them both in his mouth at the same time. Nicole bellowed.

'Ohhhh yeeesss! Yes! Oohh that feels so good.'

Luck said nothing. His only feelings were given away by the frenzied slurping of her nipples as he banged away harder against her pussy to increase her elation.

It was like a mad feast, the combined noises of Lucks' slurping and the splashing noises of his dick working away at her saturated vagina. Her moans and groans made Tony stop at the door and listen outside before knocking. Luck had a studio flat, his whole place was just one open space but for the bathroom and toilet. So it was easy to hear the noises that came from his futon which was placed against the wall, opposite from the door. Nicole was in raptures, but despite that, she placed both her hands against Luck's chest and gently eased him from off of her.

'Let me sit on you,' she said commandingly.

Luck made no objection, but laid down on his back whilst she mounted his soaking erection. She slanted towards him so that her breasts were able to fall on his face.

'Keep doing that shit baby, I love it,' she said to him.

Again Luck held her floppy breasts and squeezing them together joined her nipples once again before raising his head slightly to meet them. As she fucked him she grabbed all four pillows that were on the bed, placed them on top of each other and propped Luck's head up so that he would have no difficulty inclining his head to deal with her nipples. She worked her lower body section well, twisting, turning, sliding, pushing and bouncing with splendid rhythm so that every crevice of her pussy could feel him inside her. Steadily her motion began to increase, she became more frantic and out of control. Luck held on for dear life, he knew that she was coming. Nicole was a well shaped girl, but she was heavy and as she bobbed up and down on top off him, and increasingly, ever the more frenetically, he had to breath heavily.

'Oh fuck! Yes, baby yes!' she bellowed. 'Fuck me! Fuck me! I'm coming soon!' Luck didn't have to do anything, he could have stayed still and she would have reached Nirvana all by herself the way she rode him. She placed her hands on his chest for greater manoeuvrability. He let go of her breasts and placed his hands on her broad butt cheeks and rubbed them violently up and down as they bounced up and down on top of him, her tits slapping him unceremoniously in the face with each motion.

'Oh yes! Yes!' Nicole screamed. 'Oh shit! Ohhh!'

Her motion was now intoxicated. She had lost all sense of rhythm and simply bashing her drenched pussy as violently as possible against him.

'Oh yes! Stay there baby! Stay right there, I'm going to splash soon, I know it!' she bellowed.

It was an unfortunate time for Tony to knock, but he did, he was fed up of waiting for them to finish. Nicole ignored it and assumed that Luck would also, but when she saw him slightly raise up and look towards the door she pressed her hands more firmly against his chest to hold him down .

'No! Don't you fuckin' well dare! Not now!' she ordered as she rode him even more recklessly.

Luck had lost interest in the fuck, even more so when Tony bellowed at him.

'Luck, open the fuckin' door man, it's me.'

Nicole was worried.

'Don't you fucking well dare answer that fuckin' door! Fuck him whoever it is!'

Luck paid her no mind. He stopped fucking, wondering why it was taking her so long to orgasm, so that he could get his business sorted. Tony shouted once again and so did Nicole.

'Don't move baby I'm getting mine! Oh I'm coming, I'm coming, I'm…' she didn't finish, for in seconds she was off him and off the futon that they were fucking on, and was sprawled over the tiled wooden floor. Luck had thrown her off him and had made to his way to his dressing-gown shouting;

'Soon come man, soon come.'

'Oh you fuckin' bastard!' fumed Nicole, 'I don't believe this! I just don't believe this fuckin' shit!'

She was annoyed, but quickly had to readjust her mindset as Luck raced to the door not paying her any more mind.

'Don't open the door! I haven't got any… shit!' she said as she dived back onto the bed for cover. Just in time as Luck pulled the door to reveal Tony's tall frame. Nicole was seething. She sat up in the bed and quickly dragged the duvet over her to cover her bare chest. Luck stood there dumb. His mind was in a daze from the fucking and the wild panic that ensued once Tony had knocked the door. He feebly extended his arm to allow Tony in. He wanted to offer him a coffee or something but the sight of the seductive looking Nicole sitting up in his bed looking daggers in his direction threw him.

'Want some pussy?' was all his fragmented and tired brain could muster.

Nicole aimed a pillow in his direction.

'Fuck you, you pig!' she spurted at him with poison.

'Looks like you fucked her out, or did I hear her fucking you out?' Tony inquired sarcastically.

Nicole dropped her daggers and aimed them at Tony before dropping herself back onto the bed pulling the duvet over her head.

'I really don't believe this shit,' she muttered to herself.

Tony turned to Luck.

'Where can we talk?' he queried lowering his voice.

'Kitchen.' Luck beckoned with his thumb before striding over to the enclosed kitchen area on the other side of the room.

Once inside the kitchen the two men spoke almost in a whisper.

'You see Pum Pum last night?' questioned Tony.

'Yeah.'

'What's he saying?'

'He gave me a grand.'

'What!?'

'Said that was all he had.'

'I really don't understand that fuckin' guy. So we're definitely short?'

'Yeah, I'm gonna make some moves today see what I can come up with but, yep, we're two grand short.'

'Shit. I knew that old bastard would fuck things up. How well do you know this Baron dude?'

'We need at least two grand, it's all or nothing with him.'

' OK let's see what we can raise by this evening. You gonna be at Reggie's place later?'

'Yeah, 'bout five.'

'Cool.'

'Erm, Tony I've been thinking.'

'About what?'

'We using your car?'

'Yep.'

'Well we need plates.'

'What you talking about?'

'Number plates, in case Babylon get suspicious.'

'Luck. What are you talking about?'

'Look man, that motor of yours causes a fuss every where you go. I don't want Babylon getting interested in us.'

'But if they stop us…'

'Think about it man, we can't afford no stop and search, specially if we got either grands or shit in the car. I ain't looking to get stopped, if that's what they want they'll have to chase us, but if they follow us and want to check the licence plate…'

Tony caught on.

'Good idea, can you sort it out?'

'Yeah, Chicken gonna mark some up today for me.'

'Cool, well listen I'm going down by Reggie, I'm gonna see you later.'

'OK.'

As Tony made his way to the front door he passed Nicole who was covered up in the bed masturbating.

'Looks like you got yourself a horny bitch,' he exclaimed.

'She can be as horny as she wanna be,' said Luck nonchalantly. 'She got to get the fuck out now 'cos I got runnings to sort out.'

'Listen,' said Tony stepping out of the door. 'I'll see you later. Later bitch!'

'Fuck off!' called Nicole from under the duvet cover.

The minute that Luck closed the door behind him Nicole uncovered her head from beneath the duvet and looked at him.

'Come on baby, let's finish what we started,' she said seductively.

'Shut up bitch!' said Luck, moving back to the kitchen.

He noticed Nicole's groan of disgust before filling the electric kettle with hot water and switching it on. Nicole was hot stuff he thought to himself, but his perfect woman she definitely was not. She fucked him well, but too easily. He hadn't gotten to know her personality, he figured that she probably didn't have one. That all she was interested in was fucking. He concluded that she was probably the sort of girl that would happily make a career out of posing for dirty magazines or acting in porno flicks if she ever got the break. She simply had no inhibition and probably no ambition judging by the way she was so keen to fuck him last night. She might be good for a booty call every now and then he reasoned, but then again, maybe not, as thoughts of another woman began steadily to occupy his mind.

The town centre was absolutely jam-packed on this particular Saturday afternoon. The shopping mall that the girls were in was slightly different in design to most that are found in town centres. The owners had employed a post-modern artist to design it and therefore it reeked of class. It was the smallest of two shopping malls and it was here that the girls liked to shop in the most. The other mall had all the ordinary high street shops, whilst this one was pure designer.

The four girls tried desperately to keep themselves together as they strolled through with bags of shopping in tow. Jean had completely forgotten the events of that morning and was having a great time laughing and sharing jokes with her friends, whilst at the same time fending off looks from admirers as they walked past. They had come from mainly white guys who frequented the designer mall. Guys who, upon seeing her coming would have a sad, puppy dog 'I love you' etched on their faces. They would seek to entice her with affectionate looks, but she would simply avert her eyes from them and continue her conversation with her friends. The attention was good for her. It boosted her ego and made for a pleasant feeling in her soul. A nice detachment from her present worries.

Every now and then Shakela would stop and chat to someone she hadn't seen in a while and they would either have to wait around for her or tell her to meet them in some shop. She was chatty like that. It seemed that she knew everyone in the town or at least that everyone she knew was in town on that particular day. So involved did she become in her conversations, that even whilst talking to Julie on one occasion she hadn't realised that they were going up an escalator and she was actually on the one going down. This bought a chuckle from the other three. But Shakela, undeterred, simply carried on her conversation by running up the escalator in order to keep contact with Julie so as not lose the thread of what she was saying, oblivious to the fact that she was pushing people out of the way in order to do so. She became the brunt of a few cruel jokes when after announcing that she was desperate for a pee and disappearing to the toilet, it had been nearly twenty minutes till she returned. 'Something I ate' was her excuse which ignited the piss-taking. It was Sheila's comment; 'You just can't get fresh dick nowadays,' however, that upset Shakela, driving another wedge between their already fragile relationship. Shakela swore to herself that before the day was done she would have retribution.

Julie was in her element. She had gone through nearly three hundred pounds and was about to spend more. She had a good job as a stock-broker and it paid well. She would advise prospective investors on where best to put their money and whenever she felt most confident about the information she was giving, would invest some of her own money with those companies too. Other people in her office would do the buying and selling bit and whenever they advised her, she would instruct then to buy and sell on her behalf. Her pay packet would be well boosted at the end of each quarter so she could easily spend the sort of money she was spending without it hurting her bank balance too much.

She was the second youngest of the foursome next to Shakela. They both would click together more, the obvious generational closeness between them being the reason. But she was different from Shakela. She wasn't an excitable person but was always calm. She was often silent. The sort of person that would think about what she was saying before she said it, so that everything she said meant something. She had a powerful aura. Her mother had trained her that way. She had never wanted for anything as a child, but her mother made her aware from an early age about life, the world and the bullshit therein. So she approached life with caution, steadiness, wisdom and poise. Unlike Sheila who always talked about reaching a Karmic mental state, she had actually achieved one. She was pretty too and she purposely kept herself that way. She had learnt the art of applying the perfect makeup, a skill that she learnt from a part-time health and beauty college course and looked immaculate every time. She had money to spend, so she spent it on her always-immaculate hair and nails. She wore Chanel no 5, Poison and Opium. Her underwear was La-Purla and whilst most of her friends shopped in places like Dorothy Perkins, Wallis and Etam, she wore names like Nicole Farhi, Ghost and Armani. She would often have to lend money to Shakela, who would, if she were buying clothes, spend it in Mark One. As she glided through the mall, she cast frequent glances at Jean. Seeing Jean smile, she would feel reassured that she was OK.

As well as the funny moments in the town, there had been hair raising ones too. Jean had bought some sexy underwear, but decided later that she wanted to change it in favour of some skimpier ones that she had previously noticed in another shop. After much deliberation and encouragement from Shakela they decided to go back to the shop, but an argument erupted with the assistant who refused to replace the item, on account of the fact that Jean could not find the receipt. A few choice words from Shakela and the eventual intervention of the shop manager, though, was enough to bring success to their venture. Jean eventually walked out of the store feeling satisfied that she had finally managed to purchase the item that she wanted. The girls too, were pleased with their work, leaving themselves to reflect on how rude and feisty the shop assistant was.

Evening broke and the town centre began to clear. A heavy day's shopping for the girls was at an end. Lottery tickets had been purchased. The girls figured that they needed rewarding for such a long afternoon's work and before long they had taken their places in a long queue at McDonalds, pondering which items of junk food they would purchase for themselves. Once served, they found themselves a table and began to tuck in, reflecting on the day's occurrences and looking forward to the party that they were going to go to later on. Shakela remembered the 'fresh dick' comment and picked her moment to mount her attack on Sheila.

'Think you'll find a man this time Sheila?' she asked. A question that she knew would go straight to the heart.

'What a question to ask!' commented Jean

'I'm sorry but that's just feisty,' jumped in Julie.

'She can answer it. She's a big woman,' returned Shakela. 'It was a perfectly ordinary question if you ask me.'

'Bloody cruel if you ask me,' said Julie.

'Whose side you on?' returned Shakela.

'The side of truth and justice,' giggled Julie, a comment that bought a slight giggle from at least three of the girls. Sheila though was stony faced.

'Let me say this OK?' she opened. 'I choose my men with sound and careful judgement. At least I don't go for every bloody thing in trousers. I do, after all, have at least one ounce of self respect.'

Shakela stopped eating and the other three girls, sensing the obvious insult, went silent and nervously awaited her response.

'So what are you calling me? A slag?' she asked accusatorily. Her manner now somewhat more serious.

'That wouldn't be the word that I would use.'

'But that's what you mean.'

'Listen I'm only responding to your question OK?'

'No you aren't! Are you calling me a slag?'

'Well if that's what they call a woman who opens up for every Tom, Dick and Harry then yes, I am.'

'Tom Dick and Sally in your case.'

The issue was now beyond repair, there was some damage limitation to be done, and quickly, before a full scale argument, or worse broke out. Jean intervened, reminding them that they were supposed to be friends and that they ought not to let silly throwaway comments upset each other. Julie weighed in on the side of truth and justice with a few choice words of wisdom, which managed to do the trick and diffuse the situation. But it was not over.

Both Shakela and Sheila used the following few minutes of silence as they ate, to reflect on what it was they disliked about the other's personality. For Sheila, Shakela was the young trouble maker who didn't know her place and didn't have an ounce of moral decency in her. She disliked that and was always, it seemed, having to react or respond to her often insulting behaviour. She was an ignoramus. A young sprightly thing that was living life too fast. A young girl, who was misguided enough to feel that she knew everything that there was to know about life. From her perspective she was the centre of the universe and no matter how warped her limited view was, to her, it was always right. Sheila pitied her, longed to see her in a decent job or going to college, anything that would bring a shred of objectivity into her cloudy and messed up brain. Her complete love for materialism, particularly the materialist aspirations that the youth hip hop/ragga culture placed before her had clouded her judgement and in many respects she considered Shakela a lost soul.

Sheila, Shakela thought, was probably a dyke. All that political correctness and pseudo-spirituality had no place in her world. She was too dictatorial, too judgmental and too pompous. She was the oldest of the four but she didn't have to always remind them of it with her attitude. Why didn't she have a man? Simple: because no decent, self respecting guy would want her. She probably didn't know how to treat a man. After all, guys wanted to smoke, drink, talk shit and eat proper food, not those crazy organic vegetarian concoctions that tofu-girl was forever knocking up. No, she was a world apart and Shakela wondered how the hell she had ever made her way into such a trendy crew of girls as this. It was obvious that it was only Jean's misguided allegiance to her one time school and college buddy. Sheila hung on to Jean because she was beautiful, trendy and with it. She was certainly financially secure and very independent apart from her emotional dependence on you know who. She was, at least externally, an all true woman, a nineties woman at that. Sheila, she figured, was nothing but a wannabe, a confused wannabe who worshipped Jean and wanted to be like her, and Jean, she figured, pitied her because she was going nowhere.

She kissed her teeth and continued to munch silently on her Chicken McNuggets.

While they were sitting down, David Adams stood motionless outside with his friend Speedo watching them intently.

'That's the one, the pretty one with the extensions and yellow blouse.'

'Nice. Fit too,' replied Speedo.

'Used to love that girl.'

'Really? Good fuck then eh?'

'Hmm. You know, I can honestly say that she is the only woman I have ever truly loved.'

'So what happened? Didn't dick her hard enough?'

'Things just didn't work out.'

'Sounds like you still looking to dig out that pussy though.'

'Wasn't just about that Speedo. You'll never understand.'

'Ain't nothing to understand but good pussy. You gonna talk to her then?'

'Nah, gotta bide my time, heard she's dealing with a gangster, but that might be over soon.'

'Gotta be careful boy, fucker will shoot you the fuck up if he finds out you looking to fuck his missus.'

'Nah I ain't looking to get shot, but I do want my lady back, she meant the world to me.'

'Must have been some good punanny boy! Just be careful man, that's all I got to tell you.'

'Don't worry boy, I'll be OK.'

David dropped the cigarette that he had been toking on. With a swish of his right leg it was quashed, dead on the ground.

'Come on yah,' admonished Speedo. 'Let we go sight up the pussy man. Nuff a dem bout here today.'

In an instant the two men were off. David threw a backward glance at Jean, who looked gorgeous as she laughed enjoying the moment with her friends.

'I'm coming back for you baby, trust me,' he said to himself before disappearing into the crowded mall.

The day passed off without further incident between the girls, except when Shakela opted to take the bus home rather than to ride back in Jean's car, the way that they had all come. Perhaps she was making some kind of statement, perhaps she had had enough of their company. It didn't matter to Sheila who was only too pleased to have Shakela out of her sight. Tonight they would enjoy the party, the issue would rest – at least for now. For Jean, the day had served her well. It had helped her to forget her problems.

She decided not to call Tony for the rest of the day, Lord knows how much she wanted to. But she was glad to know that in times of strife and worry such as this, her three closest friends would not hesitate to rally around and support her. It made her feel comfortable and joyous inside. So much so, that as they walked back to the car, she slung her arms around both Sheila's and Julie's shoulders, kissed them and thanked them for a wonderful day.

six

'**Pose, Pum Pum,**' ordered Tony as he picked up his dominoes.

'Ok. Here I come boy!' responded his ageing adversary slapping down his first domino on the table.

'Good shot follow this!' responded Tony slapping down his next domino with equal zeal.

'Go again!' replied Pum Pum knocking the table with a domino signifying his intention to pass.

'You got a shit hand there boy! I know you in trouble already, so follow this if you bad.'

'Bad? Is I mek the rasshole word boy, play!'

'Can't play!' replied Tony.

'Double deuce, follow that!'

Tony knocked the table. He couldn't play for the second time.

'Shoot,' he said reluctantly.

Pum Pum played again. Tony followed.

'Time for your beatin' boy!' gloated Pum Pum, dropping another domino.

'Fuck you. I ain't dead yet,' replied Tony as he played his hand.

'Follow this nuh?' came back Pum Pum with another hand.

'Can't play,' Tony said resignedly as he knocked the table again.

Reggie's shabean was busy. It was usually like this on a Saturday afternoon. Punters spilled in either from the bookies or straight from home. There were two games of pool on the go and small groups had gathered in various parts of the room, discussing virtually everything from the latest performance of the West Indian cricket team to horses, money, the most recent sound clash or women. The bar was busy as a mixture of roots and Jungle music issued from the stereo system underneath the counter. In the furthest corners of the main room, a couple of small time drugs deals were going down. A couple of dreadlocked white guys had wandered in and got into an unexpected argument with a young and feisty drug dealer who saw them coming.

A girl posse had made their way into the shabean. They were quite young and as a result didn't garner a great deal of attention from most of the men, even though they had obviously tried to attract some by dressing up as if it was Saturday night and they were going out. They kept themselves to themselves, talking mainly about how good looking Busta Rhymes was and how bad his latest tune was. Every now and then, they would each scan the room to see how much attention they had got. But heads were busy, too busy to pay them any mind. Intergalactic sounds cold be heard as punters desperately tried to crack the 'Alien Invaders' or kill the 'Mars Destroyers'. Countless games of dominoes were on the go and the cursing and slapping down of dominoes onto the well used pieces of hardboard that covered the individual tables were, apart from the music, the loudest noise in the room. Tony was about to lose his game of dominoes with Pum Pum and for him, it wasn't good, especially not with £150 on the table for the winner. Tony's worst nightmare was realised as Pum Pum stood up, raised his last domino and wildly recited another poem.

'I sit for days with my little black bricks,' he danced as he recited.

'Watching all sorts of people get up to all sorts of tricks.

'Winning is easy, but losing is hard,

'But that's your fuckin' problem 'cos I got …' then smashed his domino on the table shouting *'…key card!!'* in his distinct Barbadian accent. Tony was not pleased. He hated losing at the best of times, especially so much money on the table and he hated losing to Pum Pum most of all. He hadn't known him for very long, but had quickly grown to despise him, hating his arrogance. An old-style pimp who had been around for a long time, Pum Pum, by his late forties, had seen a lot of street action. His knowledge of the hustling game was second to none. Secretly, Tony felt like a novice next to him and what soured their relationship even more was the fact that Pum Pum would take every opportunity to remind him just how much of a novice he was.

Pum Pum shared the same opinion of Tony. He disliked him immensely. He considered him a pretender, a squirrel after a nut without a clue of how to get it. He didn't think that Tony was a smart guy, but one who thought that he could bluff his way through the world of hustlers and hustling without having the first idea of the game. He lacked brains and tact. He was only attracted to the glamour without really being prepared to pay his dues in the dark and forlorn world of dealing and puncing.

He hadn't even bought his fancy car with money that he had earned hustling, no not even that, his well off girlfriend had to buy it for him, probably on finance. He was a pretender, a prima donna that needed to take instruction or pay the penalty. For all the animosity that flowed between them however, they knew that they needed each other. Nowadays it wasn't safe to be in this game alone, hustling was no longer a game for hustlers but for gangsters. Guns and knives had replaced the ability to reason, to convince adversaries to move out or stay out off a particular patch, or even to settle an argument. Too many trigger happy youngsters, 'Aliens' and 'Space Invaders' as Pum Pum called them, had taken too much control of things and they made life dangerous. Between the two of them they had both burnt too many bridges in their time, had few people that they felt that they could really trust and now had only each other to turn to.

With both hands Pum Pum proceeded to shovel the money into his palms. Tony made a last ditch attempt to stop him.

'Where did you get that last card from?' he asked accusingly.

'What you mean?' asked Pum Pum innocently. 'I had it all the while.'

Tony raised his voice and spoke in his Jamaican accent, it seemed to help his confidence and make him feel tough.

'You cheatin' rass, you couldn't have had that card all de while,' he arraigned.

'Wha de arse you talkin' boat boy?'

'I've been reading this here game from start, man you couldn't have had that card all de while!'

'Listen man, you only sorry 'cos you lose!' shot back Pum Pum, collecting and loading his winnings into his pocket.

'Me no sorry nutun, you teef me rass man!'

'Shut you rasshole, I ain't cheat n'body!'

' I don't like you style y'know boy!'

'Who de arse you callin' boy?'

'You! You cheatin' likkle rass!'

'Listen, try come out my face yeh, if is one ting I can't stand is a bad loser!'

'Gimme back me money man, you couldn't have had that rassclaart card all de while!'

'Fuck off guy, you mad?' Pum Pum was in no mood for this, he knew that Tony was trying it on. 'Ress man, I won fair and square seen?'

'Gimme back me rahtid money!'

'Man I tell you arready, fuck arf nah?'

'Who you a tell fi fuck arf? You warn dead bwoy!?' With those words, Tony slipped his hands into the back of his trousers and produced a gun. It was a silver Magnum that shone menacingly when light hit it. That single action brought a stunned silence from everyone in the room whose attention had already been grabbed by the shouting. They all stared quietly, wondering what was going to happen next. Only Reggie, the bartender, spoke up.

'No guns, no guns, not in my place, no guns, why can't we black people live together?' he bawled before disappearing to the floor behind the counter.

Tony aimed his piece at Pum Pum who remained unimpressed. He took a step forward with his right foot and adopted a stance that signalled to Tony just how pissed off he was with this particular action. He splayed his arms out wide, gently walked up to the barrel of the gun and said;

'Put away you're toy boy. You draw that rasshole thing more times than Clint Eastwood.'

'Yeah,' replied Tony, 'and you have my fistful a dollars, so gimme back!'

'Over me dead body boy!'

Tony moved closer to Pum Pum and shoved the gun closer into his face. Pum Pum hardly flinched but kept eye contact with him all the time.

'Dat me can arrange!' he muttered between his teeth just like a Jamaican Clint Eastwood.

The onlookers stood in amazement, fear written all over their faces. They were alarmed and in complete admiration at the boldness of Pum Pum's defiance yet wondered if they might yet see his blood spill. Some of them were already decided that Pum Pum was about to get his head blown off. It was easy to picture his brains flying across the room and hitting them. So when Tony let off the shot, it bought a scream from some and made others cower and close their eyes. When those eyes opened they caught the final trickle of dust fall from the ceiling. Pum Pum was still standing and still as impertinent as ever.

'You pussyhole!' he declared defiantly.

'My fucking ceiling!!' shouted Reggie from behind the counter. 'I just artex that the other day!'

Pum Pum simply waved Tony away, sat down and continued counting his money. Tony, realising that his ploy had failed, replaced the gun, uttered a few insulting words at Pum Pum and decided to get a drink. He was interrupted by Luck, the ambitious young hustler. They called him Luck because he regularly had good luck in pulling women. His dashing good looks, his ultra-trendy funky dread-locked hairstyle which he sometimes kept under a bandanna, his thin shape and his up to the minute latest Southpole, Fubu, Hilfiger, Boff, street fashion clothing made him the perfect candidate for any young girl's affection. In fact, he had just managed to get rid of Nicole and had called on a couple of people hastily in order to get to the shabean on time.

'What the fuck is going on?' he asked, arms splayed out and with a bad boy bounce as he approached Pum Pum at the table.

'This rasshole idiot's playing with his blasted toy again,' replied an unperturbed Pum Pum.

'Not again?' probed the youngster.

'Me finger juss slip pan de trigger man,' Tony said dismissively.

Luck surveyed the ceiling.

'That was good artexing too,' he announced.

'I know!' shouted Reggie who was still behind the counter.

'Dat finger gonna slip at the wrong time,' interjected Pum Pum, waving a finger.

'Why you don't shut your shit? You small island rass!' jumped in Tony. He quickly turned his attention away from Pum Pum and focused on Luck. 'You sort out dis business ya?' he asked.

'Yep, it's all sorted,' replied Luck. He became businesslike. 'The dude wants us to bring ten Gs for the goods, we have to meet him tonight at three a.m., dockside.'

Tony became enthused, this was his first major drugs deal and he didn't want it going wrong.

'How much we got?' he asked.

'Eight,' replied Luck.

'So we gotta raise two grand by three o'clock,' pronounced Pum Pum, hand on his chin like he was concerned.

'You sharp hee?' mocked Tony.

'Shut the fuck up! Get offa my case! So what we gonna do? How the cunt we gonna do that?' fired back Pum Pum, acting like a very concerned leader.

'If your fuckin' bitches worked harder we wouldn't have this shit would we? Or maybe they just suckin' your black dick every night?'

'Shut your rasshole boy!'

'I put five grand into this shit…' shot back Tony.

'Five grand of your woman's money!'

'How the fuck do you know that? I hustle too you know!'

'Wid your woman's money!'

'The two of you, just cool it for fuck's sake! What we gonna do man?' interrupted Luck.

Tony took a step backwards, thought for a second, then retrieved his handpiece and waved it in the air. The punters, noticing this, dived for cover again, making him smile.

'No problem,' he replied in an eerily smooth voice. 'He either takes what we have, or… he takes what we have.'

Pum Pum became animated.

'Look I ain't going to jail for you. I ain't committing no murder,' he squealed.

Luck was concerned too.

'Look man,' he pleaded, 'I'm looking to cut more deals with this guy, he's a good contact, I don't wanna frighten him off first time out!'

'It's just a ruse,' replied Tony. 'Believe me, I have it all under control.'

'I hope so, just don't make your rahtid finger don't slip on the trigger again!'

Fed up with his bitching, Tony pointed the gun at Pum Pum.

'It might slip now!' he threatened.

Pum Pum threw his hands in the air and waved him on, shaking his head in despair. Tony took this as signal of compliance and replaced his gun in his trousers. Luck stepped forward.

'We can make it dockside in an hour, so we can party till two, yes?' he asked.

Pum Pum's eyes lit up.

'Party? Where?'

'Don't worry about where, you follow me, I got to meet a skirt, just one of many that will be there believe me,' replied Luck assuredly.

'Yep, I down for dat,' declared Pum Pum. 'Pum Pum is de name an' Pum Pum is de game.'

'Tony?' enquired Luck.

'Wha'ever you say man,' replied Tony, who really wasn't all that bothered.

It was agreed. They would party before they left for the docks. The prospect of getting to meet a new piece of skirt was perhaps the only other unifying factor between these three men and whenever the prospect was flagged up, they became like boyhood friends ever supportive of one another. Tony stepped to the bar and, feeling a sense of occasion, he bought them both a drink and raised a toast to the good life. The other two joined him, drank up and left to prepare themselves physically and mentally. They all had a gut feeling that after the night was over their fortunes were going to change forever.

seven

The rooms were barely lit as the many bodies that occupied them swayed seductively in their confined spaces, appearing almost dreamlike and surreal in the dim light from the kitchen and from the L.E.D lights on the sound system. The noise of laughter and over-emphasised conversation mingled with the high- pitched drum beats and the synthesised rhythms emitting from the speakers.

The room seemed to shake in such a way that enabled one to simply lose oneself in the drowning ecstasy of five thousand watts of Lovers Rock. Heavy rounded decibels of bass tore through the dense smoky atmosphere adding to the already immense heat that seeped through the house. Each individual was squashed, no more than millimetres from the next person, often inadvertently touching their neighbour as they sought to find the joy of dance and of music, of laughter, conversation, food and drink. The echoed voice of the DJ pierced through the murky atmosphere from time to time and the ringing vocals of the singers on record provided for the revellers, sweet satisfaction. The songs pierced through the very core of their being, often initiating an emotional response that drove the body in warm and relaxed seductivity. The party was simply jumping.

As Tony, Pum Pum and Luck joined the fray, their eyes lit up with expectation. It was quite a large house and a sizeable crowd was busy getting down to the swing groove emitting mercilessly from the large hi-powered speakers that were strategically placed in the four corners of both of the large rooms. The host, a tall, attractive and extremely elegant woman met them just as they slipped past the doormen who had just approved their entrance after Luck had shown his invitation and had pointed them out as his two permitted guests.

'Hi, come on in, how are you?' she shouted with a big smile as she placed her left hand on Luck's shoulder bending down to kiss his right cheek. 'Go and have something to eat the kitchen's straight through there.'

She shook both Pum Pum's and Tony's hands. Pum Pum's rather dryly and without much conviction, but Tony's quite seductively, looking deep into his eyes at the same time. She liked him. The three men moved with poise and as much swagger as the cramped space would allow, doing their best, without losing their balance, to eye the innumerable gorgeous females in the party. Females who in turn eyed them, in a bid to either stimulate recognition or to merely check them out. But soon they were to stop in surprise just a few yards from the kitchen as Pum Pum pointed out four ladies dancing closely together against a wall. It was Jean and her entourage. Of the group, only Shakela noticed the three guys, meeting Pum Pum's glance with obvious disappointment. Unnoticed by Jean, Tony took the opportunity to slip away, whilst Luck grabbed Pum Pum's arm. He nodded in the direction of Julie and said.

'That's my girl, the one with yours.'

'What, you mean Julie?' asked an astonished Pum Pum.

'That's the one,' replied Luck. 'Shakela introduced me to her last week.'

Pum Pum showed no surprise at that statement for Shakela, his lover, was well renowned for her match-making skills. His only worry was that some day she might match make herself with someone and whilst he hardly loved her, he was very fond of her and simply didn't want that to happen.

That sexy young thing represented something of a toy to him. Something that he knew, that at any time he could amuse himself with, not just in a physical way, but also in respect of the constant verbal and mental jousting that would take place between them. He knew what that was about too. They were two individuals that didn't like each other and that caused them consistently to argue, but at the same time, what they admired about each other would turn their arguments into joke and tomfoolery and that play between them was consistent and fun.

Also, Shakela wanted a man with money. She was hardly concerned with what he did for a living. Just as long as he was able and willing to spend his money on her she was happy. Pum Pum knew this. He had played sugar daddy on many occasions to many young women and he was more than happy to do that for Shakela. He didn't want to lose her because she bought a dimension to his life that many years ago he thought was gone; he needed her. He beckoned Luck to approach them, but he, ever the professional, opted to go to the kitchen to get a drink first. He wanted to savour the atmosphere of the party before tying himself down for the night.

Luck had never really realised up to now, but this was to be his first real conversation with Julie. The first time that he was about to spend any time with her and whilst he appreciated that Julie had a tight fit body, he was a realist and knew that it could easily be her only endearing quality. Perhaps for the first time in his life, he figured that he may just have found a woman that he might have a shred of real affection for so he really didn't want to spoil it by rushing. He didn't want to give her the impression that he was overly interested in her, even though he really was.

The words of the old Ken Boothe song 'Just Another Girl' came flashing into his head and he sang it quietly as he sailed past her and through the cramped group of people before him in order to reach the bar. He had heard the tune at a revival blues party a couple of nights ago and had immediately adopted it as an anthem. His boyish good looks meant that the girls flocked to him, but although he was young, he was sensible enough not to get taken in by it all.

He knew that something inside of him was yearning to meet that perfect girl and whenever he met a new one, he would always wonder if it would be her. That was only ever a fleeting thought, but one that would always sustain him and guide his actions. It made him a gentlemen, someone that knew how to treat a woman, how to serenade and romance them. It was probably his undoing. Because when those admirers began to cling and lovers started to invade his space, he would usually have no compunction in getting rid of them, comforting himself all the time that there were plenty more fish in the sea and that his search for the perfect woman would continue.

Once at the bar, which was a table that stood in the doorway between the main room and the kitchen, he eyed the pretty young ladies that served the drinks and calmly asked for can of Brew and a light dry white wine. Pum Pum approached the posse and greeted Julie, Jean and Sheila in turn, completely ignoring Shakela. Jean asked him if Tony was about, to which he replied.

'Yeah man, we always ride together see.'

Julie inquired about Luck and whether he was going to bother to say anything to her. To which he replied.

'Yeah man, don' be so eager, he gon' chat to you soon enough.'

Sheila gave him a limp handshake and said nothing. He said nothing to her in return. Then he turned to Shakela, who had been doing her best to ignore him anyway.

'What you doing here?' he inquired aggressively.

Shakela was hardly surprised by the brutality of his inquiry, she half expected it and responded in like manner.

'Same as you,' she said arrogantly.

'Hey, I don't like to see my women out on the town without knowing first. Why didn't you tell me you were coming?' he quizzed.

'Excuse me pops,' she responded, waving a finger, one hand on her hip and shaking her head, 'but I don't have to answer to you, so don't even go there please!'

'Yes you fucking well do, you're my rasshole woman ain't you?'

'Not after tonight if you carry on with this bullshit!'

Pum Pum eased his tone down, slipped into a more caring, romantic mode and put his arm around her, but she pushed him away. He tried again, and again she pushed him away. Before long they were locked in a rather farcical struggle. Their activities attracted spectators and noticing this, Shakela pulled him to.

'You see how people are looking?' she said in a manner that blamed Pum Pum for all the unwanted attention.

Pum Pum turned to one of the onlookers.

'Turn your blasted head round boy!' He shouted. 'You see any rasshole ting to look at? Fix your eyes on your woman before she fuck somebody else, you rasshole!'

The boy turned quickly to hide his embarrassment. Shakela panicked and pulled Pum Pum closer in an attempt to diffuse his short temper. She stroked the side of his face gently and began to wind herself into his crotch. This was no show of affection, but a desperate attempt to limit the damage that was already done and what evidently was about to be done. Pum Pum had a very aggressive nature and too many times their play ended up with him becoming just a tad aggressive and on a couple of occasions that had nearly ended up in fisticuffs.

She remembered how Tony had behaved the other night and she had shared Jeans' embarrassment. She wasn't going to have that, not tonight. So she gently eased him into a bumping and grinding session. So seductive was she that Pum Pum could hardly resist the temptation, particularly as it made his nature rise.

'Hole up nuh man, I can't tek dis rahtid pace man!' he complained.

Shakela said nothing but eased him gently to a space against the wall. This made Pum Pum smile. He moved her gently round so that her back rested against the wall and before long they were embroiled in an X-rated rub-a dub session that would have taken the wallpaper off the wall if it hadn't been painted.

Luck eased over to Julie with two drinks in his hands, he whispered something in her ear and handed her one. She took it graciously and stared lovingly into his eyes. She liked this guy a lot, his smooth good looks had made an immediate impression on her. When they first met, she hoped that they would soon be into a relationship. Luck was keen on her too; he was the sort of guy that had trouble sticking to just one woman, but he figured that for her, he could at least try. He wasn't quite sure what it was that attracted him to her though. Maybe it was the cute almost childish innocence that her clear dark skinned face portrayed. Maybe it was the short slitty eyes or the cutely rounded nose and wide lips that made her face look so full and generous.

Her straight elongated figure was one that during a lustful night of sexual passion he knew he would enjoy. He romanticised, in a nice way, about slipping in between those long legs. He had been won over already by the light husky voice that sounded so sweet and so sexy every time she opened her mouth, and knew that if she was as right mentally as she was physically, it wouldn't be long before he was in love.

'So how you doing?' he shouted.

'It's OK. A bit crowded though!' she shouted back.

'Nice music!'

'It's about one o'clock!'

'lots of people!'

'No thanks! You just bought me one!'

Luck giggled to himself, he knew he wasn't being heard. For

their first conversation since meeting they were getting on well. They seemed to be enjoying each other's company, which was just as well, because they couldn't hear a damned thing that they were saying to one another. Frustrated at having to shout to each other over the music, they decided to go outside into the car. This was problematic. It meant that Luck would have to get the car keys from Tony. He excused himself and began to search the party for him. Finally he found him standing outside the toilet, eyes red and hooded. It became immediately clear to him what Tony had been up to. He shouted in his ear four times before Tony was able to comprehend his request.

'What you want the damn key dem fa?' he asked in something of a drunken stupor.

'We just want to hear each other!' Luck replied. 'We're just gonna sit in the car and talk.'

'Don't mess up me seat y'know!' was Tony's reply.

'No man it's not like that.' Luck insisted.

'Sure,' said Tony 'Leather fuckin' seats in that thing mate, I don't wanna be wiping your rahtid come off them, you geddit?'

'Sure Tony anything you say, gimme the keys nuh?' replied Luck, his words riddled with contempt for Tony.

Reluctantly and rather sluggishly Tony produced the keys, admonishing him not to be too long and to give her one for him – a statement that made Luck retire from his presence in total disgust. He approached Julie again and in seconds they were heading for the door. Shakela winked an eye at her as she left and Julie raised a slight smile at her as if to say thank you.

Jean knew that Tony was in the party somewhere. He, Luck and Pum Pum always went out together and there was no reason for tonight to be an exception. Pum Pum had been slightly non-committal about his whereabouts and she wondered if Tony had told him about their argument earlier. She felt like asking Luck but had decided against it. Instead she opted to carry on enjoying the night, hoping to give Tony the space that she felt he needed. She knew he was angry with her and she felt that crowding him now might upset the apple cart. He would speak to her when he was ready. She and Sheila were happy to dance the night away, sharing a joke every now and then, and respond favourably to the music.

Suddenly, a tall, well dressed man, with a distinctly eighties curly perm, appeared almost from nowhere, placing himself directly in between the two of them facing Jean. It was David Adams. He had been watching her since he came in. She hadn't noticed him, probably because it was so dark in the room, so he had waited to pick his moment to speak to her and that moment was now. He smiled at her, waiting for her to recognise him. Jean gradually became conscious of his piercing eyes staring fixedly at her. It shook her first of all and, falling back upon her womanly instincts in such a situation, she ignored him. But David was persistent; noticing her desperate attempts to avoid eye contact, he moved slowly and sensitively deeper into her space. He smiled to himself and waited. Jean could take it no longer, she wanted to tell this guy to lay off her but it was difficult when he hadn't actually spoken to her. However, she felt that she could at least send out a signal. Turning slowly and ready to throw a dirty look at the man, she was suddenly startled. The realisation of who he was made her hands fly to her wide open mouth.

'David!' she exclaimed, 'David Adams, my God, I haven't seen you for ages!'

'It's been a long time Jean,' he responded in a clinically refined accent that was still audible over the music because of his deep bassy voice. 'How are you?'

'I'm fine. And you?'

'All the better for seeing you,' was his suave reply.

Sheila had noticed this man all evening. He was charming, handsome, tall and very well presented. Not many people in the party were dressed like him. His curly perm framed a thin, drawn-out face, one that was very well looked after and one that obviously received regular steaming as his visage was both spotless and without any sign of age. His Nehru style jacket covered a white grandfather shirt that was obviously silk, over the neck of which lay a thin but quite expensive looking gold chain. His black trousers matched the Nehru jacket exquisitely and it was only when he put his hand into his trouser pocket she realised that he was wearing an elegant matching waistcoat. His dress style was chic to say the very least, a well-cut Italian design that simply spelled 'money'.

Sheila was almost embarrassed to look at his shoes, that acid test of a man's solvency and sense of style, she knew he would pass with flying colours and he did. Black crocodile skin laced with a gold chain was not out of place with him and it was, for her, the final icing on the cake. Just enough to make her swoon. She became excited. Her heartbeat rose to a crescendo of thumping when she learned that Jean not only knew him but also was well enough acquainted that she let him to hold her hand. When her body language went unnoticed she barged her way into an introduction, which Jean noticed immediately.

'Excuse my manners,' she said curtly. 'Meet Sheila Anderson, my best friend. Sheila meet David Adams, we used to go out together at university.'

David's handshake was polite but neutral enough to inform Sheila that it was only Jean he was interested in. She tried, however, to make conversation with him.

'I'm Jean's friend!' she shouted, nearly blowing his ears off.

'I know, I heard,' he responded, hardly bothered if she had heard him or not.

'Do you live around here?'

'Yes.'

'Where?'

'Does it matter?'

'Yes.'

'Wycliff Avenue.'

'So you're loaded then?' she asked.

'What?' he asked.

'Ever been to Mombassa? I hear it's wicked this time of year.'

'Sorry?'

'Mombassa, ever been?'

'No.'

'Nice beaches.'

'Really?'

'Fancy going?'

'No.'

'Oh.'

His one word answers only helped to confirm what Sheila had felt. As far as chat-ups went she had just presided over a botched job. This guy was obviously way out of her league. She winced and gave up, excusing herself to go to the bar. David turned back to Jean.

'How about a dance, for old times sake? I remember how you used to love to dance with me,' he said, ' and that wasn't all you liked to do to me either.'

Jean was embarrassed.

'Stop it David,' she said, not looking at him. 'That was a long time ago.'

This was a difficult situation for Jean. She didn't want a repeat of her last night out with Tony, so she respectfully declined his offer. But he was persistent and asked her again.

'No David, really,' she said. 'I really don't think so.'

'Jean please, just one,' he continued. 'Just for old times sake.'

Sheila made it back from the bar in no time. Upon hearing the conversation she quickly seized the moment, thinking that in the course of doing her friend a favour she could do herself one too. She took his hand.

'Look, she doesn't want to dance with you, but I wouldn't mind,' she said slyly.

'Maybe later eh?' was his blatantly dismissive reply.

Jean prayed that Sheila would persist but her disappointment was evident. Sheila took a last, defeated look at him before moving back towards the kitchen for another drink leaving Jean alone with him. This was all a hassle for Jean, she didn't want to upset David but he had made his appearance at an inopportune moment. He still persisted and finally Jean figured that there was only one way to deal with this situation. She reasoned that Tony had not made an appearance whole time that he had been there and that she might be able to get away with one dance before he showed. The DJ changed the record and 'Caught you in a Lie' boomed out of the system. Without another thought Jean pulled David towards her, hoping to get the dance out of the way as quickly as possible. Pum Pum, however, was stood just a couple of inches away and alerted Shakela to what he saw going on. She showed her disdain at his apparent misplaced interest in Jean and soon they were embroiled in an extremely vicious exchange of words.

'Don't you dare!' she exclaimed.

'What you talkin' 'bout, girl? The man dancin' wid he woman, you tellin' me he ain't supposed to know bout it?' he responded.

Shakela held his arm trying to stop him from doing something that he was going to regret. But in seconds Pum Pum had pulled himself away leaving her most displeased. Within minutes, he appeared at the entrance to the door with an inebriated looking Tony. As he pointed at Jean, now well into her dance with David, he spoke.

'Ain't that Jean dancin' wid some fella?' Shakela dropped her head into her hands.

'You fool guy? She ain't mad,' responded Tony in his mashed up state.

'Well it looks like she gone right potty mate, cause that is your Jean…' replied Pum Pum stabbing a finger in Jeans direction '…Dancing wit' some guy! Look nah man?'

Tony looked again, rocking slowly as a result of his half-drunken half-drugged up state. He tried desperately to focus half-closed eyes before uttering menacingly;

'Hold up yah, I soon come.'

Sheila had returned to the space where they were dancing and was as disturbed as Shakela by Pum Pum's behaviour. She made pointing motions towards the door to Jean. Unable to comprehend the meaning behind her gestures Jean, rather than to try to decipher them, closed her eyes, pulled David closer, and got on with the dance.

In no time at all Tony was standing in front of them. Pum Pum smiled a conniving smile standing behind him. Onlookers, realising that there might be trouble, paid close attention to Tony who had informed everyone by his body language that he was not pleased. With a violent thrust of Jean's shoulder he separated them. Jean, surprised by the action, turned in dismay only to greet her nightmare. A furious looking Tony who seemed to be smouldering as his deep thoughtless gaze seemed to penetrate the very depths of her soul. She looked him full into his eyes, guilt etched all over her face; she knew what was coming next.

Tony turned his gaze from her and focused directly onto David who desperately fought back the heaving in his chest motored by a beating heart and a blood stream that accelerated with wild consternation around his body. He fearfully awaited Tony's first words. They were not long in coming.

'My woman you a dance wid deh you know,' he said, Jamaican accent at the ready.

'Tony please,' Jean begged 'it's not what you think.'

The words fell on deaf ears. He ignored her totally and jumped into David again.

'Didn't you hear what I just said? That's my girl you got there boy!'

David's arms opened wide and were splayed, swinging at waist length. He stuttered a response.

'Sorry mate,' he muttered apologetically, the fear of God carved in his face and trembling body. 'I didn't know.'

Jean tried to get between them again, this time physically, but was rebutted by Tony with a slight push against the wall. He had hardly applied any strength in the push but it was hard enough to send her flying and she hit the wall with a thud that hurt her back. The crowd, seeing this, stepped back. It was 'game on' as far as they were concerned. They stared incessantly and with great interest. Again Tony confronted David, this time with greater venom in his voice.

'I want to know just who the fuck you feel seh you is a dance wid people woman?' he snapped.

David became desperate.

'Look mate. Just calm down, I didn't know. It was just a dance,' he said, wincing.

'You didn't know? Well you should a rassclaart fine oat!' Tony cried.

By now the music had stopped and everyone in the party was focused on Tony and David. The DJ made an impassioned plea for peace which everybody echoed inside, but which Tony simply ignored. David made another desperate effort, a shrill cry surfacing in his voice.

'Look mate I'm sorry OK, let's just forget it eh?' he pleaded gently patting the upper part of Tony's left arm.

Let's be friends he wanted to say. Let me buy you a drink, he thought about saying. But even if he had, it would have been to no avail.

'Figett wah!?' cried Tony pushing his arm away. He slowly squared up to him and with one shake of his head David was on the floor, blood sputtering from the bridge of his nose from the violent head-butt that Tony had landed on him. Jean stood trembling, tears streaming down her face. She tried to grab hold of Tony in a bid to calm him down, a futile gesture as she too, with a backhanded slap of Tony's wrist, was sent sprawling to the ground. David, realising that he was now the embarrassed centre of attraction, tried to get up in an effort to win back some pride, fists clenched and ready to fight. But he had hardly left the ground when he found himself staring headlong into the barrel of Tony's gun and he sank to the ground again.

Everyone except Pum Pum eased back. The gasps of panic were audible as the crowd all either cowered or ran for the exit. It was like a stampede, panic had gripped the party and fear was engraved on everyone's faces, at least all but Tony and Pum Pum.

'You gwine nyam fuckin' lead tonight!' snarled Tony through gritted teeth. Jean screamed through streaming tears.

'Oh my God Tony what the hell are you doing?'

'Me a fry rassclaart dumplin'!' was his sarcastic reply.

'Put the rasshole toy away boy, he ain't worth it man,' said a composed Pum Pum.

'Fuck arf Pum Pum!' shouted Tony, who by now had lost it. But Pum Pum was undeterred.

'I told you already man, you love draw that blasted thing too much! Put it away boy you looking to go to jail?'

'Boy I could do a rassclaart stretch for this fool.'

'Yeah well when them batty boys in there hold up your fat boxy, you gon' know what a rasshole stretch feels like.'

David was a nervous and shaking wreck. He had shit in his pants, but he sat terrified, ignoring it, wondering if these were his last moments. He thought about pleading for his life but the words seemed to stick in his throat. He stared wide-eyed and open mouthed at Tony's gun, praying that it wouldn't go off, whilst sweat rose profusely to his brow. Pum Pum was mad now and he was bellowing at Tony to put the gun down. The comment about the stretch drew a few chortles from those strong enough despite the circumstances to see the joke, but it seemed to affect Tony for the better. He backed off from David who had not yet risen from the floor. Holding his gun in the air, he grabbed Jean's hand and displayed her to all the party-goers like a boxing referee paraded the champion. Jean was hopeless, realising that any attempt at resistance was futile. As Tony pulled her around the now half-crowded room she held her head down using her free hand to sob in. Gasps of disgust were heard throughout the room, not least from her friends.

Sheila wanted to shout at Tony in a bid to release her and end her embarrassment. But she erred on the side of caution and kept her mouth closed knowing full well that if the stories were true, Tony was probably now under the influence of drugs and that in this sort of state he was likely to do anything. A trickle of a tear leapt from her eyes she turned away in abhorrence at what Tony was doing to her friend. Pum Pum was less emotional about the situation. He merely rolled his eyes to the ceiling in disgust. He had never seen anyone treat a woman in this way. Sure he'd beat his hookers now and then, but they deserved that shit, he reasoned. Jean didn't deserve this sort of treatment.

'This is my woman seen?' bellowed Tony at the top of his voice. 'Mek any man put dem hand pan her…'

He let off three shots into the ceiling that sent all and sundry cowering for protection.

'Seen?' he bellowed.

Pum Pum, realising that Tony had made his play and that his act of male bravado for the day was completed, boldly stepped in.

'Come on man let's go,' he said grabbing Tony's arm. 'We got business to sort out.'

With that Tony dropped Jean's arm, leaving her standing in the centre of the room a sad and pitiful picture of sorrow. David had made his way out of the room once Tony had turned his attention away from him and was already gone. Shakela and Sheila merely looked at each other ruefully. Pum Pum and Tony made for the exit, people fell over themselves to get out of their way as they approached the door where Tony stopped, turned, and let off another shot to the ceiling which again sent the onlookers diving for cover.

'And I mean anybody!' he shouted, and with that they were gone.

Head in hands, desperately trying to hold back the tears, Jean stood in silent desolation. Sheila was the first to approach her pulling Jean's head into her chest.

'What the hell is he doing with a gun?' she asked no-one in particular.

Shakela was quiet, stunned as everyone else was. Julie came

flying in immediately noticing that the party had stopped. She saw the bewildered crowd of people muttering to each other, some holding their chests as if to bring calm. Others had not yet finished shaking. She noticed Jean in the centre of the room, head held firmly in Sheila's breast, and ran to her.

'Jean what's going on? That boyfriend of yours just threw me out of his car!' She exclaimed, turning to show the rip on the shoulder of her blouse that Tony had caused.

Jean looked up at her as if to apologise, then she quickly scoured the room for David who was nowhere in sight, before burying her head in Sheila's chest with a sob.

'Come on Jean,' Sheila said comfortingly. 'Let's get you home.'

Outside the three men were arguing. Luck was incensed at the way that Tony had opened the car door, grabbed Julie and pulled her out of the car. He wanted to square up to him, but Pum Pum had put paid to any impending squabble by holding him back and reassuring him that there was a job to be done and that after it was over, he wouldn't have to have any dealings with Tony again. Luck saw the sense in this, but warned Tony anyway of what he would do to him if he ever treated his people like that again. Pum Pum drove as Tony was clearly in no state to do so.

'Swing round by Chicken, I need to pick up the plates,' said Luck, before settling in to what he knew was going to be a difficult journey.

The ride home for the girls seemed to take forever. Sheila drove. After dropping Julie and Shakela off, she headed for Jeans' flat. Once at home, she was ever the confidante.

'It looks like you were right,' she began. 'Something's going on.'

'Yep,' sighed Jean. 'He's losing it.'

'But the gun…?'

'Sheila, I have no idea.'

'What's happening to him?'

'Drugs.'

'Drugs! So it's true.'

'Yes, drugs. Shakela tried to warn me but I wouldn't listen to her. I've been blind to it for too long. I think he's selling it too.'

'Oh shit, look maybe we can talk to him about it, maybe we can…'

'Sheila, it would be the first sensible conversation I've had with him. All the years that I've been seeing him we've never discussed his problems, he certainly won't be able to do that now.'

'Then what do we do?'

'Wait. We just wait. It's like you said Sheila, when he's ready he'll come and talk to me, I just need to give him the space he needs.'

'Do you still think he's seeing someone else?'

'It's difficult to tell. I mean what was all that about tonight? However bad and embarrassing it was for me, it told me that he loves me and I would like to respond to that, if he'll allow me to. He's become very paranoid and worried about me and I think that there's something in him driving him closer to me, but at the same time further away. If I find out that he is seeing someone else though, that will be it. Baby or no baby. I've been hopelessly in love for too long Sheila, now it's time, I think, to at least give myself a chance.'

Jean's resignation was clear. Sheila was speechless. A silence that was partly tinged with pride. Jean had finally lifted the veil of denial that had plagued her for so long. It had taken a situation like tonight for it to happen but now she was looking at a woman that had finally managed to admit the truth to herself. Where she would go with it, she knew not, but this was a triumphant beginning.

'Sheila, I'd like to be alone now please.' Jean whispered. ' I'll give you a lift home.' 'No don't worry, it's a cool night I'll hail a cab if I need to,' responded Sheila sympathetically. 'I'll call you tomorrow.'

With a gentle hug and a slight kiss on the cheek Sheila took her leave. Once alone, Jean composed herself. She switched on the stereo to play some soft music, and at once her living room was filled with mellow, settling R&B. She fixed herself a drink and could not help stepping out with it onto the large balcony to survey the fading lights of the town. Her loved one was out there, what he was doing she didn't know. She feared for him and wanted to hold him, love him and protect him. He had upset her that night but this was inconsequential to her wanting to be sure that he was safe and well. Perhaps, she thought, her motherly instincts were beginning to take over. Perhaps this was how a mother felt, protective towards her loved ones and completely oblivious to her own safety and distress.

It was her favourite CD of the moment that occupied the space in her compact disc player. Track eight; 'I'll Wait Till You Come Home,' seemed to ring its soft and dulcet tones around her living room. As a sweet female voice sang; 'You'll never find love the way I love you, those cold nights will never hug you like I do, leave it all behind, I'll wait till you come home,' she cried.

eight

The drive to the docks had been a long one. It had taken them over an hour and a half, during which time Tony had been able to recoup his fading senses and concentrate more on the business at hand. Pum Pum drove and for the most part he kept his thoughts to himself, interrupted only by Luck's occasional request for Rizla paper or a cigarette. They had put Tony in the back of the car, figuring the journey would give him enough time to sleep and come back to himself by the time they reached their destination.

As music blared from the stereo, Tony's thoughts were able to pass on a number of matters, not least his beloved Jean. He entertained no remorse for his actions at the party, he merely wanted some answers. Was she seeing someone behind his back? Was she sleeping with someone else? Was it that guy she was dancing with? Who was he? How did she know him? Or was it merely the paranoia brought on by his habit that seemed to ever-so-effectively cloud his every thought? Perhaps this was the first time that he admitted that he loved her, it must have been. His possessive spirit would not be activated in the way that it had been if she was not something that he coveted.

His mind continued to wander as he looked at his life; it was an opportune time to do this. Now at the tender age of twenty-seven, he had been through a hard life already. His childhood had been wild and frenzied and there was little parental regard for him. He had been expelled from school and was in trouble with the police more times than he could remember. He had experienced his fair share of misery, losing his mother whilst he was in his teens to a drug overdose and wasn't it an irony that now his drug habit was at its peak? But there was Jean, yes Jean who had become the answer to many of the psychological problems that he had. He was able to admit that much, that he had problems. He knew that he wasn't a mental case, but the scars of a difficult life were now beginning to tell.

Maybe, he thought, he ought to give up the game, leave the hustling profession, see what he could do about getting himself a job and settle down. But that was all bullshit. When he thought of all the money he could make and indeed all the money he had already made out of the game, he booted the notion quickly and decisively into touch. Nothing – no job, no profession, no nine to five, no shift work – could pay him the kind of money that he had become accustomed to making as a player. Nothing, at least, that he would not need a big qualification for, and fuck it, he had already been through that route at school and failed. Now he sure as hell wasn't going to have some jumped-up, educated fool telling him what to do, no way. He chupsed his teeth as he stared longingly out of the window. Slight drops of rain appeared against the window as he surveyed the bright wet roads of the motorway.

Luck's thoughts were just as jaded. He was a fun-loving sort of person generally and whilst he appreciated the dangers of the hustling game, there was a large element of fun in it too and this was its biggest attraction for him. Money, cars and women, what else could a man want in life? Through it all he had always pledged that although he was living life in the fast lane he would always keep a cool head on his shoulders. He wouldn't give in to the many gold-digging bitches that were forever on his case and he certainly wouldn't use any of the shit that he was selling. That wasn't good for business and now it seemed that Tony was proving how stupid it was to do so.

He suspected that Tony was going under. His problems with Jean were consistently being aired throughout the small community in which they lived and tonight's actions were an indication of just how far downhill Tony had allowed himself to slip. Not to mention just how much more gossip it was going to cause. Luck was a younger man than Tony, indeed the youngest of the three, and he knew within himself that up to this point he had exercised much more discretion and much more brains in the way that he had conducted his business. Hustling was a dangerous game. Whilst he always felt that he could hold his own, he recognised how important it was not to fuck with the goods, the people with whom you did business, or yourself. Tony had now broken two of those rules and he wondered just how long it would be before he broke the third one. When he did, shit would happen and things would start to become deadly serious and decidedly more dangerous than they already were.

Luck took a deep breath and focused on the wet roads ahead of him, allowing his mind to be further illuminated by the ganja stick that he toked on heavily and thoughts of Julie, to whom he was becoming increasingly attracted. He had lived a charmed life up until this point but there was a disturbing air around that seemed to tell him that things were on a downhill slope. Life was going to get tougher, the game was going to get harder and somehow he felt that he needed to gear up for it. The only light on his horizon was Julie. He concentrated on her. She seemed to supply a conscience for him. Many players that he had known had given up the game for a beautiful woman and maybe this was his time. Maybe this was the moment that would steer him down a safer route, a more conventional path upon which to base his life. Who knew? But as he turned his head to see how Tony was doing, he couldn't help but think that maybe it all rested on his shoulders. Whether or not he was going to do something even more stupid than he had already done and whether that stupid thing would be connected more to the game than to his love life. Luck sighed deeply and resigned himself, just like Tony, to the long wet road ahead.

Pum Pum's thoughts were muted; he was the sort of guy that didn't think in words, he thought more in pictures and with feelings. Uppermost in his mind was Tony. He was vexed and tried all he could to laugh off the night's events. He had tried to tell Luck a pussy-fucking story, but he wasn't interested. Even for him it was difficult. He had been a player for a long time. He was well aware that he was now getting older and whilst he had always managed a decent lifestyle from pimping and drug selling, he had never quite made what he considered to be the big time, the big money. Now he felt that he was on the verge of reaching that elusive goal and Tony was screwing it all up.

He remembered when they first met. He had been stopped by the police and Tony pulled over to give him support and curse out the police who, confronted by two angry Black men, were too afraid to pursue the matter any further. Pum Pum had invited him to the shabean after that and then they got talking about drug deals, making money, wearing gold, fucking bitches and the like. They had pooled together all the money they had and bought a large stash of drugs; it moved quickly and they knew immediately that they were headed for bigger things. Luck was a runner for them who showed enough guile and enough imagination to be cut in on the major deals. He had showed himself astute at making arrangements, had a good number of contacts and was honest, so they made him a third partner and everything seemed rosy. He was confident, Luck was busy and Tony was cool. Then the hopeless bastard started to take the shit. The fool went and bought a gun and things hadn't been the same since.

Pum Pum was never the sort of guy to try and control his partners, he had never needed to, but perhaps now the time had come to try. This was a difficult prospect. Tony was uncontrollable, a big head, an arrogant son of a bitch who just wouldn't take telling. He wouldn't take orders. The crazy bastard simply wanted to do things his own way, never mind the fact that he was probably the least experienced, the least knowledgeable and probably the least streetwise of the three. He had to acknowledge that it was Tony's cocksure character, his aggressive behaviour and perhaps his courage that gave him such a prominent position in the partnership, but at the same time this worried him. He knew that out there on the streets, at some point a big head like Tony would probably end up laying in a gutter. He trembled slightly, reflecting for a split second that if things continued on the downward path, it might even have to be by his hand. He drove on regardless and dismissed the thought from his mind. But Pum Pum was not the sort of person that could forget things. Nor did he shirk from doing whatever it took to survive. He had never committed murder, but he had silenced a few adversaries in his time by less than honourable means.

Maybe it was the fact that Pum Pum was forced to take life a little bit more seriously now or maybe he was just in that sort of mood, but sure enough, a poem came to him.

'What is death, but an entrance?
What is life, but happiness?
Show me the man that is unhappy with life or death

and I will show you the face of a fool.
For there is no death but life
and there would be no life if not for death.'

This wasn't a pussy poem. Pum Pum was surprised at himself. He realised quickly that his creative conscience was speaking to him. There was danger ahead. He took a deep breath and released a gust of air that would have suggested that he was tired. He pressed the accelerator of Tony's 840, settled himself and concentrated even harder on the empty wet road ahead of him.

It had been a long night for both Nelson and Watts. The clubs had been closed over an hour ago and the crowds had dispersed quickly and quietly. They had only received three calls all night, all for drunk and disorderly behaviour. These were hardly imprisonment cases and certainly weren't worth all the paperwork that would be required if they brought them in. So as it was, the drunks had been merely cautioned. Watts tucked into his third cheese and pickle sandwich of the night whilst Nelson drove around almost aimlessly in the Panda car. Finally they decided to stop on a street corner, lights off, front of the car peeking out from the side street just enough for them to see clearly down both sides of the road without being seen.

Somehow they managed to get into a discussion about the size of Madonna's breasts and whether they were implants or not. It didn't last very long. Madonna, it seemed, wasn't an interesting enough topic of conversation - although breasts were. Before long they had considered the assets of Pamela Anderson, Janet Jackson, Denise Van Outen, that black girl that was married to David Bowie and WPC 2658 Griffith. They had reached rock bottom. This was probably one the most boring and lifeless shifts that they'd experienced since joining the Police force. They had both joined for some action, ex-squaddies wanting to recapture the magic of life in the services. Nelson decided to drive to the docks. it was only 20 minutes away, and they figured that if there was no action there, then they'd go and peruse the red light district for the fifth time that night.

Pum Pum, Luck and Tony were getting fed up of waiting. It was now twenty-eight minutes past four, they were waiting dockside and still there was no sign of their contact. Luck and Pum Pum stood together as they recounted the evening's events. They joked about the fiasco and how Tony was losing control of his love life. But they soon became far more serious as they began to discuss his drug habits and how they were ever going to make enough money from their hustles with him sniffing away at the profits, not to mention the liability of having an addict as a partner.

The three were interrupted soon enough by the screech of brakes, the slamming of car doors and finally the arrival of their contacts. Three large men all wearing dark glasses, gold ornamentation and the latest Boff gear approached them. Tony checked them out. This was a natural reaction of his, to check out the opposition and to him, they were opposition regardless. They were all well built, which was worrying, but only one of them looked as if he had ever really seen any action on the streets. The others looked tame, almost like novices, which made him feel better. There was no visible sign that they were armed either. Another good point for if they weren't, any possible confrontation, he reasoned, was already won. One of the three, 'Baron', the obvious group leader, the one with the hardened and more experienced looks had a briefcase in his hand. Tony quickly realised that there couldn't have been enough drugs to fit into a briefcase. The guy was either stupid or he was acting out some movie fantasy, he thought.

The three men approached Luck who introduced them to Pum Pum and Tony. The six men talked for a short while, small talk really, before getting on with the business at hand. The briefcase was handed over to Luck, whilst at the same time a brown paper bag full of notes was handed over by Pum Pum. Tony watched anxiously as Luck knelt, placing the briefcase on the ground and opening it. There were the powdered drugs as promised, all wrapped up in small plastic bags. Luck pulled a flick knife from his back pocket and proceeded to cut one of the bags. Once severed, he dipped his little finger into it and tasted the speck of powder. The group waited anxiously for his adjudication. Satisfied, he looked up at Tony and Pum Pum and nodded approvingly. As if on cue the shortest of the three men proceeded to pull away the wrapping from the bundle that was given to him by Pum Pum, an action that caused great consternation amongst the three. Worried glances were exchanged by Luck, Pum Pum and Tony.

'Count it later nuh?' Tony implored.

'Count it now if you don't mind,' came the reply from Baron. Pum Pum jumped in too.

'Look man it's all there, count it later nuh? We have to make a move soon,' he pleaded.

'Too late,' said Baron. 'Him start count arready.'

There was a couple of minutes silence, whilst they waited for the inevitable shout. Tony prepared himself. By pretending to scratch his back, he kept his hand on his gun. The shout was not long in coming.

'Two grand short,' proclaimed the counter.

Baron immediately showed his displeasure.

'Ey,' he shouted. 'Wah de Bumbo claart unu man a deal wid?'

In no time at all Tony's gun was stuck in his face. Baron shuddered and stared goggle eyed as once again Tony had another individual staring down the barrel of his gun. Baron and the other two wasted no time in raising their hands to the heavens. They weren't prepared for this. Drug dealing in their part of the world had not yet become a gangsters' sport, they were just ordinary hustlers, and there was no need for guns where they came from. It bought more than a lump to all of their throats.

'You fren mussi can't count,' bragged Tony.

'Him neva went to school you know,' was Baron's strained reply as he desperately tried to bring an air of lightheartedness to the situation. He began to shake and voluntarily raised his hands higher.

'Look,' he said. 'Just tek de goods yeh, no worry man, eight grand is enough for us man believe me.'

Pum Pum and Luck looked at one another in disbelief. The ruse had worked. Pum Pum knelt down, locked the briefcase and fastened it under his arm, but Tony, now with the upper hand, held out for the whole pie.

'Leave the money too,' he said craftily.

However afraid they were, this suggestion was not beyond contesting. The two men kissed their teeth together whilst Baron held out his arm and begged Tony to reconsider. Tony laughed and grabbed the back of Baron's head with one hand.

'Open your fuckin' mouth,' he ordered.

Baron was shocked but he obliged reluctantly and Tony, sticking his gun down it with the other hand, shouted angrily;

' You warn dead?' a line that he had always dreamed of using ever since he was a kid watching Jimmy Cliff in 'The Harder They Come.'

Baron knew he wasn't going to get his money, so he said nothing, not that he could. Tony ordered them to start walking, threatening to blow their heads off if they so much as flinched. He escorted them back to their car and as they drove away Baron threatened to avenge himself, admonishing Tony to watch his back. Tony, unmoved by the idea, sent them packing with a round of gunshots fired into the air. This made their exit even more hasty and erratic. Their C-reg. Peugeot 205 convertible only narrowly missed the side of a building as they screeched away.

Once they were out of sight Tony made his way back to his partners who, elated, showered him with pats on the back, handshakes and fists. But their celebrations were cut short by the sound of a car pulling up in virtually the same spot that the three dealers had left. Cautiously Tony went to investigate and was soon running back with the news that a Panda car had pulled up. Panic gripped the three as they quickly realised that their car might have been spotted. The clunk of another car door set them even more on edge and they split up and hid. In the hysteria, no one realised until it was too late that they had left both the money and the drugs on the ground. Tony tried to make a quick dash back for it but changed his mind as PC Watts appeared around the corner.

'Stay there, I think they're gone,' he called back to Nelson who, slightly worried, had stayed in the car and kept his hand firmly on his radio in case back up was needed. When Watts walked on to the pier and spotted the stash sitting firmly on the ground he could hardly believe his eyes. He examined it, confirming the drugs were genuine by tasting them the same way Luck had done. He shut the suitcase and picked up the money. He then picked up his walkie talkie and realised in a split second that the click he heard was not his monitor but the wrenching snap of Tony's '45. He felt the cold steel of Tony's gun against the side of his head and an arm locked around his neck.

'Not so fast beast boy! Hands over you head quick,' Tony said.

Pum Pum and Luck dived from their hiding places, anxious to ensure that Tony knew what he was doing.

'Tony just be careful!' warned Pum Pum.

'Pum Pum juss cool!' was Tony's frenetic response. 'Luck me need fi tie him up! Get rope.'

Luck made off quickly, searching the ground for rope or something, anything, that he could use to subdue the policeman. Nelson watched anxiously from the seat of his car. He was too far away to see anything but the fog-shrouded figures of Tony and Watts as he frantically bellowed into his radio for back up. He could hardly get the words out as he desperately tried to give an account of the situation. Trying at the same time to give a description of Watt's assailant. Gripped with absolute fear he could only end his call with the words;

'Just get some fuckin' back up out here now! Assailant appears to be armed! I repeat assailant appears to be armed!'

Sensing that Watts was frightened enough not to struggle, Tony released him from the arm lock. Watts placed his hands firmly on top of his head and spoke as calmly as he could.

'Now just relax,' he said, desperately trying to assume authority.

Tony responded to his authority by hitting him across the side of his head with butt of his gun.

'A you want to relax, beast boy!' he exclaimed.

Tony was nervous. The gun shook violently in his hand. He tried to calculate Watt's next move. He calculated wrong, for as Watts, forgetting himself, turned to plead with him Tony let fly with the trigger. Luck came running back onto the pier.

'What the fuck happened man?' he yelled, dropping the soaking piece of rope that he had found. 'His mate, heard the shot! He's probably gone to get ...'

Luck could say no more. He stared blankly at the floor, looked up at Tony, across instantly at Pum Pum and shouting;

'Fuck! You shot him! You fuckin' shot him!'

Tony, mouth agape, stared in disbelief at the bloodied and trembling policeman lying on the ground. Pum Pum turned around and threw up. He had never seen so much blood in his life as it gushed unceasingly from Watts' stomach and it was all too much for him.

'What are we gonna do?' yelled a hysterical Luck.

Tony rested his hand on his forehead. Trembling from head to toe he tried desperately to collect his thoughts.

'Come grab de money!' he concluded. 'They'll be coming back! Grab de money and mek we bail out!'

Immediately, Luck and Pum Pum shot into action. Without a second thought they gathered the money and the drugs and sped off, leaving Tony to stare blankly at the dying Watts. Fear consumed his very being. Mentally he had entered a space that he had no idea, no experience of. It made him dizzy and his breathing heavy, almost wheezy, as if he had been suddenly struck by a bout of asthma. He hoped that he was dreaming but the constant stream of blood that issued from Watts' body was a reminder that this was all too real. He shook as he reached into his pocket. Pulling out a piece of screwed up paper he opened it, nearly spilling the contents. Once safely opened, he shoved the packet into his nose and inhaled, making the tip of his nose white. He looked like a clown; silly, comical and pathetic. Breathing heavily and trembling frantically he tried to compose himself but was unable to do so as he felt a sudden whack on the back of his head. It was Pum Pum who had come back to make sure that Tony wasn't going to do anything else stupid for the night, like stay behind.

'You stupid rasshole! Man you got to stop taking that fuckin' shit!' Pum Pum shouted. 'Come on!'

With that Pum Pum dragged him off. Tony was in a daze; he didn't know where he was. Luck did, he took the driver's seat switched the car on after retrieving the keys from Tony's pocket and sped off. After about five minutes Watts' body stopped shaking. Lying in a pool of blood, it stopped still. Tony was now a murderer and somehow it didn't feel like it did in the movies. Dazed and confused he sat in the back of the car as Pum Pum and Luck stopped the car and switched seats. They had reasoned that Pum Pum's more elevated driving skills were necessary now and once firmly in the drivers seat he let rip on the accelerator. Tony hardly knew where he was, his heart was pounding ten to the dozen. He closed his eyes, whispering a short prayer repeatedly. In his twisted and miserable state he thought of Jean and once again longed for her comforting embrace.

As they sped out of the docks, Pum Pum had to swerve desperately to avoid the oncoming police Land Rover and three pursuing Panda cars behind it. But like an experienced drag-race driver he avoided them and sped off for the motorway. It wasn't long though, before the incessant blaring of police sirens broke through the eerie silence of the motorway. The three Panda cars and the Land Rover were chasing them.

'Fuck!' shouted a panic stricken Luck. 'We've got to outrun them Pum Pum or else it's our arse!' he declared.

Pum Pum didn't need telling. He had been in a couple of car chases before and one had ended up with him being caught, accused, arrested and jailed and that wasn't going to happen again without a fight. Luck braced himself and threw on his seat belt, something that he was not accustomed to doing. He watched the road intently, urging Pum Pum to go faster and every now and then to watch out for the odd motorcar in front just before Pum Pum swerved to avoid it. He looked into his wing mirror, encouraging himself that the objects in them were further away than they appeared to be. But there wasn't much time to think. He could only watch the front and keep an eye on their pursuers, passing information as to their closeness to Pum Pum who had hit the throttle and was driving like a veteran.

Tony sat up. The frantic speed of the motor car had roused him from his reverie. It had taken a while for him to decipher exactly what was going down, but when he looked out of the back window the stunning truth became painfully obvious to him. Lights flashed and sirens co-ordinated their eerie fanfare with the fierce crescendo of turbo engines and the vicious engagement of rubber and hard wet road. Fear gripped him as the blood in his body ran ten to the dozen and his heart palpitated wildly. His breath became short as the prospect of being caught or the prospect of Pum Pum losing control of the car and crashing gripped him. He shook and closed his eyes for a minute to relax himself as his breathing became ever more erratic. He couldn't stop trembling and every now and then he would break wind as the deadly reality of the situation descended on him with increasing clarity. As the chase continued, it began to shower heavier with rain giving the whole deadly episode enhanced jeopardy. Pum Pum applied the windscreen wipers to their fullest extent and continued to accelerate for dear life.

Tony, now under the manic influence of the drugs he had taken, became wickedly deranged. The buzz that he got from the drug coupled with the adrenaline rush of the speed and the chase, had a Jekyll and Hyde effect on him. A feeling of raving insanity and absolute power flowed through his veins, contorting his very behaviour as if he were now a god. As he sat in the back of the car he began to rock, slowly at first then more frantically as if he were a head-banger at a heavy metal concert. Then he began to shout before his whole body began to shake as if a Pentecostal spirit had taken over him.

'Fuckin' pigs! Fuckin' filff fuck off! Leave me alone! Pigs! Fuckin' pigs!' he shouted over and over in a demented manner. Then, without any control or thought of the damage that he could cause, he banged incessantly on the back window and shouted obscenities at the hoard of Police motor cars that were giving chase.

'Keep that rasshole idiot down!' Pum Pum shouted at Luck, who really could do nothing as Tony's drug induced rage reached a new peak. 'This fucking heap needs a blasted service!' he complained loudly. 'Guy got such a beautiful motor an' he don't know how to take care of the rasshole!'

Luck was concentrating so hard on his reluctant role as helmsman that he did not noticed Tony pulling out his gun and re-loading. Tony had now gone completely off his head as the chasing pack grew terrifyingly close to the car, their siren noises becoming louder. Tony's natural inner strength hadn't equipped him to function within the deadly scenario that was unfolding. But the drugs helped him to confront it and that's what he was going to do. He felt like a Titan. Aggression was etched all over his face as he aimed his gun at the chasing vehicles.

'Tony! What the fuck are you doing?' shouted Luck as he noticed Tony taking aim through the rear window.

'Leave me alone bwoy!' was Tony's vicious and uncooperative reply. He laughed a wickedly maniacal laugh, directing his frenzy towards the convoy of chasing cars that were getting closer all the time. Luck knew only too well what was going to happen. Pum Pum noticed Tony's actions in the rear-view mirror and he implored Luck to make sure that Tony didn't pull the trigger, but too late, for in seconds the rear windscreen shattered into a million pieces and a rush of cold air filled the car. Tony held his arms aloft like a victorious boxing champion soaking in the praise from adoring fans, shouting incessantly at the police that were giving chase. Then he held the gun and pointed at the chasing police cars that swerved to avoid the bullets as Tony let loose a series of deadly gunfire at them.

'Ya think ya can cyatch me, bitch? Fuckin' Babylon! You nah catch me!' he shouted with crazed passion. Tony was now living in reality a fantasy that he'd had so often in the past. He was Al Pacino in 'Scarface', or O'Dogg from 'Menace to Society'. He released another volley of gunfire, less focused this time, but as the windscreen of the Land Rover shattered he cheered.

'Fuck you pig! Fuck you!' he bawled madly as the driver, no longer able to control his motor car, ran alongside the crash barriers, destroying the side of it. The impact eventually caused the car to swerve. The driver lost control, the vehicle skidded and fell on its side. As the Land Rover lay horizontal across the motorway, it was hit by one of the cars behind causing an almighty smash and disabling both motors instantly. Wheels, windows and pieces of shattered metal flew across the motorway in vivid destruction.

'Woooooeeeee yessss!' cried Tony, arms raised in triumph. Neither Luck nor Pum Pum could believe what they had just seen, they looked at each other blankly for a split second then concentrated on the road again.

'I must be fuckin' dreaming!' cried a defeated Luck eventually. Tony had raised the stakes once again. This was, for both of them the most horrific moment in their lives. They might as well have been in a war zone, for they were having to draw on the same depth of mental strength and agility to live through it. There were now two cars left. Tony was enthused.

'You warn come agen!?' he screamed. 'Come den nuh? Unumuss warn dead! Unumuss warn dead!'

Another hail of gunfire let rip from his piece, again the chasing Panda cars had to swerve to avoid being easy targets. The drivers were inexperienced and unarmed. Finally, in a vain attempt to avoid yet another volley of gunfire they hit each other, lost control and just like the other two police cars went sprawling across a wet but thankfully empty motorway.

As the BMW sped off, Tony, gun still in hand, held his arms aloft once again, half in praise of himself and half in celebration. The atmosphere became less tense in the car. Pum Pum and Luck were furious with Tony but relieved to have escaped. Whether or not all they had done was delay the inevitable and add more charges to the ones that they already had, they would have to wait to find out. Tony slumped back into the seat, a glint of excitement written all over his face.

'You see dat? You see dat?' he screamed excitedly. 'Bad bwoy you know, bad bwoy, me save de fuckin' day!' he ranted, beating his chest like Tarzan.

Pum Pum was downright angry at the way things had gone down, but he could not hide his elation at the fact that they had all gotten away. Luck though was more pensive.

'Suppose them fuckers are dead?' he asked grimly.

There was silence at first then Tony spoke up.

'Then they burn in fuckin' hell!' he concluded. Pum Pum and Luck's reaction was instant.

'Shut the fuck up!' they bellowed simultaneously and as they sped away, still cautious that they probably weren't out of the woods yet, they considered what they would do once safely back in town. The drive back was steady and watchful. Their minds were littered with questions as to what would be their next play. As Pum Pum guided the car through the streets they considered themselves lucky not to have passed any other police. Luck directed Pum Pum to his friend Chicken's house who ran a car repair shop from there. As they pulled up, Luck jumped out of the car and rang the door-bell. It took a long time for Chicken to answer the door. His fat stomach swelled over the top of his boxer shorts. His big frame filled the doorway as he directed a grim tired look at Luck.

'Just tell me what the fuck you doin' at my house so late, or should I say so early? I got fuckin' kids trying to sleep man,' he opened aggrievedly.

Luck's tone was nervous and apologetic.

'We've got trouble man,' he opened.

'So what the fuck that got to do with me? You fuckin' dealers always got rahtid trouble, what the fuck that's got to do with me? I don't need your fuckin' trouble.'

Luck had a look of resignation on his face that helped his plea once it eventually came out.

'Fuck it, Chicken man I need your help man, big time.'

'I helped you once already, why I got to help you again?'

'Chicken, please.' Luck didn't want to say it, but he had to.

Chicken was quiet, he looked at the tense, pitiful sight before him. A young boy, who had much better life prospects than those that he had allowed himself to get into. He took a final glance and allowed his good nature to take over.

'What is it?'

Luck looked up at him eagerly.

'We need to re-spray that thing and get the original plates back on it,' he said pointing at Tony's motor.

'You need a rear window too!' said Chicken sarcastically.

'Oh … yeah … we do,' replied Luck, hoping that Chicken wouldn't ask how it had happened.

Chicken eyed the car with affection. He liked the look of it and was somewhat humbled by the challenge ahead.

'I don't wanna know what trouble you in. Far as I'm concerned you're another customer. I will help you out with the little things. Anything else, that's where I draw the line. I'm gonna open the garage, leave it in there with the keys and check me tomorrow night.' Luck's face brightened. He was about to thank him, but Chicken had little time for it.

'It's gonna cost you too,' he said, closing the door. 'Pull up to the garage front.'

Luck hurried over to Pum Pum who was waiting anxiously to know what had transpired.

'What that fat fucka gon' do?' Pum Pum queried.

'Leave the car here,' Luck said. 'Chickens' gonna re-spray it.'

Upon hearing those words Tony jumped up.

'You fuckin' crazy?' he moaned. 'Re-spray my fuckin' motor? No fuckin' way man!'

Luck threw him a look that would have pierced his heart if it were a knife.

'Look you fuckin' ignorant fuck!' he raged 'I'm trying to save your tired arse. What the fuck do you want? You wanna do a fuckin' bird? We're re-spraying your precious little number here and that's that! Either that or I go to the cops now, and give my arse up, me and Pum Pum get a couple of years you get fuckin' life! What's it to be?'

Tony had no quarrel. The young soldier was right once again. He laid back into the leather seat and exhaled loudly.

'You can pick it up back tomorrow OK?' Luck reassured him.

Pum Pum said nothing as he manoeuvred the car into Chicken's garage, which by now he had opened. Once inside, the three men solemnly left the vehicle, thanked Chicken and walked gingerly and in total silence back to their respective homes.

nine

As Detective Inspector Kirk stepped out of his car he surveyed the scene at the docks with anger. Plastic 'POLICE. DO NOT CROSS' signs were arrayed around the fatal area where Watts had fallen. His body lay covered by a blanket. It had not yet made its way into a body bag. Six police cars were on the scene as onlookers tried their best to peer over the shoulders of the officers who were shielding the body. A couple of news cameras were rolling and reporters were giving their comments. Other reporters spoke into mobile phones or made notes and as Kirk stepped over, he was accosted by four of them who shoved their microphones and dictaphones in his face, begging him for a statement.

'No comment!' he growled as he brushed past them to the death scene.

'Do you have any information regarding the officer's death?' pressed one reporter.

'Not a fuckin' pig's bollock!' replied Kirk. 'Broadcast that and fuck off the lot of you!'

As he approached a team of five plain-clothed officers, one a woman, his words were issued with outrage.

'Hennessy!' he stormed at one of them. 'What the fuck is this? A fuckin' fairground? Get these fuckin' paparazzi wankers away from here now!'

Hennessy, a fat man, jumped to it instantly and in seconds was ushering the reporters away. Kirk turned to the woman next, who anticipating his next words, broke in first.

'PC 3478 Clive Watts, 33 years old, married with two children. Good record, few black marks against him. Died of a single gunshot wound to the stomach,' she said.

'His family know?' enquired Kirk without looking at her,

preferring to gather as much information as he could from the scene of death.

'Not yet sir,' she replied.

'Get onto it!' he ordered.

'Yes sir.'

Hands in pockets, he walked to the centre of the scene and surveyed the area once again then his eyes settled on the dead body that lay before him.

'Gimme all you got Pritchard!' he shouted.

Pritchard, another member of the homicide team, walked over to stand beside Kirk. He knelt down next to the body and began his appraisal.

'Looks like our man walked in on a drugs deal. Slight marks around his neck tell us that he was probably held in an arm lock before the shooting took place. Took a knock to the back of the head too, probably got a bit shirty. Looks like it was done with the butt of a gun. We may be trying to find two suspects, a piece of rope was dropped just over there. We'll be looking for prints, but it was wet so we may not be very successful. His partner, a PC Nelson, was in the Panda. Says he thought he heard our assailant shout to someone else. Pom Pom's the name that he heard, probably a Rasta, we reckon that's an alias, referring to a pom pom hat probably. Looks like they didn't want to kill him, maybe just tie him up. Watts was standing about here. His partner was sat in the Panda just over there, couldn't see much. Watts turned to him and ...' Pritchard was now standing and mimicking Watt's last movements. His movement took him to the spot where Watts was felled.

'Blam!' he continued. 'Single shot to the stomach. Our hero falls'.

'Murder? Manslaughter?' enquired Kirk.

'Too soon to tell. Guess courts are gonna have to decide that one,' replied Pritchard.

'The assailant?' Kirk asked.

'Not enough information to tell at this stage but we're probably looking for a nigger. About six-foot, well built. He would have to be to handle poor old Watts, as you can see he was a big fella,' responded Pritchard. 'I'll have a full report in the morning for you sir.'

As Pritchard walked away, Kirk looked around the spot some

more, his mind working all the time, trying to picture the scene. There was little evidence around, but Kirk didn't need much. His professional experience had taught him to make the most use of what information he had. Inspector Hatchet was next up and Kirk motioned him over.

'Profile,' he said. Like Pritchard before him, Hatchet got to work with regimented efficiency.

'Not much to go on yet sir, but I'll give you my thoughts,' he opened. 'Drug dealer probably Black, most likely a novice. He got away with the goods but he bungled this one. Might have been a big score, but the fact that he bungled it suggests that he's probably new to the game. Carried a gun but doesn't seem to be a killer, probably the first time he's ever used one. Probably uses it as a bit of bravado but nevertheless keeps it loaded, 'cos he's never sure when he may have to use it. A professional would have probably killed him outright, to ensure that there were no witnesses. But it looks as though all he wanted to do was tie him up again suggesting that he's a novice, probably watches too many movies. We're tracing the gun, looks like a magnum. Not a yardie thing, but it looks like our friend has ambitions in that direction.'

'What about the other guy?' asked Watts.

'Zilch at this moment sir. Pom Pom's the only name we have, probably a Rasta.'

'Ain't no fuckin' Rasta,' corrected Kirk, slightly angrily. 'Those guys don't wear fuckin' pom poms on their hats. Kids do. Fuck that idea off.'

'Yes sir,' replied Hatchet slightly embarrassed. 'We picked up a local informer, a dealer, name of Baron. He's being interviewed at this moment. Says he's had dealings with one of the guys. We'll have his statement soon.'

'Good,' said Kirk.

'Full report tomorrow sir,' added Hatchet as he walked off to continue his investigation.

Kirk began to rack his brain some more. He tried to recall everything he'd learned during seventeen years on the force, particularly his experiences of dealing with Black people. The name Pom Pom disturbed him. This was no ordinary name. It was, as his inspectors had surmised, probably an alias, but no Black person would take on an alias like Pom Pom. No. He reasoned that Nelson had heard wrong. Or at least that he had heard right, but being unfamiliar with West Indian patois had allowed his own English perceptions to get in the way of what he had heard. His mind raced desperately for an answer. He studied what he knew of Black street culture as his mind drifted through the various phrases and meanings of the terms that Black peoples' lingo offered. Then in an instant it hit him. He took centre stage, called to his inspectors and regardless of who was listening made a statement.

'OK, listen up. We're looking for at least two people,' he began. 'Black. Drug dealers. Novices. One or all of them armed. They picked a shitty spot for a major drugs score. An open space with places for concealed viewing. The leader doesn't know much about the game. He's a dreamer. Probably scared shitless right now. Probably on the run. Soon as we get a description we should scour the airports. He'll probably be looking to get out of the country soon. Jamaica, Barbados or some fuckin' jungle bunny country. He's probably a drug addict too. We've got one suspect, name of Gapford Maycock. I nicked him five years ago. Goes by the name of Pum Pum, Jamaican slang for pussy, vagina, cunt - call it what you want. Sort of name you'd give to a guy like him. He's a pimp, that's what I pulled him in for and he still hasn't learnt his lesson. I want him brought in.'

'Have we got a recent address?' shouted the female investigator.

'Probably not, but I know where we can find him.'

Kirk turned to walk back to his car.

'Where?' shouted the female cop eagerly.

'Elisha Road,' came the chilling reply. 'I want the works. Anderson; organise it. When we go in I want total back up. I want those cunts to think that Desert fuckin' Storm hit them. No shit. When we go in, we go in hard. See you all in the morning with your reports.' Kirk said no more, but got into his Vauxhall Vectra and drove off. Anderson, the female cop, turned to Hatchet with a worried look on her face.

'Think he wants you to second on this one,' said Hatchet. 'Might be good for you, could lead to a promotion maybe.'

The words gave Anderson no encouragement.

'Yes I suppose it could be good,' she said, blowing a gust of nervous breath from her mouth. 'Let's just see if we survive Elisha Road first huh?

Evening. Jean was subdued. She had been like this for two days, not having heard a single thing from Tony since the party. She had spent the first day wallowing in a pit of misery and had, in that period, cleared more bottles of Thunderbird, Babycham and Lambrusco than she ever had in her life. Normally she wasn't a drinker and the events of the last few days hadn't turned her into an alcoholic, but she was practising hard. The words of her mother rang once in her head, an admonition not to drink alone, because people that drank alone had problems. She heard her mothers voice once, then ignored it. Halfway through the day she had figured on progressing to the heavier stuff. The Gins, Vodkas, Brandys and Rums were all lined up ready and waiting for her to start on them, but the latest instalment of 'Coronation Street', then 'Eastenders' and then 'Brookside' had halted her flow. Since she watched those shows, she drank no more, got her head together and carried on with her evening as best she could. As she stared almost blankly at the T.V., the shrill noise of the telephone echoed throughout her living room. It was Sheila.

'Hiya babes,' she opened. 'How's it going? Ready to make some conversation now?' Jean was clearly stopped in her tracks.

'Yes Sheila, it's confirmed, I got the tests back today. I'm pregnant,' heaved Jean, knowing that this was the reason for the phone call. 'I knew anyway… no I haven't seen him for a couple of days now, not since the party… no sign of Luck or Pum Pum either? Gosh. I wonder if they're in trouble?… Yes you're right, I'd better call him and tell him… so you're coming over later?… OK, well I'll be here, not going out at all… see you later.'

No sooner had Jean put down the phone than there was a knock at the door. She shuddered and took a deep breath before approaching it. Something told her that it was Tony. Her intuition was confirmed as she pulled the door open. There he stood, soaked through by the rain. He hung his head. She did too before whispering;

'Come in.'

Cautiously, Tony entered. He took off his long trench coat and laid it carefully on the back of a chair. Jean immediately removed it and headed for the small cupboard next to the kitchen where her immersion heater was, she hung it in there. Cautiously, and half whispering an invitation, she motioned towards the settee. Hardly able to speak himself, he humbly took a seat. She sat next to him, not as closely as she usually did, but close enough to send a signal that things were OK and that she was ready to talk.

'Haven't seen you since the party,' she said tensely.

'Yeah, I was busy y'know,' he replied.

'You could have called.'

'So could you. You forget I had a pager?'

'It's been off.'

The air filled with silence once again. They had almost set off on the wrong foot, by immediately engaging themselves in a difference of opinion and neither of them wanted to continue with that. Jean got up.

'Want a drink?' she asked.

'Yeah, a double whisky please,' he replied.

Jean walked thoughtfully across the room to the kitchen, where she kept her drinks. She couldn't remember the last time Tony ever said please to her and wondered why he was suddenly being so polite. She prayed that it was maybe the start of something good. Tony played nervously with the sovereign ring on his middle finger while he waited, concentrating more on what he was going to say to her than anything else. He hardly noticed that he had pulled it off. Jean was back in an instant with the drink. Without realising, he placed the ring on the coffee table in readiness for the arduous task ahead of him. He took the drink from her nervously and took a sip before placing it carefully on the table. They must have had the same mindset because the next words they spoke were the same.

'I've got something to tell you,' they both said in tandem.

'You go first,' Tony said, almost apologetically.

'No you go first,' Jean insisted. She was more keen to hear what he had to say than to tell him her news.

Tony straightened up. It was clear to Jean that his next words were going to be difficult for him to say so she did her best to make him feel at ease by holding the silence and staring at the ground. Tony arose from the settee, took an almighty deep breath and walked across the room, slowly pacing up and down as if in a desperate bid to compose himself. He too, staring at the ground and nervously rubbing his hands together, did his best to avoid eye contact. Finally the blood rush was under control. His heart seemed to skip a beat as the moment descended upon him. In the instant that it took to send a signal from his brain to his mouth, he could have easily abandoned the words but he didn't, he took the plunge then spoke.

'About the other night, the party,' he began sheepishly, 'I just want you to know that I'm sorry for what happened. The drugs, it kinda spun my head you know?'

'So the rumours are true?' Jean queried.

'Yes, but it wasn't serious. I mean I wasn't addicted or anything, but I went to a rehabilitation centre anyway. That's where I've been the last couple of days. I'm over it now.'

'How long have you been taking drugs for?'

'Oh I had just started. It was like a fascination thing you know? Luck is well into that sort of thing and he ... well ... he made me try it out and I got kinda hooked y'know?'

'What about the gun?'

'I threw that away. Jesus Christ I don't know what I was doing with a gun. Drugs can really make you do some crazy things. Jean, I just want you to know that I'm back on my feet. I was stupid, believe me, I'll never treat you like that again. Jean, I want to try again, forgive me nuh please.'

Jean was taken aback. Never before had Tony displayed such remorse. But she erred on the side of caution. After the events at the party she wasn't so easily convinced that he was for real. After all, he had revealed a new side of himself to her then and he was doing so again now.

'Hear what I've got to say, then we can talk,' she said matter-of-factly.

Tony looked at her coldly, not knowing what to expect. Jean motioned for him to sit down. As he reached the settee she reoccupied her seat next to him, but this time a little closer than she had been.

'Tony,' she started. 'I'm pre ...' he was cut off in mid sentence as the shrill pitch of the telephone echoed around the room. She was embarrassed and not wanting the din of the phone, nor the possibility of a long conversation with whoever it was to disrupt what she was going to say, she begged Tony to hold on as she reached to answer it. He could barely make out the voice on the other end of the phone, but was soon convinced by the way that Jean spoke that it was male. He listened intently, paying particular attention to Jean's voice patterns all the time. He detected that she was nervous and was very conscious of his presence. Even her evasive manner was not enough to discourage the caller from inviting himself round sometime. Jean reluctantly agreed and made quick arrangements with him before replacing the receiver, much to Tony's disquiet. He noted that it was a phone call that she did not want, but for what reason he didn't know. It made his blood boil, but under the circumstances he did his best to remain calm. The only problem was, that his best, was at best, only ever a few seconds in duration.

'Anyway,' Jean said returning her attentions to him. 'Like I was saying ...'

'Who was on the phone?' Tony questioned in a troubled tone of voice.

'Oh no-one,' she replied in a dismissive manner. 'Just an old friend. Anyway like I was saying ...'

'Which friend? What's his name?' Tony was persistent.

'No-one, honestly he's not important.'

'What was his name!?'

Tony had begun to shout. Jean knew that the Jamaican accent was on its way. She tried to calm him down but Tony had already gone too far. She stood centre of the living room massaging her fingers and staring at the floor and spoke softly, trying her best to remain relaxed. She was filled with trepidation and it showed on her face. She didn't want another argument with Tony, particularly over such a clearly unfortunate turn of events as this.

'David,' she said softly.

Tony erupted.

'Was it that bat face likkle bumbo-claart wah me nearly kill de odda night?'

Jean remained silent.

'Was it!?'

'Yes.'

'I see.'

'Tony, believe me, there's nothing in it. He's just an old friend. Someone I knew from college, that's all. I mean, I even think I told you about him. He's an ex boyfriend.'

Jean's last three words were said quietly as she dropped her head, realising the mistake she had just made. She realised that her receiving a call from an ex boyfriend was just not going to sit well with Tony. Nervousness had overtaken her and the constant blood rush had caused her thoughts to falter. In trying to be honest and in trying to make the situation seem a little less suspicious, she had only made it worse and aroused Tony's very mixed passions even more.

' Ex man? Ex boyfriend? Gyal, you know what time it is?'

'What? It's nine o'clock.'

'Look man it late. No man, no friend, no ex don't suppose to ring you so rahtid late!!'

'Please Tony don't get the wrong idea, it's all perfectly innocent.'

'Innocent? The way he was feeling up your batty while you were dancing didn't look very innocent to me.'

'He wasn't feeling up my bottom.'

'You mean you didn't notice? What? You were enjoying it too much too notice, or is that what you always do when you go out?'

Tears began to well up in Jean's eyes and her face contorted as she fought to control them. Those words were unnecessary and uncalled for.

'Tony no, please don't do this,' she managed to say.

'So him a come roun' ya?'

'Yes, just for a visit, not tonight though. Look, you can be here if you want when he comes. Jesus Christ Tony, please don't get the wrong idea, please, darling, it's not like that at all. Please I don't want you to start getting ideas.'

'Me nah get ideas.'

'Good, then let's forget about that, it's not important. Look what I wanted to tell you was …'

'How did he get your number?'

'Oh Christ.'

'Me ask you how him get your number!?'

'I don't know.'

'You don't rassclaart know?' Tony said sarcastically.

'Honestly. You know, I forgot to ask him. It didn't even cross my mind. Look I'll sort it out OK, something's not right. I don't know how he got my number. I swear I'll sort it out but now let's just deal with this matter OK?

'No it's not OK, I don't like guys ringing my woman OK?'

'Tony it's nothing really. Please let's just …'

'You know what time it is?'

'You asked me that already. Yes I know it's late but ...'

'Nobody don't supposed to ring you so late!'

'Tony I got the message the first time, I ... I'm sorry, OK, it won't happen again.'

'You heard what I said? I don't think you heard what I said, it too fuckin' late man.'

Jean couldn't take much more, she put her hands to her ears and went wild.

'Tony please!' she bellowed 'I can't take this! You are so paranoid! Look there is nothing going on. Jesus Christ! I get one lousy phone call and ...'

'It only tek one phone call.'

'One phone call for what?'

'You know wha me a talk boat.'

'Oh please Tony don't be stupid!'

'Don't call me stupid!'

'Tony please calm down.'

'Me calm!!'

His last words were bellowed at the top of his voice. It bought an excruciating silence that for Jean was unbearable. Tony approached her and stared coldly and menacingly into her eyes. It seemed to last forever, a beam of madness shot from his red, almost bloodshot eyes before he threw a punch so hard that when it connected she fell back, toppling over the glass coffee table behind her. Glass shattered into a hundred pieces and Jean hurt her back as she fell with great force onto the stem of the table.

'Tony! Oh my God! No! Jesus Christ no!' she screamed, frantically crawling off the sheets of glass that had been smashed beneath her, the very image of fear and total shock etched on her face. She pleaded with him again but to no avail. Tony grabbed her hair and pulled her to him. With flailing arms she struggled desperately, trying to fend him off, but he was far stronger than she was and it was no trouble for him to hold her by her hair with one hand and slap her face with the other. She bellowed with pain as each slap, first the palm and then the back of his hand connected with terrifying rhythm. More screams of pain blended with the violent thud as he threw her headlong into the wall. Her shrieking was clearly audible and so too were his insults;

'Bitch! Slag! Slapper!' he bellowed as he tore into her once again. Thunderous fists of pain rained their heavy punishment down on her face. She kept struggling though and he, tired of having to wrestle his way to her, stood over her and let his feet do the work. Her head, back and stomach were the easiest to reach and just like his football heroes, he worked her like a penalty shoot-out, one deadly kick after the other. It became almost enjoyable for him, particularly as she no longer fought back. She merely curled her body up, trying desperately to shield herself and particularly her head from the onslaught. A hopeless idea it turned out to be as Tony put his hand in his back pocket and pulled out his gun. He turned it around in his hand and holding the nozzle proceeded to beat her with the handle. Time and time again he struck her with it until the blood from her face and head began to stain the cream carpet of the living room.

Breathing heavily and with the devil in his eyes, Tony took a step backward intently eyeing the pathetic picture of helplessness that lay before him. She was no longer crying now but coughing. Holding her mouth and lamely trying to catch the blood as it issued forth. Shaky though calm he moved toward the small table next to the settee that the telephone was sat upon and with a knife drawn from his back pocket severed the wire. Breathing quite heavily he moved over to the airing cupboard where his coat was hanging and without even a backward glance he lifted it up, slung it over his shoulder and headed for the front door where he stopped, thought for a moment, then headed back to the kitchen. He took the bottle of whisky, twisted off the cap, and took a long slug of the spirit before staggering back into the living room to take a last glance at the twisted shape of Jean. Another swig of the whisky and he was out of the house, not even bothering to pull the door after him.

Jean was barely conscious, unable to open her eyes for the blood that trickled steadily over them. She lay twisted on the floor, aware only of the morbid silence and the faint hum of traffic outside her open front door. Her head spun and amid all the agonising pain she tried to negotiate her way to the telephone. Her desperate attempts to stand were hopeless as the agony in her stomach forced her back to the floor. Eventually she managed to crawl her way to the settee and use it as leverage to pull herself up. She reached for the phone and held the handset to her ear only to be met by a chilling silence.

Her breathing became more strained and her chest heaved as she fought for breath. Her senses were becoming duller and struggle as she did, she soon realised that nothing she could do would stop her from fading. Her mind was too dulled to sustain any form of revolt, any form of normal activity. Her body shook and eventually she could do no more. She sat in hopeless repose before slipping limply onto the floor as her mind faded to black.

ten

It had been a long day and was becoming a longer night for Detective Inspector Kirk as he waded through endless files and various bits of paperwork. This was the aspect of his precious job that he disliked intensely. He was an action junkie who liked to live life on the edge. His wife and children hadn't seen him for six days and although he knew that she was upset about it, he didn't give a fuck. His work was more important to him and hey, it brought home the dough, put bread on the table and helped her seduce the milkman. So what the hell was she complaining for?

The rush of excitement that his job could often provide was, in his opinion, better than sex, or at least better than sex with that hag that he called a wife. Whenever he fucked her she would moan and groan for a while, probably shake her fat pussy for a second, scream, light up a fag then fall asleep. She had grown fat too. Sex with her felt like fucking a pregnant whale nowadays. It was not something that he looked forward to. The kids were always moaning as well, wanting to know when they were going to go on holiday and where to. Toby wanted to go on a boat across the sea and Genevieve wanted to go somewhere that had cliffs. A trip to the Isle of Man would please both of them, he reasoned, and it would please him no end if they all fell of the fucking cliff, then he might get some peace about the house. As he pulled on his cigarette he sat back in his chair to try and recollect his thoughts.

He mused over the recently labelled docks killings. If he could get a result with this one, it would increase his chances of getting a promotion no end. The Chief constable was on his case too and this worried him. It was beginning to look bad for the force, the fact that they hadn't yet produced an arrest. But there was a certain pleasure that he derived from this case too and it was the fact that he was chasing a nigger. This made his work all the more exciting because to him, he was finally doing some good.

All policemen join the force to do some good, he reasoned. Sure, many became corrupted after being in the force for a while, but he believed that essentially a copper's objective was to do society a service and to rid society of all its inherent evils. Black people were an evil as far as he was concerned. Fuck the Chief Constable and his Equal Opportunities bullshit. Fuck all those lefty do-gooders, they were wankers and tossers. Pulling their average-sized plonkers in front of a bunch of professional piss artists who had nothing to do but dream up ridiculous policies that didn't mean shit to anyone but them. As far as he was concerned the police shouldn't have an Equal Opportunities policy statement or a stinking department and fuck the Black Police Association too, what the fuck was all that about? A bunch of wogs join the police force and automatically they start talking about having their own little apartheid. What was the fucking world coming to? The force didn't need it. What it needed was more officers ready to take on the Black invasion, rid the country of these no-good ignorant niggers and lock them all up.

He had felt this way since he was a child. His father was a policemen and had been caught up in the Notting Hill riots of '58 and the experience had left him mentally scarred and had ruined a promising career as an officer of the law. He had spent the rest of his days dealing with the post traumatic stress disorder that the occurrence had left him with. Kirk had grown up having to care for his father and the tormented years spent watching him become more and more of an emotional and mental wreck took their toll. Kirk didn't consider himself a racist, he didn't know what that was. He never cared very much for the term, it meant nothing to him. He was just a good citizen who, like his father before him, simply wanted to do some good by joining the force.

The docks case held more than a passing interest for him. A Black man had killed a police officer. There was a great deal of animosity around the station and indeed across the county because of it. He knew that there were officers out there that were itching to take revenge on the culprit, and if he could deliver him it would be one of the proudest moments in the whole of his career. It would certainly earn him a few brownie points in the upper echelons of the force, that was for sure. His thoughts were interrupted abruptly by a feverish knock on his office door.

'Come in,' he called.

It was Anderson. She stepped in nervously carrying a bundle of files underneath her arm and gently pushed the door behind her.

'The docks case sir,' she said.

'Sit down,' he replied. 'I was just thinking about that. What have you got for me?'

'Well sir, we feel that our informant seemed to be holding back a little, but we think we got enough from him to pursue another suspect.'

'Go on.'

'Baron says he was at the docks that night, to meet a guy who wanted to deal some coke.'

'By the name of …?'

'Tony something. He didn't catch the other name.'

'One of our set-ups?' asked Kirk.

'No sir.'

'So how the hell does this Baron geezer get to deal coke without us hitting him for it?'

'It's a trade-off we have with him sir, he gets to do what he wants in exchange …'

'… For information,' interrupted Kirk

'Yes sir.'

'Carry on.'

'He's says that there was only one person there that night. This guy that he hadn't seen before. They met via a mutual acquaintance.'

'And that mutual acquaintance wasn't there on the night?'

'Nope, not according to Baron.'

'Would he say who this mutual acquaintance was?'

'No. He mentioned that he was a kid, no-one important.'

'Where's the kid now?'

'He doesn't know. He only had a mobile number for him and now it's cut off.'

'He's protecting him.'

'We don't know that sir.'

'Page him, get him back here.'

'Sir, Baron's a reliable informant. We've grown to trust …'

'Trust? Don't ever trust these niggers Anderson. Never.'

The atmosphere became silent and heavy.

'Go on,' relented Kirk. 'But if we run short of leads, I'm bringing him back in.'

'Yes sir. Anyway, this guy fucked him over, put a gun to his face and told him to leave. Left him with no money, no drugs, no nothing.'

'And?'

'He left.'

'He left?'

'Er yes sir, he left.'

'Did he get a look at the guy before he left?'

'Oh, yes, er yes he did. Graphics have issued a photo-fit to the press. It's going out on the news tonight and will be in the papers tomorrow.'

She tossed Kirk a copy of the picture. He studied it, wondering where he had seen the cunt before.

'Good work,' he said.

'It perfectly matches the description of the guy that shot at the Pandas during the car chase.'

'What fuckin' car chase?' enquired Kirk with surprise.

'Er what? You don't know about the car chase?'

'For fuck's sake Anderson. I wouldn't be asking you if I knew about the damned car chase now would I? I mean for fucks' sake, I'm leading on this fucking case, how come I wasn't told about this?'

'You've not been around sir.'

'I've got a fuckin' phone haven't I?'

'I left a report on your desk yesterday, sir.'

'What? Oh.'

Kirk picked up an unopened envelope marked URGENT from beneath the pile of unopened envelopes that lay on his desk.

'This one?' he asked humbly.

'Yes sir,' replied Anderson. 'PC Nelson, Watts' partner, radioed back in once he heard the shot. A squad hit the scene and gave chase to the suspects.'

'What were they driving?'

'A dark blue BMW 840.'

'Shouldn't be hard to trace.'

'The licence plate turned out to be dud.'

'Probably re-sprayed the fucker now too. Pull in every nigger seen driving one and contact the DVLA. Get addresses of everyone named Tony that has one within a hundred mile radius.'

'We've already started sir, we've got two thousand names to go through.'

'Start with the nigger sounding names, like Marley, Hendrix, Brown ...'

'Kravitz sir?'

'Don't be smart.'

'Anyway the suspect fired at the officers in pursuit.'

'What!?'

'Through the rear window!'

'I do not fuckin' well believe this.'

'He was probably drugged up sir.'

'Oh really? I thought that shooting at a police car was an everyday occurrence. Any fatalities?'

'A few injuries only, thank God, but we lost the vehicles.'

'Fuckin' bastard! Bastard! Now this investigation's costing us money!' shot a sickened Kirk. He mellowed quickly. 'Elisha Road?'

'We move in tonight.'

Kirk smiled.

'Good,' he said sharply and with venom. 'Good'.

Luck and Julie were by the river enjoying a perfect, pleasant evening. It was warm with a cool breeze, slightly more humid than other nights that week as the early evening rain had stopped, but nonetheless peaceful, quiet and ideal for an evening stroll. Luck was enjoying a wonderful respite from the mental hell that he was enduring. Each time he looked at Julie's sublime and simple features, he ached.

From the moment that he had returned from the docks, he had sworn to put the hustling game far behind him, regardless of whether or not he escaped punishment for Tony's deadly mistake. Julie was a way out of the game for him, so it had been quite an easy thing for him to draw closer to her. Thus, the couple of days had been filled with a night out, a meal at a restaurant, long walks, much conversation and something of a bonding between them.

Spending time with Julie was also useful because it enabled him to lay low. He had changed his hairstyle and now sported a fashionable faded 'skifful', as his father used to call it. He had also grown a moustache and a goatee beard brought together by thin strands of hair either side of his mouth. In Julie's eyes, it made him look more handsome and appealing. She had wondered, if only for a minute, why he had gone through such a sudden and drastic change. She asked him, but he shrugged it off with 'Oh, cos I felt like it,' and she pondered the matter no more. She had taken the opportunity to tell him how she felt it had made him look. His response to that was a single and rather strained smile. Julie was in heaven. Luck had been so good to her over the last couple of days that she wondered whether this was merely a dream or whether it was happening for real. She felt a real surge of devotion to him, sensing that this precious young man was in need of help. She wanted only to love him and care for him and Luck had certainly appreciated her efforts thus far.

As they leaned across the edge of the bridge, he having suddenly disappeared in deep contemplation, she once again sensed that he was troubled. So she placed her arm gently across his shoulder and kissed his cheek.

'What's wrong? You've been quiet this evening. Got something on your mind?' she asked quietly and with special care.

Luck desperately wanted to tell her his problems, in the hope that they would go away, but he sensibly reasoned that they wouldn't and therefore swore that no matter how difficult it was for him, he would to keep them to himself.

'No, nothing,' he replied. 'I'm fine.'

She looked at him, desperately wanting to press the issue. Luck was clearly finding it difficult to handle something. She didn't know what it was, but it played on her. However, not wanting to upset Luck by pursuing the matter too aggressively, she waved away the notion. She figured that when he was ready to tell her what his problems were, he would and when he did, she would be right there to give him all the comfort she could. A second thought shuddered its way across her mind, why not at least say something to him now? Hell, he was evidently troubled now. He needed comfort immediately, right this minute she thought. Speak to him. Speak to him now. Let him know how much she cared. With a slow intake of breath she turned to him and held him firmly with both arms locked around his neck. She took her time to speak again and when she did, her deeply internalised emotion for him found the words.

'I think it may be a bit too soon for me to say this, but who cares, I think I'll take my chances. I love you. I've never met anyone that I've cared about so much in such a short space of time. I want you to know that whenever you have troubles and whenever you have worries, I will be here for you. Right here, right by your side. Understand?'

Luck had no words. He merely took a gentle intake of breath himself and nodded. He closed his eyes and gently allowed his lips to meet hers. He had been worried about being seen, being noticed. He was on the run and it nagged him, but in the moment that they kissed, he was free. A slight gust of wind caressed his face and bought up goose pimples, across his cold cheek. But before the cold could settle, the warmth of Julie's hand caressed his face, warming his cheek once again. It was a strange moment, but one which seemed to signify that from the whole sordid mess that was now his life, something wonderful had arisen. As the kiss came to a tender halt Julie whispered 'I promised I'd go and see Jean this evening, care to accompany me?'

Luck shuddered at the sound of the name, realising that if it wasn't for her, or at least because of Tony's misplaced affection for her, he probably wouldn't be in this situation now. But he reasoned quickly that he would be wrong to hold it against her. He gave a quick nod.

'Sure, anything you want to do,' he said quietly, and they turned back in the direction of the car. As they held hands and walked in a sombre yet comforting silence, a tiny tear fell from his eye and rolled slowly down the side of his face. Luck looked up to the sky and prayed for his life and for his freedom. He wiped the tear away then looked at Julie who, fortunately, had been giving her attention to negotiating the slightly wet grass rather than looking at him. He smiled inside to comfort his soul and continued his walk.

Sheila had had an uneasy feeling about Jean's welfare ever since the events at the party, which was why she frequently called her and often paid her impromptu visits. Though they had recently spoken on the phone, she felt that – especially with the news of her pregnancy – another visit was due sooner rather than later. On the way to Jean's place, she met Shakela who was also on her way to the flat to show off her new mobile phone and to give Jean the number. As the two ladies approached Jean's building, they made polite conversation with each other. Jean was the only thing that brought these two women together. Under other circumstances they may not even have looked at each other in the street.

As they passed through the main door to the building they felt no suspicion about the fact that it was wide open. The residents of the other flats in the building often did this, regularly ignoring the security arrangements and allowing visitors the opportunity to bypass the intercom system. Sheila, as she would often do, showed her disgust and Shakela, as she would often do, told her not to panic or worry for Jean was a big woman and could easily look after herself. Sheila's misgivings increased though, when they reached the top of the stairs and found the door to Jean's flat wide open. She darted across the short pathway to the door.

'Something's wrong!' she shouted as she approached the door.

Shakela was unmoved, prepared to count this only as a momentary lapse by Jean, or even that she had left the door open to allow the cooking smells to leave the flat. The fact that she didn't even smell any cooking had hardly registered with her. Shakela, now only a yard away from the door, shuddered from a frantic cry of;

'Jean! Oh my God! Shakela! Quick!'

Once inside the flat she beheld a bloodied and slightly flinching Jean lying sprawled in her best friend's arms. It only took an instant to register the absolute bombsite that was once Jean's living room. Broken glass and furniture informed her immediately of what had taken place. She quickly sprung into action. Sprinting past the frenzied Sheila, who by now had Jean rocking in her arms as though she were a baby, she ran to the kitchen, filled a bucket with hot water and disinfectant and dumped a clean rag into it before darting back into the living room and placing it in front of her friend.

'Call an ambulance,' advised Sheila as she held the wet rag and gently dabbed it in the water, wiped Jean's forehead and the bruises on her face with it. Shakela turned to the telephone, noticed the line was cut, and whipped out her mobile. Desperately she gave the address and described the situation whilst once again surveying in absolute horror, the scene of total devastation and carnage that used to be a living room.

'What do you suppose happened?' she asked tensely, clicking her phone off.

'I don't know,' replied Sheila with a trembling voice. But she feared the worst; that Jean had informed Tony of her pregnancy and his reaction to it was a battering. 'Where's the fucking ambulance?' she cried as tears rolled down her agonised face. Jean opened her eyes for a second and stared blankly at Sheila who, rubbing clean the side of her face, repeated;

'It's OK baby, it's OK.'

Within minutes they were joined by Luck and Julie who had made good time to Jean's flat. They too were quick off the mark after noticing that an ambulance had pulled up outside the building, bolting upstairs and seeing Jean's front door open. A frantic exchange of ideas and observations ensued before Luck pulled Jean and threw her left arm over his shoulder whilst Sheila took the other arm. Jean was hardly able to walk so they both took a leg each before carrying her out of the flat to the waiting ambulance, the occupants of which were still trying to figure out which flat it was that Jean lived in. Julie followed them but Shakela stayed, saying she would wait at the flat and straighten it out.

Soon the ambulance had gone. Luck and Julie followed it in his car. It was quiet again. Shakela once again surveyed the room, desperately trying to get a picture of what had gone on. She exhaled deeply, wondering where on earth she was going to start with the cleaning up. Amid the carnage that was once a coffee table she noticed a glittering object. She moved towards it and right away recognised that it was Tony's ring. She picked it up and looked at it thoughtfully. It was sufficient evidence to inform her that Tony had been at the flat and that realisation brought a wry smile to her face.

Mickey and Jacko were irritated. It was one o'clock in the morning. They were pissed and were down to their last bottle. Jacko turned out his pockets.

'Fuck bloody all,' he slurred. 'I got fuck all in this 'ere l'il pocket o' mine. Naff all. What're we gonna fuckin' do now? You got any?'

'I dunno. Fuckin' 'ell. Les 'ave a fuckin look shall we?' replied his equally befuddled partner.

Mickey struggled to keep his balance as he dug deep into his both his trouser pockets.

'Fuck all there,' he declared.

'Thas' it then ...'

'Hold on a fuckin' minute, I gotta try me other pockets first.'

Mickey swayed dangerously as he surveyed his shirt, back and jacket pockets.

'Fuck bloody all. Nothin' 'nout, zilch, nil, bugger fuckin' all,' he declared. 'Bastard.'

'Les fuckin' go to Elisha Road, you know where all the Blacks are, got to be somebody there who'll buy us a fuckin' smoke.'

'Fuckin' good idea that one Jacko, some nice Black totty round there too, got arses comin' out their fuckin' ears. I'd like to bang one o' them,' he declared, lips protruding and fists clenched, elbows bent and punching the air whilst crudely thrusting out his crotch. 'Jacko you're a fuckin' genius mate, a fuckin' genius.'

'Don't tell me what I fuckin' already know fuck head, I'm the fuckin' dogs bollocks round 'ere mate.'

As the two poor excuses for men staggered down the street, they hardly noticed the whirring of police riot van engines behind them. Elisha Road was only two blocks away and as they walked, the first riot van slowed down even more to keep pace with them. A policeman, armed and in full riot gear, stuck first an elbow, then his head out of the open window.

'Going to Elisha Road fellas?' he asked.

'Yes. So fuckin' what if we are then ya silly cunt?' replied Mickey.

'I wouldn't. Not tonight,' the policeman returned.

'Why fuckin' not then?' asked Jacko, completely ignorant of whom he spoke to.

'Gonna be hot round there tonight,' replied the policemen holding up his gun. 'I'd go home if I were you.'

Mickey shuddered. So did Jacko.

'Home it fuckin' well is then,' Mickey decided, common sense prevailing over his inebriated brain. 'Now, which way is it?'

'This fuckin' way nugghead,' said Jacko pulling his shirt in the opposite direction to that in which he walked.

'Night fellas,' laughed the policeman as the van drove on.

'That was some fuckin' idea goin' to Elisha Road wasn't it?' said Mickey sarcastically.

'A slight error in otherwise sound fuckin' judgement,' was Jacko's arrogant reply. 'Which way we fuckin' goin' then?'

The two drunks sombrely wandered off down the street only slightly aware of the horror that was to befall the occupants of Elisha Road that night.

As usual the place was busy. The hookers displayed themselves in scanty clothing smoking, chatting and leaning up against walls and lampposts, waiting eagerly for business. Dealers sold their ware relentlessly. Trade was good tonight. The brothels were busy too and the blues parties, two of them, were just beginning to attract crowds. Both Reggie's and the other shabean were busy with people buying food to sit and eat in their cars or to savour the early night air.

In an instant the relative calm that was Elisha Road became pandemonium as eight riot vans pulled up. Behind them three other police vans blocked off one end of the road. Onlookers panicked as the riot vans ground to a halt and what seemed like hundreds of armed police poured out of them. There was barely time for people to move as they were immediately struck or beaten with the butts of the guns or with batons, irrespective of who they were or what business they had there. The hookers pulled off their stilettos or their high heels and ran for dear life, but most ran straight into the lines of police officers that crowded the end of the street. Even the other side of the street was a no go as three other vans blocked that off too. Some ran through alleys and were chased by dogs that mercilessly savaged anyone they caught. Others tried to hide or drive off, again to no avail.

Mr Singh had heard the commotion and had made his way out onto the street in his pyjamas. He raved. As he watched the brutal actions of the police he jumped, danced and sung with delight.

'Get them! Get them! Those Black bastards ruined my business!' he shouted repeatedly. 'Clean up the area, lock them up. Electrocute them!' He tried to help out the police too. 'There's one running away, get him, get the Black bugger!' he called. As he delighted in the blood sport that was taking place, the excitement got the better of him. He had brought his walking stick with him and started swatting imaginary people with it as if he were doing the beating.

'Kill! Kill!' he shouted incessantly.

One police officer mistook his actions as aggression and noticing his swinging action thought that he was being overly hostile. So he pounced on him, knocked him too the ground, and beat the shit out of him with his baton before hauling his smelly bloodied carcass into a van.

More batons swung in the frenzied violence. Regardless of gender or age, those confronted by a policeman were mercilessly beaten down. In one instance a man was felled and upon noticing this, three policeman joined him to beat the crap out of the helpless victim. A dog jumped up and tore into a woman's face scarring her for life. A young girl, an innocent bystander who had come to Elisha Road to meet her boyfriend, slipped and fell to the ground in an attempt to evade a riot cop. Once on the ground, he too belted her repeatedly with his truncheon. In another incident a large man felled an attacking policemen with a fierce right hook and seeing this, fleeing crowds stopped running and without remorse or fear began to kick shit out of the fallen Babylon.

But there were few stories like that to tell. Elisha Road was on the wrong side of a massacre. The police wasted little time herding injured people into vans, shouting obscenities and racial slurs at them. Other policemen broke into the houses, and the road filled with the noise of screams and shattering doors. The music stopped and the hullabaloo of panic and violence once again filled the air. Some people fought back but were felled instantly. More and more people were herded into the vans. Those that were indoors, partying, eating, or playing dominoes had locked themselves in upon hearing the bedlam outside. But again it was futile. Police men simply kicked doors off and once in, a few choice words and pointed guns were sufficient to inform their captives of what was required.

After a while the six vans at the end of each street pulled into Elisha Road and were immediately replaced by another six. The force needed more vans to carry more people back to the station and as they closed up exits and entrances to the road, one gave way to allow a single unmarked Vauxhall Vectra to make its way onto the street.

It drove hurriedly to Pum Pum's brothel skidding violently to a halt as it reached there. Immediately, Kirk and Anderson jumped out and after briefly surveying the carnage behind them they headed inside. Two officers were already perfectly positioned there, guns aimed at a solitary figure that was lying on the ground. Kirk greeted them with a commanding 'Well done boys,' before leaning down to the person lying with his hands behind his head and his face wallowing in carpet. It was Pum Pum. Holding him by the hair, Kirk lifted up his head to view his face.

'Gapford Maycock. Pleased to make your re-acquaintance. How you knockin' 'em then our kid?' he said arrogantly.

'You fuckin' rasshole, I know you?' was Pum Pum's defiant reply.

'You don't remember me then? Never mind, let's get to know each other again. Bishop Street, August 14th 1987, remember me now fuck-head?'

'Kirk you bitch!' replied Pum Pum. 'Still ain't fucked no good pussy yet?'

'Fuck you Maycock, you're nicked.' Kirk dropped Pum Pum's head and got up to speak to the officers.

'Interview room two as soon as the duty officer signs him in,' he ordered.

The officers obliged by picking Pum Pum off the ground and handcuffing him as soon as he was up on his feet. They marched him out and as they pushed him past Anderson, he winked at her, smiled, then blew her a kiss.

eleven

Shakela had fallen asleep. She had left her mobile phone on, waiting for a call. It hadn't arrived and after doing her best to put Jean's living room back together, a wave of tiredness came over her and she had nodded off in front of the television. Her sleep was interrupted by the muted noise of the intercom. She jerked awake and raced to answer it. It was Sheila. She buzzed her in. There was nothing said as Sheila entered the room. Shakela broke the silence.

'How is she?' she asked.

'She'll live. She needed a few stitches. She's also badly bruised, but she'll live, thank God,' was Sheila's downbeat reply. 'Why didn't you call the police?' she asked quietly.

Shakela started.

'Sorry?' she asked.

'Why didn't you call the police?' repeated Sheila. 'When you called the ambulance, why didn't you call the police?'

'I'm not too sure that that's what Jean would have wanted,' replied a hesitant Shakela.

'How do we know that this was Tony's doing?' Sheila probed.

'Well I guess we don't, do we?'

'All the more reason to call the police, don't you think?'

'Well, maybe, but I think we can assume that Tony did this. Look, when Jean's better she can always call the cops if she wants to. Let's not make premature decisions for her OK?'

Sheila was still puzzled by Shakela's actions, but she laid off her quizzing. There was another pressing matter that she had to deal with. She sat on the settee next to Shakela who sat up to accommodate her. Leaning forward she rubbed her eyes, stared blankly at the T.V. for a few seconds, then turned to her.

'Shakela I've got something to tell you,' she said gloomily.

'What's that then?' Shakela asked.

'Jean was pregnant.'

The ferocity of Shakela's response startled Sheila.

'What?' she bellowed angrily. 'For who!?'

'I'll give you three guesses!'

'Oh Tony you bastard!' cursed Shakela under her breath.

'What did you say?' queried Sheila.

'Nothing. So?'

'What do you think? She wasn't just bleeding from her head and nose, darling.'

Shakela took a sharp intake of breath and cursed even more. As she swore through gritted teeth it was difficult for Sheila to make out what she said, though it wasn't for want of trying. Shakela's reaction to the news seemed to suggest a more personal involvement in the whole affair than perhaps she was letting on. Her suspicions were further aroused when a call came in on Shakela's mobile. It was the way that Shakela picked up the phone and ran to the kitchen before even answering it that nailed it for her and as she sat alone in the living room her misgivings began to steadily get the better of her. It hardly made sense, but she had a gut feeling that Shakela was somehow involved.

In a last ditch attempt to find some clues she moved over to the kitchen door to try to catch an earful of what Shakela was saying and to whom. But again she struck out. Shakela was too far away and talking too softly for her to pick up anything. What she did pick up though were Shakela's footsteps walking back across the kitchen towards the living room. She darted back to the settee, grabbed a cushion, and pretended as if she hadn't moved. Without a word Shakela grabbed her coat, slung it over her back and headed for the front door.

'Where are you going?' asked Sheila

'Home. I've stayed here long enough. Look I'll see you tomorrow. Going to the hospital?'

'Yes, I'll be there in the evening.'

'OK then, I'll see you tomorrow.'

With that Shakela was gone. All very quickly. All very mysteriously and all very dubiously, Sheila thought. In an attempt to calm her thoughts she picked up the remote control, pointed it at the television and aimlessly began channel hopping. She settled on the local news, watched a couple of reports and pricked up her ears at the latest news about the now infamous killing of a policeman at the docks just a couple of days ago. The news report unveiled a photo-fit picture of the alleged killer. It was based upon evidence that they said was given to them by a local drugs dealer. In an interview the Chief Constable of the Area Police Authority stated that a large manhunt was taking place for the killer and that if anyone should see him, they should not approach him but call the nearest police station. They showed the photo-fit picture again, this time adding a description of the renegade's height and possible weight. This gave Sheila a second chance to study it. This time it made her heart jump. Her eyes widened and her jaw dropped. She raised her hands to her gaping mouth in complete and absolute shock. One piece of this terrifying jigsaw puzzle was now in place. It made her wince with fear, for the stakes in this particular game had now risen to a height that neither she nor anyone could ever have imagined. Her heart raced within her breast.

'Tony,' she whispered to herself. 'Oh my God. Tony, you bloody stupid fool, you damned stupid fool.'

Pum Pum had been waiting in interview room two for nearly an hour. He was very pissed off. He sighed, folded his arms on the table and rested his head on his hands. He began to create new names for his hookers to pass the time but soon got bored of doing that. He tried to force a poem from his tired brain. That too was ineffectual. Fuck it, he thought. He was tired and it was late and if they were going to keep him in the damn cell for so long, he might as well sleep.

He had just closed his eyes when he heard the latch turn on the door. It swung open and in stepped Kirk and Anderson. Pum Pum sat up and leaned back in his chair, staring blankly at the two of them. Kirk was tall, a typical looking policeman with an arrogant swagger. Pum Pum remembered their first meeting now, and noted how much he had changed. Five years was not such a long time but Kirk had seemed to have aged by fifteen. He had a beer gut now and his once muscular frame had now drooped. He face was fatter too, his moustache was still the same, as was the inherently evil look in his eyes. Kirk was a copper through and through. The lack of uniform only made him seem more grotesque and more unbearable.

Anderson, on the other hand, was much more appealing. He had fancied her the moment he had laid eyes on her. A blond with long shoulder length hair, she had a slight pretty face with large rounded eyes. She was unblemished save for a couple of wrinkles under her eyes, obviously from working too hard. She was busty too. Pum Pum imagined that they were soft titties which would feel like jelly in his hands. The bra that she wore under the white blouse did not complement her enough and he figured that she was deliberately playing down her size. Like most fashionable white women, she had thin legs, Pum Pum thought, but as she turned round to get a chair he noticed that she had a cute, pert butt that sat well underneath her short skirt. She was fuckable, he concluded. He also noted that she was slightly nervous. He judged from the way Kirk was watching her that she was probably a trainee. That was an obvious advantage. Kirk and Anderson drew separate chairs and sat opposite him. Pum Pum continued looking at them, watching their every move intently.

'So what?' he opened. 'I don't even get a rahtid tape?'

Kirk and Anderson said nothing. Pum Pum tried again.

'Ain't y'all supposed to have video cameras in these places?'

Again they said nothing.

'Well what about my damn phone call, duty solicitor or some shit! Y'all just fuckin' about man!'

'Where were you in the early hours of the twelfth?' opened Anderson.

Pum Pum abhorred their arrogance, so he ignited his.

'Fuckin' shit out my missus, what were you doing?' he said with a slow smile.

Anderson looked at Kirk nervously. Then she turned her attention back to Pum Pum and proceeded with her questioning.

'Her name and her address please,' she said starting to write.

'Edwina Hot Pussy.'

'One of your girls?'

'I've got 13 lovely kids, nine of them are girls, I don't fuck my girls.'

There was an intense degree of honesty in that statement.

Anderson wondered for a second if she could make something of it, but resisted the urge.

'I mean your hookers,' she responded, trying to remain calm.

'I ain't got no hookers, I ain't no pimp'

'Really?'

'Really.'

'So what do you do for a living Mr Maycock?'

'Write.'

'Write what?'

'My name.'

'That so?'

'I write my name, Her Majesty's government pay me. That's my living. I also write poetry too. Want to hear one?'

Anderson was stuck. Kirk was unimpressed with her interview technique. Pum Pum was taking the piss.

'You're looking at ten to fifteen for accessory to murder. I'd answer her questions if I were you, you jumped up little fuck!' he warned.

Pum Pum looked at him slyly.

'Tell me something,' he said to Kirk in a friendly voice, leaning forward for effect. 'When you're both out in your squad car, late at night with nothing to do, do you fuck her? 'Cos I would.'

Anderson winced, her eyes agape staring at Pum Pum, completely shocked at his total insolence.

'Fuck you!' she burst with fury.

'Yes please, right here?'

'I wouldn't fuck you if you were the last man on the planet, you stinking pig.'

'I ain't the last man, I'm the first man, original man, Black man. W'happen you don't want no pokey from the big Black dick?'

Anderson shuddered.

'Go on, rub it on your lip first, then …'

Kirk had heard enough. He shot up resting both hands on the table and towered over Pum Pum.

'You fuckin' wog!' he exploded. 'Do you know, I could get ten of the biggest members of Her Majesty's filth and do you over right this minute?'

'You definitely won't find what you're looking for then, will you? Another dead Blackie on your hands. You guys might yet have to answer for what you did at Elisha Road. You might get riots for that, but another dead Blackie in custody? What you think's gonna happen? You want to be responsible for that? Get your li'l boys in. I can play martyr, why not? I arready playin' the arse wid you.'

Even Kirk was amazed and slightly impressed at Pum Pum's guile.

'Where were you on the twelfth?' he repeated. 'Refuse to answer and I'll do you for withholding information.'

'See Edwina. 21 First Avenue, call her now if you want. Look see, I know you want that guy that killed the cop. But you already up the wrong tree man 'cos it ain't me. Check Miss Hot Pussy, she won't forget what I gave her that night, not for a long while and neither would you madam,' he closed, winking at Anderson.

Kirk and Anderson exhaled in tandem, looked at each other, then fell silent. Kirk stood up and Anderson followed. They left the room and stood in the corridor, whispering.

'Let him go,' said Kirk.

'Sir?' replied an astonished Anderson.

'Let him walk.'

'But why? Sir we ...'

'We what? What the fuck do we have?' Kirk was irritated. 'Edwina Hot whatever-her-name-is will alibi for him whether he was there or not. His hookers aren't going to let him down. We can't book him for anything else. Jay walking? He didn't have a penny on him according to the duty officer. Being in a brothel? He had his fuckin' trousers on. Fuck it! Let him walk.' Kirk's fist hit the wall as he said those last words such was his agitation. 'I need a fuckin' coffee.'

'Sir we can raid his house,' suggested a desperate Anderson.

'Anderson, did he sound like a fool to you? He displayed more guile, more common sense, more fuckin' nous in that five minutes than you'll ever do in a lifetime in the force. His house will be clean. We won't even find a stick of fuckin' weed. I said let him go and meet me in the canteen. Now!'

Pum Pum sat in the office, proud of his performance, but worried about what they were planning to do with him now. In moments the door opened and in stepped the duty officer. Pum Pum flexed and geared himself up for trouble but his worry was soon abated by the duty officer.

'Looks like you're free to go,' she said.

Pum Pum was marched in silence to the duty officer's desk where he was handed the few items that had been in his possession at the time of his arrest. He stuck them in his pocket, gave the officer a quick 'Thanks,' and in seconds he was walking down the steps of the station, inhaling the cool night air. He looked up at the sky, buttoned up, then pulled the hem of his jacket down and smiled.

twelve

Shakela was happy that it hadn't taken very long for her to get home. The taxi was on time and made good progress as there was not a lot of traffic about. No sooner had she stepped through the door than she was peering out of the window waiting anxiously for her caller to arrive. She seethed as Tony's car, now sprayed a subtle grey, pulled up rather hurriedly outside her flat. He got out of the car looking around him cautiously and was soon knocking at the door. She ran excitedly down the stairs, opened the door quickly and beckoned him inside. Her anger got the better of her and she immediately tore into him.

'I thought I told you not to drive here?' she said.

'Don't worry man,' he replied in an effort to calm her down. 'Pum Pum's lying low for a while, he's out of town.'

Though she hardly understood what he meant by 'lying low' her tension eased.

'Why did you re-spray your car?' she quizzed.

Tony looked at her, wondering what to say.

'Felt like a change,' he lied.

They locked the door and climbed upstairs into her living room. Without another word she sealed herself in a desperately passionate kiss with him. He responded in like fashion. It seemed to last for hours, both of them savouring the moment as if, before setting off to eternity, these were their last moments together. Shakela gently pulled away and looked worriedly into his eyes.

'What'd you beat her up for?' she asked quietly.

Tony hesitated, his eyes moving quickly from side to side as he searched for a reason.

'She was getting on my nerves man!' was the best he could do.

Shakela paused for effect. Stroking his face with one hand, she kissed him again gently this time, then spoke.

'Did you know she was pregnant?' she asked venomously. Tony was stunned. He released her waist and gripped her tightly by her arms, not knowing if she was playing a joke on him or whether she was serious. It only took a moment to register the seriousness in Shakela's eyes and he realised that this was no joke.

'What!?' he bellowed. 'She… She didn't tell me… and what?'

'She lost it,' said Shakela calmly. 'You beat it out of her. Proud?' Her eyebrows were slightly raised, arms splayed and her voice was like acid. 'You told me you weren't sleeping together! You lied to me!'

Tony was dumbstruck and stood in silence, remorseful, gathering his thoughts before he pulled himself to. Shakela too was silent; she wanted to press the issue, wanted to make him know how badly that piece of news had hit her, but she reasoned that it was not the best time. There were all sorts of explanations that he needed to provide and rather than frustrate him any more she decided to let him deal with the obvious shock. He seemed to recover from it surprisingly quickly.

'Nothing I can do about that now anyway,' he shrugged.

'What do you mean?' asked a confused Shakela.

There was another silence, this time much longer. Shakela breathed heavily, realising that Tony was about to drop a bomb. He looked at her tensely, and began pacing the room, passing the palm of his hand nervously from his forehead to the back of his neck. Shakela's attempt at patience with him was short lived and finally she could take no more.

'Tony what is it?' she inquired anxiously.

Tony stiffened. For the second time that night he needed to take himself into an emotional sphere that he was hardly used to. First he had had to express remorse, and this time he had to give a simple explanation and admission of guilt. Whatever was to happen as result of his misdemeanour at the docks, he figured that Shakela, if anyone, should know the truth.

'You know that policeman that got shot at the docks last week?' he began, 'Well ...'

He couldn't say any more, choosing rather to pull his gun from the back of his trousers, and display it clearly for her to see. Shakela's heart skipped a beat when she realised what he meant. She shuddered.

'You're not serious?' she asked in a cold, terrified voice. 'Please God, tell me you're not serious.'

He had no more words for her. He looked away and said nothing. She darted towards him and grabbed his arms the same way he had done to her just a few seconds ago.

'You've got to give yourself up!' she cried. 'They'll hunt you down like a dog!'

Tony shook himself angrily out of her grip. He turned away, thought for a second then turned back to face her.

'I can't do that,' he whispered desperately.

'Then what will you do?'

'I've booked a flight for Jamaica. I'm leaving the day after tomorrow.'

'You're going to leave me?'

'What else can I do?'

'Take me with you, please, I love you Tony please, take me with you.'

He was taken aback by her devotion. She didn't seem to care that there was a price on his head, she just wanted to be with him. The tears streaming down her face reinforced the notion. He could do no more than hold her.

'Let me settle in first,' he said calmly. 'Then you can come out there and join me.'

Once again they locked themselves in a long kiss, a kiss that now more than ever seemed to signify their devotion to each other.

Pum Pum had been standing outside Shakela's flat for some time. Lying low had meant spending some time at Elisha Road but what a brilliant idea that had turned out to be. Shakela was the only person that he knew that wasn't a frequent visitor to Elisha Road, so he had wandered by with the intention of staying with her. He was surprised to see Tony's car outside her flat and wondered what business he had with Shakela that was so urgent it couldn't wait until the morning. He seethed as he beheld them at the window kissing in each other's arms. The first time he was unsure what he had seen, but when for the second time they became locked in a passionate embrace he had no doubts. His temper flared and it took all his self control to stop himself from going up there when, shortly after the second kiss, the lights went off. He would like to have thought that was it, that Tony was going home now for the night and that he would soon appear at the main door and get into his car, but he knew better. Nonplussed and angry, his thoughts were interrupted by a car pulling up closely to him. It was Luck.

'Yo! Man I've been looking all over the place for you,' he said, hurriedly winding his window down.

'W'happen Luck,' responded Pum Pum in a depressed tone of voice.

Luck had come to tell Pum Pum of the evenings proceedings with Jean, but saw straight away that there was a more pressing matter. When he saw Tony's car he feared the worst. He enquired as to why the car was outside the flat. Pum Pum responded in a deadpan voice, indicating that he hardly cared.

'What do you think?'

There was a silence.

'No!' was Luck's shocked reply. 'What the fuck? I don't believe this, you mean that crackhead sonofa bitch is fuckin' Shakela?'

Pum Pum would have appreciated a little more subtlety from Luck under the circumstances, but he remained realistic.

'If I know her, his head she probably between she rasshole legs by now,' he shot back.

Luck didn't need a degree to understand that and immediately challenged the notion, but was silenced at Pum Pum's eye-witness account of the earlier proceedings.

'Does this guy not having a fucking clue?' he asked in disgust. 'What you gonna do?'

Pum Pum was silent, calm, and in little mood for more words. He made his statement in much the same way as Tony had done earlier with Shakela and pulled out a small handgun.

'Got my li'l toy yesterday,' he said.

'You're not going up there now with that thing are you?' snapped an anxious and now very worried Luck.

'No. I gon' to let them have their fun,' he laughed. 'Fuck it, it's the last night they gon' be together anyway. I'm going to the shabean. I'll sort this shit out in the morning.'

'Pum Pum look, relax, think about the consequences.'

'Luck, fuck the consequences. I never liked that fuckin'

pussyhole anyway. I'm sorry I ever pardy wid he. Look at all the trouble he bring down pan we. Shoot rassclaart policeman, have we on the run like fuckin' darg and now this. No man that fuckin' rasshole. He got to die.'

'Pum Pum please, don't do nothing stupid.'

'All that is stupid been done arready, now I gon' do something sensible. I comin' back here in the mornin'.'

With that Pum Pum strolled away, ignoring Luck's muffled pleas to think again. Soon, Luck gave up hope. He butted his head against the steering wheel in sheer and total frustration. 'Shit ... shit,' he repeated over and over again to himself, before starting the engine and driving off into the cold night.

Tony and Shakela were in the bedroom. Pum Pum was absolutely right. Tony was eating pussy. This was how they started making love. It was their foreplay. Shakela was fully clothed but for her panties which were always the first to hit the floor. She lay down on the bed and moaned with sheer pleasure as she held the back of Tony's head, positioning him carefully between her legs so that he could lick every quarter of her soaking pussy, whilst gyrating her waist to meet his tongue. She became animated and raised her legs to rest on Tony's' shoulders so as to work her way deeper into his mouth. Tony licked, got into it more then kissed and before long was sucking her. Increasingly passionate groans announced her orgasm. Afterwards, Tony stood up and shook off his clothes as did she hers, before holding his now erect nature in his hands and entering her. The fuck was long and passionate. Whilst they would usually start off their sex in wild 'get down' nasty fashion, this time it became a blissful serenade of lovemaking that was more emotionally charged than was usually the case. The telephone surprised them but they ignored it and carried on fucking regardless, hoping the caller would give up. But the answer phone clicked in and Shakela's recorded voice rang out through the heavy atmosphere.

'THIS IS SHAKELA,' it said 'CAN'T GET TO SPEAK TO YOU NOW. LEAVE A MESSAGE, I'LL CALL YOU BACK.'

They both stopped fucking to hear the message. It was Sheila. She sounded cold and embittered as she spoke.

'Shakela, this is Sheila,' she began. 'It's all starting to come together now. Bitch!!' Then she slammed the phone down.

Shakela was startled. As was Tony.

'How the fuck does she know?' asked Tony.

'I don't know. I don't know,' replied a slightly worried Shakela. 'Who cares anyway?' she continued. 'Fuck me.'

Morning had come too soon for Shakela. She had made love to Tony with a vengeance the night before and she could have done with sleeping for a little longer. But there were many things she had to do today, so she rose early and pottered around her kitchen preparing a hearty breakfast for herself and her lover. She pondered Sheila's message, but only for a moment. So she knew, big deal. Right now a lot of things were coming out in the open and under the circumstances, little of it really mattered anymore. No-one could have told her, because no-one knew. Sheila was probably quite a smart woman if she had managed to put two and two together. But what the hell? Who the fuck was Sheila? That fucking dyke would probably give anything to be where she was right now, fucking Jean's man.

Her thoughts turned to Jamaica and the wonderful life that she and Tony were going to have together. Lost in her daydreams, the last thing that she expected to hear was the twisting of a key in her front door, which was visible from where she stood. She knew that it could only be one person and the very thought of it terrified her to a point where she had no control. Motionless she faced the door, realising that it was locked from the inside and that there was no way that Pum Pum could get in with his key alone. She realised that Pum Pum would be none too happy seeing Tony's car outside. She might be able to cover herself in that respect but she couldn't justify her half-naked state and a naked Tony asleep in her bed. Her heart pounded as she waited to see what Pum Pum would do. Within a split second the brutal thud of snapped wood and broken locks signified his entrance. The door was off in an instant and it came crashing into the living room. The thud made her jump and the fiercely vengeful look in Pum Pum's eyes made her scream. He darted across the room towards her. She pleaded with him.

'Pum Pum it's not what you think honest,' she said, terrified to death.

'No? Then what is it bitch tell me? What the fuck is it? Man been here all night, you two kissing by the window, what is it?' he argued.

No sooner had he opened his mouth, he had gripped her by the neck and with a sweeping flow of his right arm sent her sprawling. She hit her face against the table. Her mouth was cut. She wiped away the blood, shouting obscenities at him. Pum Pum raised his voice too, pouncing on her again and fiercely feeding her with boxes. Shakela had little choice but to scream for help. She put up an admirable defence, doing her absolute best to trade punches and kicks with him, often successfully, but eventually she realised he was too strong for her. He had her by her hair and on her knees by the time that Tony emerged from the bedroom. The initial noise of the door being kicked in had awoken him and he had been hurriedly scrambling around the room for something to put on. He faced Pum Pum and the hapless Shakela, barefoot with nothing on but panties and an open shirt.

'Wondered when you was going to come out!' yelled Pum Pum aggressively.

'Pum! Pum!' pleaded Tony. He was witnessing a side to Pum Pum that he had never seen before. The years had obviously tamed him, but when he had to he could get raw. Now he was at his most impossible, at his most ignorant and his most aggressive. Now Tony would find out just what Pum Pum was capable of and the lengths that he would go to when the gangster came out in him.

'Don't Pum Pum me you piece of shit, how the fuck could you do this? We had nuff runnings together man, nuff runnings and this is how you treat me? I know you never liked me man, I never liked you, but why you got to bring woman into it?'

'Well you never treated her right ...'

'So what does that have to do with you? This is my fuckin' woman. You fuckin' my rasshole woman!'

Shakela broke in. 'No I'm not your woman! Look how many women you've got and how many off them prostitutes of yours are you fucking anyway?' she screamed.

'Shut the fuck up bitch! N'body ain't talkin' to you you rasshole!' yelled Pum Pum, slapping her across the side of her face. Shakela bawled in pain.

'Listen man cut that shit out now! Look man just let her go!' interjected Tony

'What? You want me to let her go, tek the bitch!'

With that, Shakela was hurled towards her lover. A kick across her back helped her on her way. She crawled on the floor for a yard or so before scrambling to her feet and racing over to Tony, who immediately embraced her and kissed her gently on the cheek.

'It's just one thing I want to know. Bitch just tell me one thing,' said Pum Pum, 'How long has this been going on?'

Shakela gave Tony a worried glance and he nodded reassuringly at her.

'Six months,' she said quietly, head bent towards the floor.

'Six months? Six fuckin' months bitch you've been fucking this piece a darg dee dee fuckin' shit behind my back?'

'Well I don't think that you were ever faithful to me once love!' snapped Shakela.

'You know what I should do?' said Pum Pum, reaching into the deep pocket of his long leather jacket. 'I should fuckin' kill the rasshole two a you!' He pulled out his gun and pointed it right at the couple. Shakela started, recoiled then found a place behind Tony who took a sharp intake of breath, keeping his eyes firmly fixed on Pum Pum. At that moment Luck arrived. He ran into the room taking a deep breath as he surveyed the scene. Pum Pum spoke to him first.

'Fuck off Luck, you're too rahtid late!' he bellowed.

'Pum Pum, for Christ's sake put the gun down. We're wanted for murder already man don't make the shit any worse for yourself just put the gun down nuh?' he pleaded.

There was a deadly silence that Tony quickly exploited. Slowly he raised his arms out wide just as Pum Pum had done to him at Reggie's. An image that made him look like Christ on the cross which was apt given what he was about to say. He moved slowly, almost gliding towards Pum Pum. Once very much in Pum Pum's space he moved right up to the gun, allowing the barrel to rest gently on his forehead. Still keeping his eyes locked into Pum Pum's he spoke gently.

'No,' he whispered. 'Don't put the gun away, shoot me, blow me away, shoot me nuh? Blow arf mi head. Me nuh fraid fi dead. Never have been, never will be.'

The gauntlet had been thrown. Pum Pum froze, realising that the onus was on him to either put up or shut up. The gun began to tremble in his hand, everyone seemed to hold their breath as the tension rose.

'For Christ's sake guys,' pleaded Luck. 'Don't be so fuckin' stupid!'

'Got a pussy story for you,' Tony said teasingly. 'Fucked your bitch last night.'

Shakela winced, embarrassed and not amused at what Tony had just said. Pum Pum became angrier. The trembling of his hand became more noticeable. Tony smiled. His psychological gambit had worked. He knew that Pum Pum had never used a gun, perhaps never even held one; these were empty threats. He arrogantly turned his back on his aggressor and his laughter grew louder. It was cut short immediately by a bullet hitting the ceiling. Shakela screamed and everyone but Tony shuddered. Pum Pum slowly aimed the gun at Tony.

'Next bullet that leaves this gun,' he said with menace, 'is yours if you don't leave town.'

'Fuck Arf!' replied a furious Tony. 'Me walk weh me warn walk seen?'

'I'm warning you,' replied Pum Pum, walking to the door. 'Leave town. Don't show you face at the shabean or anywhere round here. Leave town.' With that Pum Pum was out of the door giving Shakela the most threatening stare as he left, a stare that she returned with a single middle finger pointed straight in the air and a tongue poking out of her mouth. Luck tried in vain to get Pum Pum's attention by calling him as he made his way past a group of frightened onlookers who had heard the commotion and gathered, still in their pyjamas and night clothes, in the corridor. Quickly he turned his attention back to Tony, squaring up to him in immediate confrontation.

'What the fuck did you think you were doing man? Screwing with the guy's woman? You never got on with him anyway, how could you do that?' he asked.

Tony was in no mood for a lecture or for any further confrontation. He merely remained quiet, staring blankly out of the window.

'Best thing, you can do now is leave town man,' Luck advised.

'Not before I reach that gambling house,' replied a defiant Tony. The comment startled even Shakela who sat staring at him open mouthed.

'What?' shouted Luck. 'Didn't you hear the bredda? He was serious, if you go back there there'll be blood man!'

'Yeah!' replied Tony. 'His!'

Luck and Shakela exchanged a despairing look. She raced to the door where the onlookers had gathered and went berserk.

'Can't you fuckin' people mind you're own business?' she screamed. 'Go on piss off, the lot of you. It was a fuckin' blank anyway, now piss off!' With that the onlookers were quickly gone, not knowing if any more guns were to be fired that morning and not wanting to find out either, just in case a bullet might be for one of them. Luck gathered his thoughts. He was angry and disgusted.

'So, this is what it's come to, eh?' he said calmly. 'All the runnings, all the drugs, the gold, the cars, for what, this? I got to laugh man, I really got to laugh. You could have had it all man you know that? You could have had the whole wide world in your pocket. But now, check it, you know what you have to look forward to? Hmm? Shall I tell you? Hell. That's all you've got man. A one way ticket to fuckin' hell. Remember Jean Samuels? Hmm? Remember her. The girl loved you man, she'd have done anything for you man, anything you would have wanted her to do, she would have done it, but wha? Love? Shit man, you even cheated yourself out of that. Good luck to you boy that's all that I can say. What ever happens to you, you just forget I ever lived OK? Fuck it! I can't help you, I've got my life to save and you know what? I'm going to do it. I have a beautiful woman beside me who I love and who loves me and I sure ain't stupid enough to think that I need any more than that. Good luck to you boy, good luck, hope you find what you're looking for.' Luck allowed his eyes to move quickly from Tony's head to his feet in a swift glance. He gave Shakela a pitiful glance as he walked past her to the door. Within seconds, like Pum Pum before him, he was off out of the flat and out of their lives, for good.

Luck's words had pierced Shakela. She pictured Jean in her minds eye and placed herself in her position. She imagined Jean's pain and the sheer anguish she must have been going through. She pictured the good times that they had had together over the years and remembered that at one time they had been friends.

Tony continued to stare blankly out of the window. The air felt cold. A single tear fell down his face as Luck's final words to him echoed repeatedly in his brain. He thought of Jean, but only briefly as Shakela approached and faced him.

'He's right. I can't let this go on,' she said solemnly to him.

He looked at her, almost dazed.

'What?' he muttered.

'I can't let this happen,' she repeated 'I have to ease my conscience, I'm going to see Jean, I'm going to tell her everything.'

Tony was startled.

'What?' he growled. 'But a minute ago you ...'

'Yes I stood by you but ...' Tears once again filled her eyes as she desperately struggled to finish what she was saying. '... I can't do this to Jean. She loves you and soon you'll be dead and she won't even know why!' Shakela broke down. Tears streamed down her face as she cried, 'God this is all my fault.'

Tony grabbed her by her arms, shaking her as he spoke.

'Don't do anything stupid. Look, today we can sort out your flight. Come with me. Believe me we can forget this, start brand new.'

'No,' she replied, tearing herself away from him. 'We can't. If Sheila knows, Jean will know. She probably knows already, but it's my responsibility, it should come from my mouth. It's over Tony, Jean loves you and I know you love her.'

'Don't be stupid!'

'No! Tony, please, don't you be stupid! I know you love her – you always have. Why else would you get so paranoid over innocent phone calls, why'd you beat her up eh? Did you think she was screwing around?'

'That's what you told me!'

'Well I lied! Fuck it Tony I lied! God, I had to do something to get you away from her. Yes even if it meant lying! Jean's not seeing anyone! Christ almighty she would never do that across you, never. She would have been happy to have your child, she would have been happy to have you. Now I know that it's her you love. Tony do what you can to patch it up. Head for Jamaica, take her with you, she wants you, she loves you and you love her.'

'Shakela, it's you I love.'

'Don't play that shit with me Tony, you never loved me and you know it. Anyway, you shouldn't talk in your sleep. I know you love her. It's over between us Tony, I'm going to tell her everything. I really didn't want it to turn out this way.'

There was nothing left to be said. Shakela took a step backward, angling her body so that Tony could see the front door. He looked at her, she looked away.

'Good-bye Tony,' were her final words. He made his way quietly to the bedroom, emerging in a few short minutes fully clothed to the sight of her, head in hands, sobbing on the settee. That was his last glance. He left the flat, stepping over the broken door lying in the living room.

thirteen

Jean's first evening at home since leaving the hospital was not a happy one. Shakela had arrived in sombre mood and had just begun to explain to her the fact that Tony and Pum Pum had been at loggerheads and how Pum Pum had threatened to kill him. They were so angry that someone was going to end up dead. She explained that Tony was the murderer the police were pursuing for the killing of the policemen at the docks. Panic got the better of Jean and even in her still very painful and handicapped state, she wanted to leave the flat and try to track Tony down. Shakela asked her not to go, explaining that things were just a bit more complicated than that. This made Jean prick up her ears. She concentrated harder on her breathing in order to calm down quickly and wait for Shakela's explanation. It came as no surprise that Shakela had more to say on the subject. She almost expected Shakela to turn round and confess her own involvement in the matter.

Once Jean was calm again and had re-taken her seat Shakela, having composed herself as best she could, began to talk. Through a stream of tears and with a shaky and nervous voice, she recounted the tale of just how she had tried to lure Tony's affections away.

'I've been jealous of you for a long time Jean,' she began. 'You're a successful, intelligent, beautiful Black woman and you have Tony. I loved him too because in him I saw the embodiment of all my fantasies about my ideal man. He was the sort of man women dream about. Wesley Snipes, Blair Underwood and Denzel Washington all rolled into one. Maybe it was his suave and debonair good looks, maybe it was that bad boy ruggedness, I don't know. All I knew was that, after meeting him for the first time I became obsessed with him. The desire within me was so fierce, I just could not rest until he was mine. I decided that by hook or by crook he would eventually belong to me. Even the thought of having to share him with you Jean, it filled me with no dread, no fear whatsoever. I would rather have settled for half of him than none at all.

It only took a few choice words, the right clothes, a blues party, a good rub-a-dub session, a sly invitation to my flat, and a steamy seduction and a passionate night of sex to convince him that seeing me behind your back would be good for him. That running the risk of messing with me, even though I was Pum Pum's woman, would be worthwhile and add an edge of adventure to his lovelife. I don't know, maybe the same kind of adventure that he craved for out on the street. At least that's certainly what it did for me. He revelled in that thought Jean and even though he knew that I belonged to Pum Pum it was no deterrent for him. He hated Pum Pum anyway and he was pleased to have one over him. Now that I think about it, it was probably that which motivated him more than anything. But that wasn't a problem for me. I mean I would have been happier if he had truly loved me, but whatever his motivation for sleeping in my bed and holding me tightly on a twice weekly basis it was god enough for me.

Still, even though things were working well after few weeks of nervous but determined sneaking around on both our parts, I found it too difficult to deal with the fact that although I had won him over, he still loved you Jean. He would always talk about you, always give you priority and even in his sleep Jean, you never left him.'

Jean heaved. A single tear ran down her cheek. She looked away once, not bothering to wipe it away, then continued to mind Shakela's testimony, staring at her coldly and with venom as she spoke.

'I worked night after night on this,' she continued. 'Finally, I came up with an idea. My plan was to destroy your relationship. I figured that this was the only way to ease the agony and I thought hard to come up with something that would work. So one particular night after we made love in the back of Tony's car, the night after you bought it for him, we were talking, and I told him that you were seeing someone else. That I had been hearing rumours for weeks now and they had become too consistent to be ignored. I convinced him that I felt that for his own sanity I had to tell him. I told him that you had been acting quite strange towards me, especially this one particular night, when you were talking to someone on the phone.

You were talking to a guy and you called him your telephone love. Yes, I know that's what you used to call Tony Jean, he told me.'

Jean seethed, but held it in check.

'I told him that you had been off with most of your friends and that you would never take a phone call in front of us and that maybe this was the lover that I had been hearing about.

Tony's response to all of this was frightening and it wasn't what I had expected. He had gotten himself involved in drug trafficking and that wasn't just another rumour that I had heard, I knew first hand. He had met Pum Pum and Luck. They had made some new contacts and he was on his way to making bigger deals and more money. But the streets had become much more dangerous and he knew that drug dealing was no longer just a means of survival, a means of hustling out a living, but more a gangster's profession. Gangsters kill to secure their livelihood and God knows he had made enough enemies in his time. So he figured he needed a gun. He knew that an ex-forces school friend had left the army with a stash of guns and he was selling them off. He said that he was planning to buy one and that when he did, he would kill you and your lover if he ever found out that it was true. I was scared stiff by what he said Jean and I wondered if he really was going to buy the gun. But even if he did, I knew he'd never do a thing like that to you Jean, not the way he loved you. I reasoned that although Tony did have this bad boy, rebellious streak in him, he was never the kind of person to kill anyone.'

'Not even in one of his drugged up states?' accused Jean.

'No, not even then,' replied Shakela ruefully. 'I dismissed his rantings as bravado and persevered with my plan. The next phase was to find a lover for you. I agonised over this one but it seemed that either God or the Devil was on my side because one day the perfect candidate showed up.'

'David,' pre-empted Jean.

'Yes. I knew that David used to be your lover at university. So when I had a chance meeting with him in Desdemona's wine bar – you know the one on the High Street? – I took advantage of the situation by talking about you. On top of that, to my absolute amazement Jean, I learned that he still harboured feelings for you and would have loved the opportunity to try to win you back. So I gave him your phone number and encouraged him to call you. However I nearly regretted that action the night that you, me and Tony went out together. The phone call that you got that night came from him and I was worried for you because I had not yet told him about Tony and I feared that had if he answered the phone that night, David would be frightened off.'

'I've got news for you,' Jean interrupted. 'He called the next day and Tony answered it.'

'He didn't tell me that. Is that what caused the argument the next day when we went shopping?'

'Yes.'

'I'm sorry.'

'Sure. Keep talking.'

'I had another chance meeting with David in the shopping mall that day, when I went off to use the loo. I brought the conversation over to the subject of you again. I told him that you were in a relationship now, but that you were unhappy, and that the meeting must have been an act of fate for only the other day you had been talking about him. Reminiscing on how you should not have ended the relationship then and that you might be a happier woman now if you hadn't. I noticed the excitement in his eyes and I implored him to continue calling you. I told him to ring, because you would be thrilled to hear from him, but to be cautious for your boyfriend was a gangster and a bit of a hothead and that if he answered the telephone he must hang up straight away. For good measure I gave him an invitation to the party, explaining that if he had no success trying to reach you by phone he would definitely see you there. I remember the absolute joy on his face as I left him.'

'That's why you were so keen for me to go to the party?'

'Yes?'

'Keep talking.'

'As you know, the party was disastrous. I had no idea that Tony was going to show up. I was angry with Pum Pum for not telling me. I certainly had no idea of what Tony was going to do that night. It was then that I learned he'd bought the gun and I cursed Pum Pum, because it was him that had alerted Tony to the fact that David had been dancing with you. I really thought I'd had blown it, but fate was to give me another throw of the dice. Purely by chance, I bumped into David again at Desdemona's. He'd got a plaster over his nose after the head butt that Tony gave him. We talked about what had happened at the party and I told him that as a result of what had happened you and Tony were no longer an item. I told him you had been so sad and afraid that you might never see him again. Once again his eyes lit up. I advised him to contact you again and not to give up, for love would truly conquer all. I surprised myself at my ability to talk so much crap and almost pitied David for being so gullible, but once again the plan was back on track and I would only need to wait and hear the outcome.'

'Well you saw what the outcome was. He called back,' said Jean, pointing to her black eye.

'Jean, I don't know what to say.'

'You just keep talking.'

'Well really, that was it,' continued Shakela. 'That was how I did it, and now,' she said holding back the tears, 'it's all gone horribly wrong.' Shakela could hardly look at Jean, who stared at her with a blank expression. She continued.

'Tony seemed to be consuming more drugs recently. I see now that it was all getting to him, it made him more and more paranoid. That's why he paid particular attention to the phone calls that you were getting, that's why he erupted at the party and that's why ...'

'... He beat me,' Jean interrupted.

Shakela was silent. She stared at the floor before flipping her tearful eyes to the ceiling. She just could not look at Jean.

'Yes,' she responded, head now hung low in shame.

Jean was nonplussed. She hardly knew what to say. She thought hard, confused as to what to do next. She looked hard at Shakela desperately trying to hold any feelings of malice or hatred in check. She hardly knew where to place her feelings, but somewhere in the midst of all the emotion there was pity for the snivelling little sorry-looking figure that sobbed hopelessly before her. Shakela had stolen her man, lied to him about her, ruined their relationship and now as a result, endangered his life. To hold her emotions in check showed an almost angelic quality that really only a situation such as this could ever reveal. She thought about Tony and cried inside for him. She loved that man but she loved him too much and not wisely and that was the root of her pain. Her musings were cut short by a cautious notion.

'Shakela,' she said calmly. 'Did you explain all this to Tony?'

Shakela raised her head, a complete look of horror emblazoned right across her face.

'Oh my God, no, not all of it.' She replied. 'I was so caught up in thinking how I was going to explain this all to you.' She leaped up. 'I'll see if I can find him.'

'I think you'd better. Tell him to call me when you find him,' said Jean in a cold and sinister voice the likes of which Shakela had never heard. She headed for the door. Jean accompanied her and showed her out. Jean looked at her one last time. Shakela's make up had messed up her face now that it had mingled with the liquid of her tears. She brushed more aside as she whispered to her.

'I'm so sorry.'

'Go,' was Jean's only response. 'Don't ever come here again.'

Shakela stepped out of the door and turned with a pleading gesture.

'Forgive me,' she sobbed.

This was the last straw. Shakela should have gone when she was first asked to. Her plea for clemency aroused Jean's wrath. With a mighty swing she bought the palm of her right hand across the side of Shakela's face.

'How can I forgive you? You've destroyed my life and my home!' she erupted. 'Everything I ever wanted in life is as good as gone. Get out you bitch! Go! How can I ever forgive you?' she screamed, slamming the door in her face, her angelic, loving quality gone. As the front door slammed behind her, Shakela fell helplessly against the corridor wall. She rolled her eyes to the heavens, took a deep breath, wiped her tears and headed timidly into the night.

She hardly felt the rain as it pummelled down on her uncovered head. She hardly felt the tears that streamed down her face and became mingled with rainwater. A passer-by tried to talk to her but she didn't hear him. Another passer-by got angry and shouted at her for almost bumping into him but she didn't hear him either. Mickey and Jacko, drunk again for the night, staggered passed her, eyeing up her seductive shape as the rain saturated her clothing making it more evident. She didn't notice them. Her head was in a stupor. She felt dizzy from the myriad of confused thoughts that ran through her brain. Her sobbing became louder, more extreme. Another passer-by wanted to say something to her but he changed his mind – her torment was too great for anything that he, a stranger, could do.

Her sobbing became so hysterical that she could no longer maintain a normal step. She had to either sit down or she had to run. She chose to run. Faster and faster she went. The chaotic pain in her gut and the disconcerted thoughts than ran through her mind caused a tidal wave of images that reflected her tormented conscience. She was no longer fully in control of her faculties. The noise of the night traffic faded as she ran ever faster. Running seemed the only release for her. It seemed the only way to escape from the omnipotent grip that her conscience was held in. There was simply no escape. She stopped, clung to a lamp-post and screamed more tears, like a pitiable child scolded for doing the wrong thing. Shakela flung her head back and wailed. The hand that held her conscience gripped tighter and tighter; there would be no respite for her this night. She thought of God as she viewed the majesty and overwhelming splendour of the heavens above her. She might have sought His forgiveness, but now it was too late. Her heart had eaten her out. Her gut wrenched tightly and fear gripped her being. A passer-by, overwhelmed by watching her anxiety, exercised his compassion and walked over to her. The feel of his hand on her shoulder frightened her and she screamed.

'No!' she bellowed agonisingly shrugging the hand away and running off into the road.

The man screamed, so did Shakela. Who knows if she had seen or sensed the oncoming motor car that hit her. Like a matador's bull, crazed with a sense of freedom from its tormentor it tossed her into the air and the first part of her body that connected with the concrete was her head. It smashed. The awkwardness of the fall severed her spine also. Now there was no more pain, no more anxiety, no more conscience, no more tears, there was simply silence. The man ran to the road as did the few onlookers that were around. He knelt before her and examined her. He took off his coat, revealing a white collar around his neck. He was a vicar. He cried as he lay his coat on her twisted body. Then prayed.

Pum Pum was at Reggie's. He was in a grim mood. Monkey, Slice and Veteran, his domino-playing buddies, were tired of cussing him for not concentrating hard enough on the game. He had been through five bottles of Dragon Stout and was about to start on the spirits and they believed that the drink had gotten the better of him. Veteran, his partner in the game, would look at him sadly whenever it was his time to play, knowing that he was going to make a stupid move. He and Veteran had lost three games on the trot six-love and they had thrown away a lot of money. It probably didn't matter to Veteran because he was a long-time gambler and always had money. It didn't matter to Pum Pum either, for he had other things on his mind. A dose of creative inspiration hit him again and he hardly noticed the increasing poignancy with which his heart spoke.

'Who can truly speak of love towards his neighbour?
'Few.
'Who can truly speak of antipathy towards his brother?
'Many.
'Who can truly speak of compassion towards his sister?
'Few.
'Who can truly speak of hatred towards his friend?
'Many.
'Is not death life then? And is not life death?
'For in life there are no answers and few clues.
'But in death there is light and revelation.
'The man that seeketh the truth shall not be afraid to die.
'But shall abhor life, for within it we lie.
'And though we live, should we not die?
'For when we die, Then do we live.
'Death is merely of the body.
'But life is of the spirit.
'Fear not death my humble heart
'And embrace the truth that comes with life.
'For who shall truly speak of love towards his brother?
'Few.
'And who shall truly speak of loathing for his neighbour?
'Many.'

Pum Pum slapped down his final domino, then left the table to the utter disgust of his fellow players. He headed for the bar. He emerged with a straight double brandy, sat down and simply waited.

fourteen

It was two o'clock in the morning. Tony was alone. Just lying on the single bed of his hastily-rented room made him realise the extent of his loneliness. He was more alone now than he ever had been in the whole of his life. It wasn't just a physical presence that he felt was missing, but a spiritual one. He remembered someone telling him in his youth that God would protect no one from death, that he would take the spirit away so that death could inhabit; it felt like that now. Lying prostrate and staring blankly at the ceiling, he knew it would be a long night.

He had managed to rent the small room after deciding that his own flat was not the best place to be at the moment. The only trip that he had made there since the shooting was to collect the things for his flight to Jamaica. Those things, clothes and a few odds and ends, were now locked away in a single suitcase waiting to board the plane to freedom. The flight was only twelve hours away but it seemed like an eternity. He wondered what he ought to do, just lie low, or get out and try to forget all that had transpired. He was afraid. Perhaps going out might get him caught. Maybe a strange twist of fate might cause him an injury, maybe God might judge him and take his life for all the things that he had done and for what he had put Jean through.

Gripped by an overwhelming sense of fear and depression, it became painfully evident to him that his life was very much in tatters. He had nowhere to go and no one to run to. For a split second he considered taking his gun and blowing his own head off, but no, that was too simple a solution, too easy a way out. He still had one hope. The 14.00 hours flight to Kingston. He consoled himself with the thought of the beautiful island that he was once fortunate enough to visit as a child. He switched on the small remote television for the second time that night. Local T.V. had news bulletins all night and it was with consternation that he saw his photo-fit picture. He shivered. When the news reporter reiterated that the description had come from a local informer, he raged. Baron, he thought, that bastard had sold him out to the police. This was bad news. The photo-fit image bore a striking resemblance to him. His trepidation grew.

He stretched over his bed and reached for the quarter ounce or so of cocaine. He sat up, poured out a small bit of the snowy powder and took an old rusty razor blade to separate it into tiny rows. He then searched for a piece of paper which, when he found one of adequate size, he rolled to make a small straw. Holding one end to his nose and the other to the first row of cocaine he slowly moved along the lines of white powder, inhaling strongly as he did so. He felt dizzy for an instant and as the effect began to settle he felt an immense power surging through his blood. It was all he needed. His emotional disposition was instantly changed. He confidently but rather stiffly rose off the bed, staggered over to his shoes and with trembling hands proceeded to put them on. Following this he put on his long black mac, grabbed his gun and his keys and headed for the door.

His first stop was at an all night petrol station. The attendant heard Tony's booming system pumping out TuPac's 'Only God Can Judge Me Now' way before he pulled into the station. He waited patiently as Tony staggered out of the car and filled his petrol tank. He adjusted his seat to face the window expecting Tony to come up and pay for his petrol. He never did. Instead he sped off without even a thought of paying. The attendant, shocked by the action, immediately rang the police, angrily describing both the car make and registration and giving as vivid a description of Tony as he could manage.

The night had become pleasant. Traces of the earlier rain were evident on the roads but it had become warm and tranquil. The driver's side window was wound right down as Tony cruised the desolate streets of his home town. This was the most peace that he had experienced over the last few days and it was worth savouring. His tape had moved on and TuPac, his rap music hero, was now singing 'Holla at Me' and as the tune went on, he thought of Pum Pum. Hatred swelled up in his breast. The thought of being insulted in such a way by that maggot consumed him. It took a near head-on accident to bring him back to his senses when he strayed into the wrong lane and was forced to swerve out of the way of a oncoming motor car. He relaxed once more, and concentrated a bit harder on the road. His his last bout of drug taking had clouded his brain, it was hard to think straight. Eventually he pulled up into Elisha Road. His intake of drugs may have fogged his senses but it had also put him on quite a high. His mind had gently drifted onto thoughts of the opposite sex, his dick began to tingle and now he was feeling decidedly horny and wanted a fuck. What the Hell? It was his last night in the country anyway, why not? He thought.

He drove slowly and with vacant expression surveyed the prostitutes that paraded their half-naked bodies before him. Some knew him and others didn't, there were new faces around. Some hookers, the new ones, posed quite elegantly as he passed them, others ran up to his car. He passed Doreen, who recognised him and looked away. One prostitute, an ugly misshapen thing obviously bereft of business actually stood in the road before the car in an effort to stop him and banged her hands hard in frustration on the bonnet, before jumping out of his way when she realised that he wasn't going to stop. A couple of them even came up to the window, but he didn't like those.

He stopped beside a voluptuous young lady that had grabbed his attention. With pouting lips and sharp shiny fingernails she lent over the automatic window that Tony had lowered and asked him what his preference was. Her heavy dark cleavage rested firmly on the car door and he hardly looked at her for the view he was getting of her ripe and tender breasts. He said nothing, looked at the girl and sat transfixed by her evident youthfulness and her obvious beauty. He wondered for a second as to why such a beautiful well-set thing like that should want to choose such a means of making a living. For a second he half thought of paying for her services but realising that he would need as much money as possible in Jamaica, he decided not to. From his inside pocket he whipped out his gun and pointed it in her face. She stood still, shell-shocked.

'I don't want any trouble, please don't hurt me. Please I have a child,' she said nervously.

'Then get in the car,' was Tony's cold reply.

She thought for a second to consider her options. There weren't many. Reluctantly she slung her small handbag over her shoulder and walked around the bonnet of the car. She was conscious all the time that Tony, following her with the gun, could blow her away at any moment if he was mad enough, and in truth she had no way of determining that. He had done a very good job up to now. She opened the door and got into the car. She looked at him tensely, with cold fear in her eyes, and said nothing.

'Just be quiet and you'll be OK, believe me,' said Tony softly but in a matter-of-fact tone. He liked the girl and certainly didn't want to harm her, but he was in no mood for messing, he wanted his business sorted and that was it. If she did what he told her to do she would be OK, he pledged to himself.

'Please, I'll do anything, you want me to do, just don't ...' she began. But that was all she could say. Tony's fist across her mouth made blood splatter from it and put paid to any conversation. As her head fell against the car window she winced. He was serious and although frightened out of her wits she would say nothing else.

'Bitch, I told you to be quiet. I didn't wanna hurt you, just want my shit deal wid seen?' he bellowed at her. With that Tony accelerated and they were off.

After some fifteen minutes of driving Tony pulled up in a common. It was a hilly area, one that lovers would often drive to when a car was their only means of provision for love making. It was a spot that Tony knew well. He had taken Shakela there many a time, and she had once christened it their 'beauty spot'. The sight of the dark field bought a swell in Tony's breast as he recollected those passionate nights with Shakela. Nights when they would fuck then sit in the car, watching the other lovers in their cars and trying to work out which position they could possibly best do it in. They would laugh at the sight of cars gently bobbing up and down, or the sight of a leg exposed from an open door because there wasn't any room. Heat would gush around the car with the radio quietly going on in the background and they would enjoy what Tony now realised were precious moments. But he soon snapped himself out of his unexpected moment of reminiscence and got down to the business at hand.

This particular night the field was empty and it made Tony feel a little more comfortable, but the prostitute was even more nervous. The night-shrouded field and the quiet still of the warm air complemented the awe inspiring view of the star-ridden dark blue sky. Slowly Tony pulled down his zipper, loosened his belt and undid his trousers, allowing a his half-erect penis to surface. The prostitute needed no prompting – she knew what he wanted. She inclined herself across the handbrake, allowing her lips to settle comfortably on the tip of his cock. She stroked and kissed it repeatedly, before running her tongue up and down it like it was a lollipop. Before long Tony was hard as a rock and it was at that moment she gently peeled back his foreskin and dropped her gaping mouth on it. She worked him professionally.

Fearing that she might bite him in an attempt to free herself Tony stuck his gun against her head, even removing the safety lock, so that all he had to do was pull the trigger. It would mean a bloodied and shattered skull all over his dick if he had to shoot, but he wanted no funny tricks. The prostitute became terrified and soon enough the sound of her slurping away at his cock became combined with nervous breathing and eventually sobbing. She didn't worry about being killed for trying to escape, because she wasn't going to try to, but that at the time of his orgasm the rush of excitement might cause him to let fly on the trigger. She admonished herself to be careful not to get too carried away, to do her best to control his orgasm and move out of the way immediately he came into her mouth and it was over.

When he did come, the orgasm alone wasn't the only inspiring sensation that Tony was feeling. As she sucked him off, he had fixed his stare at the beautiful night sky arrayed majestically before him. It seemed to provide comfort, a serenity that he had never before experienced. Reassuring him that all would be well, whether in life or death. It took away his fear and as he came, he closed his eyes and wallowed in the absolute delectation of the moment. When it was over he opened his eyes to behold a terrified young lady, with running mascara and mouth dripping his sperm shaking and staring anxiously at him. He leaned across to her and taking a handkerchief from his jacket pocket gently wiped her face and her mouth. She cried some more, this time with relief. It appeared from Tony's seemingly compassionate action that she would live through her experience.

'Told you it would be alright,' he said to her reassuringly. 'Just needed my shit dealt with.'

Silently they drove back to Elisha Road. He pulled up at the spot where he had picked her up and motioned for her to leave. Hand fixed on the door handle, before leaving the car, she turned and gave him a final glance. All the time they had been together she knew that he was troubled, she almost felt as though she wanted to help and certainly the look in his eyes at that moment was a call, a plea. But she knew that what she had done on the common was all she could do for him. As she dropped her gaze to the floor, he looked away, staring fixedly through the windscreen until she got out of the car. As Tony sped off she stood and watched him leave.

Three of her prostitute friends approached her. They were all eager to speak to her, wanting to know how it had gone with a client driving such an expensive car or to tell her of their exploits whilst she'd been gone. She shrugged them off and once again began to weep. With tears rolling down her face she began to walk away swearing to leave the profession for good. It would be hard to make ends meet, but the nights activities were enough to convince her that rather than repeat the experience she would try somehow to eke out a living.

Tony's head was awash with a myriad of thoughts as he sped along the motorway. So full was his mind that he took no notice of his speed or the direction in which he was travelling. He had reached 110 mph and was still looking to go faster. The motorway was empty. At that time of the morning few cars travelled along it, so when a couple of traffic policemen, parked along the hard shoulder, noticed Tony's motor speed past them, it brightened up an otherwise dull night. They gave chase. They figured that the flashing blue light on the roof of their Panda car would be enough, but when they realised that their assailant was taking no notice of this they radioed for help and turned on their sirens. This was all just an irritating nuisance for Tony, who eventually slowed the car down and brought it to a halt.

As the officers pulled up behind him, he got out of his car and slowly walked towards them. One officer jumped out of the Panda car and walked authoritatively and rather angrily towards him. The other stood by the Panda, hand poised on his radio. Tony was relaxed and he appeared menacing, almost demonic, as he walked slowly towards them through the slight mist created by the combined efforts of fog that was building up and his car exhaust. His long coat billowed behind him in the breeze. As he got closer to the first officer, who rather worriedly prepared himself to do some talking, Tony reached into his pocket for his gun, pulled it out and shot him right between the eyes. Without pausing he proceeded to the next one, stepping over the body of the first officer. The second one tried desperately to get back into the Panda car, but was too late. Tony unleashed a deadly series of three shots that hit him in the back and felled him instantly. Tony stood motionless over the body, took careful aim at the policeman's head and fired. Satisfied by the gush of blood that spurted forth from the shattered head of the policeman, Tony turned back to his car and continued his journey without so much as another thought.

Maybe it was the absolute feeling of power that killing gave him, or maybe it was his frustration, but Tony began gingerly at first, but then eventually almost obsessively to thirst for more blood. He changed direction and headed towards the docks. He remembered Luck telling him that he met the drugs dealer, Baron, at a gambling house not too far from where he had killed his first cop. It wouldn't be difficult to find a blues house or a shabean, and the likelihood was that Baron would be there. Had it not been for Baron opening his big mouth to the police, Tony thought, he wouldn't be in this situation. His mission was set.

He reached the docks in no time at all and after driving around the only Black neighbourhood for a good half an hour and after a couple of wrong turns, he pulled up outside a big house with lights on and music blaring. There were people outside, standing up against walls or leaning up against their cars chatting, smoking ganja and flirting with the opposite sex. Tony surveyed the area. Baron was not around. He shuddered slightly at the thought of having to go inside but he dismissed it quickly by reminding himself of the man responsible for his grievous situation.

He got out of the car and slowly walked into the house. Curious glances followed him as he made his way up a short flight of stairs and through a wide open front door. He treaded carefully past people holding up the walls in the corridor, the smell of marijuana scenting every crevice of the house. He stopped by one room and looked in. Bodies were crowded round a pool table anxiously discussing the outcome of what Tony immediately realised was a tense game – and with a wad of notes on the table, no wonder.

A brother stopped him as he moved through and shoved a flier in his hand. It was advertising a blues party just a few miles away, actually not far from the single room that he was staying in. He pushed it into his pocket without even folding it and steadily moved through the hallway. He stopped at another room and looked in. The stares of strangers pierced him once again as he made his way to the middle of the room where a game of dominoes was in session. He eyed the four players. One was slightly older than the rest with an uncombed beard and a balding head. He was a large and quite robust-looking figure who didn't look out of place chomping on the large cigar that protruded from his mouth. The other was a bit young, thin and well dressed. He wore an open-necked shirt that exposed three or four large gold chains around his neck. He was cursing loudly and banged his dominoes onto the table with more gusto and enthusiasm than the other players. The third player was a short man, who, judging by his tropical-style beach shirt, seemed to think that he was somewhere in the Caribbean. He smoked only a cigarette and coughed violently whenever he took a pull on it. He seemed like a cautious sort of person and was evidently more worried than any of the other players about losing the game. The fourth and final player he hardly needed to check out. The gold rings and the fiercely smart and contemporary street gear gave him away instantly. Sure enough it was Baron.

Baron hadn't noticed Tony as his gaze was firmly fixed on his hand. He pulled his dark glasses down to hang on the tip of his nose to view his hand better, barely hearing his name called over the bassy music that blared from the massive speakers situated around the room. When he finally looked up he beheld an avenging angel. Majestically Tony stood above him, legs slightly astride with a stance like a cowboy ready to draw. The cold look in his eyes confirmed his intention, but Baron's reaction was sharp. He turned over the table, sending the money, dominoes, cigars, cigarettes, spliffs and ashtrays flying everywhere. Quickly he untangled himself from the carnage and bolted for another door on the other side of the room that would lead him to the kitchen and out through the back to safety. He never made it. Tony didn't have to give chase, but rather coolly held his stance, pulled his gun and let loose a hail of bullets that felled him in an instant.

The crowd erupted in a frenzy of panic. There was a stampede as everyone, screaming and shouting, bolted for the doors. People tripped up over each other but still desperately dove for the exits. Tony stood still. He didn't have to move, for those people that were trying to get past him and out of the door did their utmost to avoid even touching him. Shortly he was alone with Baron who was still moving slightly. Blood spurted from his back and legs as he desperately sought to gain ground, but his feeble crawl along the floor did precious little to assist him in this. Tony stood over him pointing his gun at the back of his head. Baron pleaded incessantly for his life to be spared, crying weakly through his pain.

'W'happen man?' he pleaded. 'You took the money and the drugs, why the bomboclaart you doing this man!?'

'I don't like infarma,' Tony said in a cold voice.

'Shit man. I didn't do that, believe me man it wasn't me… please spare me… it wasn't me!' These were Baron's last words.

'Bastard,' Tony whispered to himself before unleashing a single deadly shot that ripped Baron's head completely apart releasing a pool of blood and freeing his brain from a fragmented skull that had shattered on the impact of the bullet. He turned slowly, held his gun aloft and walked cautiously out of the house. He needn't have worried for there was no one else around. Where once there was a veritable beehive of activity, there was now nothing and no one. They had all disappeared in fear for their lives. Climbing into his car once again, he surveyed the flier that had been handed to him. Careful to avoid the stretch of road where the had killed the two policemen, he set off once again.

As before, Tony pulled up outside a busy house. The heavy bass tones of the sound system were quite compelling, as on his journey to the blues he had loaded himself back up with drugs. It was taking effect now. His eyes were red and he was tired. He needed to rest and as he approached the blues his head began to get heavier and heavier. He had hardly eaten all day and the weariness was beginning to show on his face. He approached the door and knocked. Two burly Rastas greeted him as one pulled the door open.

'Five dalla fi come in,' said the other one.

Tony was unimpressed and simply took his gun from his pocket and pointed it at them. It was payment enough. Humbly, they opened the door and beckoned him in, whispering to each other as he walked past into the crowded house. The noise was deafening, and soon he began to experience difficulty focusing. Pretty women with fearful eyes glanced him as he shoved his way past. He stepped on a man's toe, but just the look of Tony's red eyes informed him not to pursue his grievance. Soon Tony was against a wall. He fell back and allowed it to prop him up. With a deep breath he raised his eyes to the ceiling before shutting them and allowing the music to consume him.

Within the hour it was light again. Tony, seemingly refreshed, stepped out of the house and welcomed the singing of the birds. It was a new day and one that he believed would soon herald his freedom. He remembered Pum Pum's admonishment to leave the town, it hurt him, the way that he had allowed himself to be dealt with by that scum. He kissed his teeth, took out his gun and headed for his car. He would make one last stop before making his way to the airport. He knew exactly where Pum Pum would be now, so he drove towards Reggie's shabean to settle his final score.

Kirk stepped gingerly out of his car. The stretch of motorway where Tony had killed the policemen was cut off. Another homicide. But this one was different from most. Kirk's face betrayed his anxiety as he surveyed the scene. Much the same as he expected. Squad cars, a medical van, a forensics van and loads of police officers both uniformed and plain clothed milled about doing their jobs. He had received the news on his way home and it had sickened him to his stomach to hear that another two officers had gone down in such brutal circumstances. He walked towards the death scene. He had somehow lost much of his edge, much of the aggression. He knew that he wasn't going to like what he was about to see. Anderson saw him and hurried over.

'The Chief Constable's here sir,' she warned.

'Shit, that's all I need,' replied Kirk. 'Where?'

'Just over there,' she responded, pointing to where one of the bodies lay. Kirk hoped that the Chief Constable he hadn't noticed him. He was alright for now.

'What have you got?' he asked, turning to Anderson.

'Looks like our man. The two dead officers radioed in that they were chasing a grey BMW. Looks like he resprayed the car. Licence plate checks out though. Belongs to a Tony Morrison. We've sent a squad to his place, heard nothing yet.'

'The officers?'

'PC 4527 Jennings and PC 3769 Taylor. Jennings was a veteran 15 years on the force, Taylor …' Anderson dropped her head. 'It was his second week on the job. He'd just left training school.'

Kirk turned to the nearest car and kicked it.

'Fuck!' he shouted.

Anderson respected his vibe.

'I'll be in touch with their families later sir,' she said solemnly as she left.

Kirk walked over to Pritchard who stood by the squad car where the second dead officer lay. Pritchard was just about to do his thing, when Anderson interrupted.

'Sir I've just received a call. He's killed Baron.'

'Jesus fuckin' Christ he's on a fuckin' killing spree tonight enee!?' exploded Kirk. His agitation had not reached its peak, but it was about to.

'Detective Inspector, can I have a word with you please?'

It was the Chief Constable.

'Fuckin' 'ell!' moaned Kirk under his breath. He walked over to the Chief Constable who had not yet moved. The people that were talking to him moved away. Kirk couldn't help thinking that he had sent them off. As he approached the Chief Constable's space he knew what was coming. It came with swiftness.

'Detective Inspector, what the hell is going on? Haven't you caught this chap yet? Jesus Christ, the man's on a bloody mission. How many officers do you intend to let him kill?'

'Sir we're doing the best we can …'

'Well it's not good enough Detective. I don't want to lose any more …'

He was cut off in mid speech. Anderson had made her way up to them hurriedly, mobile phone in hand.

'Sir,' she said eagerly. 'You're needed back at the station. There's someone that claims to know who our man is going to kill next.'

Kirk turned immediately to his car.

'Detective, I haven't finished with you!' shouted the Chief Constable.

His words fell on deaf ears, for in seconds Kirk had hit the accelerator of his Vectra and was gone.

fifteen

Seven o'clock in the morning. Jean's eyes opened at first light. She had been tossing and turning all night on the settee and had hardly slept for worrying about Tony. She sat up and immediately reached for the telephone, picked up the handset but replaced it instantly fearing that anyone she spoke to just might be the harbinger of the inevitable bad news. She thought about calling Tony's pager but that was usually a fruitless exercise as he would never call back until he felt like it. This time she feared that he might never return her call. But she had to try something. As she lifted the handset and dialled the number she could hardly think of what to say. But in no time at all she was speaking to the operator.

'Can I have your message please?' she said.

Jean shuddered.

'Erm er,' she began nervously 'Tony call Jean.'

'Is that the end of the message?'

'I love you.'

'Tony call Jean I love you. Message sent thank you for calling.'

She sat motionless wondering what to do next. Even sending that pager message had been something of an ordeal, but once she had gone through with it she was encouraged to try something else. She began to think of Tony and what had possibly transpired between he and Pum Pum during the night. Desperately she hoped the nightmare would end and that Tony was safe and would be back in her arms as he had been so many times before. But she knew that this was a fantasy now. She resigned herself to the worst. Her heart pounded with nervous frustration. Almost aimlessly she switched on the television in a desperate attempt to calm herself down. The early morning news had just begun. She sat with one elbow resting on her thigh and her chin propped on her clenched fist, watching anxiously for news.

'Two men and two policemen have been shot dead this morning in the local area,' began the newsreader. 'The two policemen, PC Jennings and PC Taylor, both from London, were both mercilessly shot dead at point blank range when they stopped a suspicious car in the early hours of this morning.'

Jean shuddered as once again her heart began to pound. Her eyes widened as she stared at the television set. The newsreader went on and she learned of that night's killing spree by Tony.

'In a separate incident, a local drugs dealer was also shot this morning as mayhem ensued at a local crack house in Elisha Road, a notorious part of town,' continued the reporter. 'A man believed to be part of the gang responsible for the shooting of a policemen in Southampton last week was also shot. Police believe all four killings to be somehow connected.'

Jean prayed that it was not Tony that the newscaster was talking about, but it was evident that a major catastrophe had intruded upon her life. She just could not stop worrying about her loved one. A number of thoughts ran through her head as she listened to the closing statement of the newscaster's report.

'I must repeat that the Police believe the killer to be part of a gang that killed a policeman at the docks last week. They have issued a warning that he is highly dangerous and is not to be approached. Over now to Gavin Arnold at the scene of the fourth murder.'

As the report cut to Reggie's shabean, the recognition of it as Tony and Pum Pum's favourite hangout overwhelmed her. She could take the anxiety no more and without even listening to the rest of the report collapsed in a mad crescendo of tears. Her bawling became louder and louder as the realisation of Tony's death became all the more real to her. In a vain hope that it was not he that had been killed she shot up and headed for her bedroom to quickly dress herself and head for the shabean. She was cut short by a knock at the door. She ran cautiously over to it, wanting desperately to see her lover before her safe and sound, but instinct reminded her that there was trouble in the air and thus she erred on the side of caution. Her heart throbbed with expectation as she cautiously leaned towards the door handle. She drew back the lock, praying once again that Tony would be standing there before her.

'Who is it?' she whispered nervously.

There was no answer. She asked again, before a faint 'It's me,' greeted her. She was sure that the deep sensuous voice belonged to her man, but as she hastily undid the locks and opened the door, she saw David standing before her. He quickly grabbed her, asking her if she was all right, explaining that Sheila had remembered his address, located his phone number from the directory and had called him in the early hours if the morning, explaining that she was in trouble. He had also caught the hourly news reports in the night and suspected that Tony might have been involved in the killings . It had taken him the whole night to muster the courage to come over. He held her and this time she did not ignore, fight or contest his advance. She clung to him.

'He's dead,' she cried. 'I know he's dead. The news… they said there was a killing on Elisha Road. I know he's gone.'

They moved to the middle of the room where David calmly sat her down. She was inconsolable. He stood up and moved the curtains to look out of the window and would almost have sworn that he had seen a tall figure not unlike Tony make its way off the street and into the building. But he figured he was paranoid – he would probably be seeing Tony everywhere and in everything that he did. He shook his head, composed himself and turned once again to Jean. She had stood up to gather her composure, approached him and asked him politely to leave. Passion overcame him as he swore that he would not leave her until he could be sure that she would be all right. He hugged her once again, informing her of his undying love for her and that, if she could now forget Tony, he would revive her fortunes and give her the kind of life for which, he knew, she had always longed. She too was overcome with emotion and in that moment they realised that perhaps out of the ruins that was now her life there might arise a new beginning. They kissed, slowly at first then ever the more passionately. Jean knew that it was not love that caused her to do it, but his words had come just at the right time. She was a wreck and was desperately in need of some form of comfort. Tony had never told her that he loved her and now whilst she wanted to hear those words from him, that they came from David was comfort enough.

Neither she nor David heard the door as a key twisted once in the lock and with a slight push gently opened. In stepped Tony, his clothes drenched in blood from his night's work. He stood in total shock as he watched David and Jean locked in burning embrace. He shuddered, unable to gather any thoughts but the acknowledgement of the sudden plunge of jealousy straight to his stomach. He rested both of his hands on the back of the settee to support his tired and failing body. Still they kissed and as they did so tears filled his eyes. The whole episode had culminated in this. What Shakela had told him was true. He saw the evidence of her infidelity with his own eyes. Jean was kissing another man. He remembered his words to Shakela about what he would do. His eyes blazed and the heartbeat within his chest was no longer evident. His body was beset with the same coldness that had taken four lives that night. There would be more bloodshed. When they finished, Jean was the first to notice him. Instantly stricken with a nervous mix of happiness and fear, she shook visibly as did David upon noticing him. She quickly left David's embrace and started towards Tony, desperate to convince him that things were not as they appeared. Tony stopped her in mid-stride by pulling his gun from the back of his trousers and pointing it straight at her, an action that made her recoil in absolute terror.

'No,' he cried, 'no fucking way.'

'Tony please,' came Jean's distressed and now familiar reply.

David lunged towards Tony in a valiant effort to disarm him but to no avail. That action cost him his life as Tony instinctively let fly with the trigger. Three shots let rip and David was on the ground, his stomach and lungs punctured. His stomach spurted blood as the life force slowly ebbed away from what eventually became an empty dead shell on the living room floor. Jean screamed in frustrated panic. She didn't know what to do as fear held her rooted to the spot trembling and in tears. Tony aimed the gun at her. She screamed again, begging for mercy. He shouted at her, hurling obscenities and insults as he ordered her to confirm that David had been her lover all along. Her vain attempts to convince him otherwise were futile, he would not have it, the evidence was clear. In a mad rage Tony pulled the trigger and fired a shot, raising the gun just above her head as he did so, just enough to miss her. She jumped holding her ears and, realising that he had deliberately missed her, hurtled towards him and flung her arms tightly around his neck. He squeezed her as tears filled his eyes. He dropped the gun and hugged her tighter, as if hanging on for dear life.

The embrace was a long one. Jean wallowed in it, whispering words of comfort to him and stroking the back of his head. It seemed to relax him. But as they were joined, he reached slowly into his back pocket. Steadily he raised his fist revealing a small flick knife, which he instantly engaged. He raised his hand and with a swift movement plunged it mercilessly into Jean's gut. She released herself from him in shock. As she took a step back she realised that he had pierced her. The blood poured from her stomach as she looked at him. He moved towards her again and with a mighty thrust stabbed her again. This time it was enough to finish her. She leant forward, cupping her hands as if to catch the blood that flowed from her, her face contorted with a mixture of pain and confusion. She dropped to her knees then fell, face first into the carpet, where she lay completely motionless.

Tony dropped the knife and slowly began to walk backwards as he surveyed the dead body of his loved one. He was cold and emotionless. His rapid moral and mental deterioration had bought him to this. She was once his whole life and his very reason for living and now she was gone, dead but deservedly so he thought. Few other thoughts ran through his brain as he looked down at her and then David. He had done what he said he would do, killed them both. This chapter of his life was closed and that was all that mattered. Now it was time for him to skip the country. But as he turned towards the door, he was halted in his tracks by a confusion of car lights and sirens. A police helicopter hovered only yards away from the balcony, filling the room with light and noise. He quickly ran to the window and saw at least eight police cars and two vans as crack shots armed with rifles and garbed in bullet proof vests jumped out and took their positions behind the cars, aiming their rifles right at the flat. He was close enough to see the pilot of the helicopter and the marksman that occupied the other seat, his gun squarely aimed at the flat.

Tony ran into the kitchen to view the backyard from the window and sure enough noticed three armed policemen scale the fence and enter the garden. He realised that they were out to cut out all of his escape options. He figured that they would be coming up the stairs to the front door as well. He froze, but quickly and nervously collected his thoughts as he ran back into the living room and picked up the gun that he had dropped and hid, back to the wall next to the large bay window. He breathed heavily as he considered a strategy, but soon the realisation dawned on him that he was completely surrounded and that there would be no way out. He dug feverishly into his pocket and taking out his last portion of drugs sniffed for all he was worth. When he reached a sufficient high to lose his fear he loaded up his gun with as many bullets as he could and waited.

'You are completely surrounded!' came a voice through a loud hailer. 'Come out with your hands in the air, I repeat, you are completely surrounded!' Tony turned, flicked the large doors open and took pot-shots at the brigade, who simply returned a hail of automatic gunfire at the window, shattering it and the surrounding frame into a million pieces. The helicopter took off as the pilot moved out of the firing line. Tony dived for cover and when there was a break in the gunfire, returned his comparatively puny firearm at them. They fired again, this time more consistently as Tony hid again. For the third and final time he returned fire and he was greeted with a monstrous crescendo of gunfire. A bullet caught him on his right shoulder and he was felled. Before he was able to regain his ground another bullet hit him in the arm. Searing pain ran through his body and as he staggered up to return fire he was hit again. Blood gashed from his many wounds. Losing consciousness fast, he was unable to hear the kicking in of the door by armed police officers, who raised their guns. Tony turned, raised his hand to fire at them and was greeted with a monstrous hail of gunfire that soiled what was left of his dying body. He fell a yard or so from where Jean had fallen. The commander, sensing that the danger was over, spoke into his radio then approached the window shouting

'Hold fire! Repeat hold fire! Aggressor immobilised! Aggressor immobilised!' informing their colleagues that the job was done.

Tony lay on the floor, blood dripping from every crevice of his body. He could not feel pain. He drifted slowly into unconsciousness no longer able to assess the situation around him. Speeded-up images of his life raced through his mind. He saw through the eyes of the unborn child and relived the terror of his birth, hearing the screams of his mother as she delivered him. He felt the surge of faeces leave his tiny gut as he instantly warmed to his mother's pained cries of joy and beheld the world for the first time. He recalled his joy at learning to crawl and the further joy at learning to walk. He remembered his little friends at nursery school and he remembered the primary school at which he spent so many dreadful years of his young life. He remembered hating the teachers and them hating him and how at secondary school he would smoke behind the bike sheds, get caught and caned. He recalled the endless trips to the Headteacher's office for the many fights that he ended up in. He would hide bad reports from his mother who thus far had raised him single-handedly. He recalled being suspended from school for bad behaviour and hanging out on the streets with the bad boys, stealing and mugging to make ends meet. He recalled his one journey to the Caribbean with his mother at the age of 15 and remembered how much he longed to stay there. He remembered seeing his mother, an emotional ruin, a drug addict by the time he was eighteen and how by that time he was taking drugs himself. He recalled the dancehalls and the night-clubs, the pretty girls and wanting to be like the local celebrities that were the hustlers, pimps, gangsters and drug dealers of his neighbourhood. He remembered being constantly in trouble with the police. The funeral of his mother who died from an overdose of cocaine. Finally he remembered meeting Jean, who, in an instant, shrouded in a haze of azure blue shining light appeared before him as an angel looking more beautiful than she ever had. He noticed her drift elegantly before him and take his head in her hands and gently kiss him. He blinked once, then became still, forever.

Outside, Detective Inspector Kirk surveyed the carnage before him. None of Tony's bullets had found their targets and none of his men had been hit. Policeman congratulated each other whilst others sought to control the crowds that had gathered. Others were sickened and just wanted to go home. News cameras rolled and reporters either recorded or gave live coverage to their respective stations and programmes. Amid it all Sheila stepped up and looked up at the flat. A tear trickled down her face as a consoling arm came around her shoulder. It was Detective Inspector Kirk.

'Thank you,' he said. 'We couldn't have done this without you.'

Sheila winced. Tears welled up in her eyes.

'Fuck you!' she said agonising through tears. 'Just fuck you! You have no fucking idea, you never fucking will.'

Those words initiated a thrust within her breast that made her feel faint. As she struggled to stay on her feet, she lowered her head from the gaze of the Detective Inspector and walked off. She knew that the news reports would portray the episode as gang warfare and drugs-related activity. That Tony's actions were those of a disreputable drug addict. They would be partially correct she thought, but by and large they would be wrong. These were no yardie killings, no gang warfare retribution, no territorial shoot-outs. These were crimes of passion. Initiated by one man's overindulgence with the dust of death and another's selfish heart that wouldn't lay still for the love of somebody's man. Chickens had come home to roost this day and death was the sad and woeful outcome. May they all rest in peace, she thought as she cried.

epilogue

It had been a wonderful day. Sheila was bridesmaid and Luck's eldest brother had been best man. When Julie stood at the alter and said 'I do,' a tear rose in Luck's eye. When the pastor said,'You may kiss the bride,' they didn't stop kissing. At the reception Sheila made a speech and dedicated it to Jean's memory. It made Julie cry. No-one talked about Tony, Pum Pum or Shakela. They had become names that few people wished to remember or discuss. During the reception, Sheila, Julie and Luck left for a short while to share their happy moment with Jean. The drive was a short one for they had married at the same church that had housed her funeral. A big funeral it was too. At the graveyard it was Sheila that placed the wreath on her grave. The tombstone read:

OUR BELOVED JEAN 1969–1999 SHE KNEW ONLY HOW TO LOVE.

Sheila knelt down by the grave and smiled. She told her friend of the wonderful day she had because Julie and Luck fallen in love and had got married. She was happy for them and hoped that Jean would be happy for them too, that their union met with her approval. As she rose the three held each other tightly. There were no tears and as a slight gentle gust of wind surrounded them, they sensed Jean's approval. Then they cried.